CARDINAL SIN

Dan turned and banged on Yvonne's door. "Ms. Rice? This is Dan Sutton. Open the door, please."

I hesitated with my fingers on the door handle of my van. "She's not answering, Dan. I tried."

He looked at me. "You're supposed to be in your vehicle. With the doors locked and the windows rolled up."

I moved even closer until we were shoulder to shoulder. "I tried the back door, too. Besides, with all the commotion we're making between talking and your siren, if Yvonne could answer, don't you think she would?"

Dan blinked, then jiggled the front doorknob. "Locked. You say the other door is locked, too?"

"Yes."

Dan nodded. "Stand back."

I took a step backward and slipped off the porch. As I rose and dusted myself off, I heard the sound of splitting wood. Dan had kicked the door in.

"Wait outside." All business now, Dan drew his gun and stepped inside.

The doorjamb was splintered. The front door dangled on its hinges. I tiptoed closer and peered inside. The fire was nearly out.

Yvonne Rice sat in the easy chair closest to the fireplace. Spools of embroidery floss rested on the table beside her. An unfinished magenta and gold feather lay in her lap. Her chin sagged, and her eyes were slits.

And, oh yeah, there was a red wound in her chest that needed patching…

Books by J.R. Ripley

DIE, DIE BIRDIE

TOWHEE GET YOUR GUN

THE WOODPECKER ALWAYS PECKS TWICE

TO KILL A HUMMINGBIRD

CHICKADEE CHICKADEE BANG BANG

HOW THE FINCH STOLE CHRISTMAS

FOWL OF THE HOUSE OF USHER

A BIRDER'S GUIDE TO MURDER

CARDINAL SIN

Published by Kensington Publishing Corporation

Cardinal Sin

J.R. Ripley

LYRICAL UNDERGROUND
Kensington Publishing Corp.
www.kensingtonbooks.com

LYRICAL UNDERGROUND BOOKS are published by

Kensington Publishing Corp.
119 West 40th Street
New York, NY 10018

All Kensington titles, imprints, and distributed lines are available at special quantity discounts for bulk purchases for sales promotion, premiums, fund-raising, educational, or institutional use.

Special book excerpts or customized printings can also be created to fit specific needs. For details, write or phone the office of the Kensington Sales Manager: Kensington Publishing Corp., 119 West 40th Street, New York, NY 10018. Attn. Sales Department. Phone: 1-800-221-2647.

Lyrical Underground and Lyrical Underground logo Reg. US Pat. & TM Off.

First Electronic Edition: May 2019
ISBN-13: 978-1-5161-0622-6 (ebook)
ISBN-10: 1-5161-0622-9 (ebook)

First Print Edition: May 2019
ISBN-13: 978-1-5161-0623-3
ISBN-10: 1-5161-0623-7

Printed in the United States of America

1

It was a quiet afternoon in Birds & Bees, and I was enjoying being lazy. Then again, they say that it's always quietest before the storm.

They were right.

I was half-drowsing in the sun with a patchwork comforter over my knees—a gift from my aunt Betty—feeling much like a lounging lizard in late August, kicking lazily back and forth in the rocking chair. I'd moved it to the window to be nearer the warm, sleep-inducing sunlight when the bell tolled, announcing a customer.

"Hello," I said, struggling to control the yawn that was working its unladylike way out of my mouth. I stood, balled up the comforter, and tossed it on the rocking chair, setting it in motion once again—either that or a ghost had taken up residence. "Welcome to Birds and Bees."

"Hi." A lovely, auburn-haired woman smiled at me. "I was across the street when I saw your sign."

"Awesome. Welcome."

I examined my new customer the same way I would a new bird. There was an exotic quality to her features, including the deep-set brown eyes that were revealed when she pulled off her sunglasses and stuck them atop her head. There might have been some Polynesian or Hawaiian blood coursing through her veins. Arteries, too, for that matter.

"This is your first time in our store, I take it?"

"Yes." The woman was dressed casually in blue denim pants and a sweater the color of moss that fell to just below her hips. Her shoes were dusty leather work boots that ended at the ankles and looked like they might have a story or two to tell.

"Is there something particular I can help you with? We stock our own blends of birdseed and locally made birdhouses."

"Do you sell bees?"

"Bees?"

"You know, buzz-buzz." The vibrating of her fulsome lips sounded remarkably beelike.

"Sorry, no."

"I suppose I should have known. I was hoping..." She glanced at the window. "Because of your sign."

"Birds and Bees?"

"Yes."

"Again, sorry. You aren't the first person to get confused. I sell a few beekeeping supplies but not much else. And Mitch Quiles is pretty much my only regular customer for those. In the spring and summer, we also carry plants that are beneficial to bee and butterfly populations."

"Mitch Quiles?"

"Mr. Quiles is a beekeeper. He owns an apiary at the edge of town. I've got jars of his honey for sale on the shelf there, if you are interested in some local honey." I pointed down aisle two. "It's organic."

The woman was disappointed. "When I saw the sign, I just assumed you sold bees. Silly of me, I guess. I didn't even know I was in the market for bees until I saw your sign from the diner window."

I followed her gaze out the window. Ruby's Diner, once a gas station, stood directly across Lake Shore Drive from the Queen Anne Victorian house that served as my home and the center of my business operations. A dusty, matte-black pickup truck sat at the curb.

"Follow me." I motioned for her to accompany me to the sales counter.

The house is three stories plus an attic and a basement. The store occupies the first floor. The main stairway in the middle of the store leads up to the second floor, which was currently occupied by a couple of renters. One of them being an employee of mine, Esther Pilaster. The other unit was currently occupied by the co-owner of Brewer's Biergarten, which was immediately next door. His name was Paul Anderson. My mother and I had the third floor to ourselves. Paul's partner was my ex-partner—in bed, not beer, that is.

Being over a hundred years old, the house needed constant repairs and upkeep. Then again, I was only a little more than a third that age, and I needed constant repair and upkeep, too.

"Here." I rummaged through an old-fashioned Rolodex under the counter. "Let me give you Mr. Quiles's contact information. Maybe he can sell you some bees. A starter set, as it were." I grabbed one of our store's business cards and flipped it over to write on the back.

"Thanks. That's very helpful of you," she said, taking the card from me. I watched her lips move as she read the back of the card, then flipped it over to examine the front. "Amy Simms. That's you?"

"Yep. All five foot four and hundred and five pounds."

The woman was polite enough not to call me out on what was clearly an underrepresentation of my weight. She flapped the business card repeatedly against her opposite hand, then stuffed it in the front pocket of her jeans. "Thanks again."

"My pleasure, Ms....?"

"Yvonne Rice. Call me Yvonne."

"Pleased to meet you, Yvonne. I haven't seen you in Birds and Bees before. New to town or visiting?"

"I arrived about a month ago. I bought a cabin on five acres."

"Wow. I envy you."

"Yeah, I love it. I came from the city, so the solitude and the space are a real treat."

"Tell me about it. I live here."

"Here?" Her brow formed a V.

"Right here." I spread my arms. "This is not only my place of business, it is home sweet home."

Yvonne chuckled. "At least it's convenient."

"But there's no getting away from work," I replied. "Or my tenants."

Yvonne Rice flipped through the pages of a well-worn bird ID guide I kept on the sales counter. "Now that I think about it. Maybe you can help me with something else."

"Sure, name it."

"There's this bird that's been hanging around in the bushes around my cabin."

"Can you describe it?" I was always up for a challenge.

Her finger stopped on a page near the front of the book. "It looks like this."

"A cardinal?" The northern cardinal was a common bird in these parts. "I'm not sure I understand your question." And I didn't.

She ran her thumbnail over the picture of the bird. "You see, it looks like this. I mean, the shape, that thick bill, and that black around the face..."

"But?"

"But the bird I have been seeing is yellow."

I tilted my head. "Yellow? How do you mean?"

She turned the book to face me. "The feathers. They are yellow, not red."

"OMG. I heard about this a couple of times. I think somebody in Kentucky reported a sighting a few years back. Then a woman down in Alabama or Louisiana, I forget which, she actually filmed one visiting her bird feeder."

"What is it?"

"It is a northern cardinal. But it's a genetic mutation. Very, very rare," I explained. "Don't quote me on this, but if I remember correctly, its yellow feathers are due to a rare mutation that blocks its ability to assimilate red hues. You know how flamingos get their rosy pink color from the shrimp they eat?"

"Yes, I've heard that."

"Cardinals normally eat foods that are carotenoid-rich, too. That's what produces these red and orange feathers." I indicated the vivid red cardinal in the book. "Because of this mutation, the yellow cardinals are incapable of metabolizing those carotenoids, or something like that."

I scratched my head. "I'm no scientist."

"I think I understand."

"And you got to see one." I sighed and planted my elbows on the counter. "Wow."

"So they are relatively common around here then?"

"Only if you consider one-in-a-million common," I said with a laugh. "I've never seen one. I've never personally known anybody who has."

She smiled coyly. "Except me."

"Yes, except you."

"Would you like to see it?"

"I would love to!"

"No problem. Give me a couple of days to figure out a good time."

"Of course." I pulled her closer as a familiar customer crossed the threshold. "Mind if I give you a friendly piece of advice?"

"Okay."

"I wouldn't go spreading the word around about the bird."

"Why not?"

"The last person to do that had people *flocking* to her yard trying to catch a glimpse."

Yvonne put a finger to her lips. "Mum's the word." She did a slow turn. "Maybe I should think about getting a bird feeder or two." She rubbed her hands together. "Some birdseed, too."

"I like the way you think, Yvonne." Smelling a sale, I hastened from behind the counter to assist my new friend.

* * * *

Three days later, I found myself invited to a housewarming and bird-watching party.

Yvonne Rice had popped into the store a second time—and that time I had not been snoozing—and invited me to supper at her house. "Nothing formal," she explained. "In fact, we'll use the big picnic table in the backyard. I set up the bird feeder there. Hopefully, the cardinal will show up for us."

"Have you seen it since we last spoke?"

"Once or twice."

"That's good." It was a sign that the bird was staying in the area.

"There will only be a few other neighbors. Being new to town, I don't know a lot of folks. Feel free to bring a date." She paused. "Or are you married? I don't see a ring."

"Single." I looked at my empty ring finger. The only ring I had was around my bathtub. Mom kept it clean, and Mom was out of town. I tended to let the whole cleaning thing slide. "But I have a boyfriend. His name is Derek."

"Bring him. You should come too, Kim." Kim was on duty at the time. "In fact, bring your mother and anybody else you like."

I explained that my mom was in New Orleans with her twin sister, my aunt Betty, enjoying the sights. "But I will tell Esther." She hadn't been working in the store at the time. Whether she would be interested in attending was anybody's guess.

In the end, Esther declined the invitation, telling me that somebody had to stay and keep the store open and the dollars coming in.

It was a barbed commentary on my habit of abandoning the store for more pressing matters. I couldn't help it that the Town of Ruby Lake was a hotbed of activities other than bird-watching.

Although in this particular instance, bird-watching was exactly what I hoped to do. Catching a glimpse of the rare yellow cardinal would be a real coup.

Yvonne and I had agreed that if we saw the bird, we would photograph it and post it on the Birds & Bees bulletin board and web page, without mentioning its exact location, only that it had been sighted in the county. That would preserve her privacy and the cardinal's peaceful existence.

On the way now to Yvonne Rice's cabin, I had my camera and binoculars with me. Kim rode along with me in the minivan. Her boyfriend, Dan, was meeting us there because he was working up till then. Ditto my own boyfriend, Derek Harlan. He's an attorney in town, and he can examine my briefs any time he wants to.

Don't ask me to explain what that means.

I slowed and turned off the main road onto a bumpy gray gravel drive leading up to a modest log cabin with a stacked river-rock chimney.

Several other vehicles were parked haphazardly on the gravel and patchy grass between the cabin and the road. The smell of pine filled the air.

"There's Dan's car." Kim nodded at a vintage Firebird Trans Am, Dan's pride and joy. I didn't see Derek's little import model.

"I'm glad he could make it after all."

Dan originally had said he was scheduled to be on duty and would be unable to attend. At the last minute, he had called Kim to say that he had worked out with Chief Kennedy to take the evening off.

Following the sounds of animated voices, we found that everyone had arrived before us, including Derek. He had exchanged his business suit for a pair of nice-fitting jeans and a green flannel shirt. All were seated around a redwood picnic table draped in a pale red and yellow gingham cloth that fluttered in the breeze.

At the edge of the yard, I spotted Yvonne's new red tube feeder dangling from a lower limb of an old oak.

Yvonne waved and hurried over to greet us. Introductions were made.

"I brought you a little housewarming gift." I handed her my gold-wrapped box.

"You shouldn't have," Yvonne protested. Our hostess was rocking a pair of form-fitting sand-colored corduroys and a white sweater. A compact, rainbow-colored knit cap sat atop her head. I was in my best denim and a silky-soft flannel shirt.

Yvonne had said there was no need for formality. Not that that had stopped Kim, who had decided to flaunt her good looks in a tight, knee-length blue skirt and matching top, along with a sequined jacket she had purchased at a designer outlet shop out by the interstate near Charlotte.

"Me, too." Kim thrust her offering on Yvonne as well, and she carried the packages to the picnic table.

Mine was a birdhouse. Kim had refused to tell me what was in her own box. "You'll see when Yvonne opens it," was all she would say.

After introducing us to the others seated at the table, Madeline Bell, Ross Barnswallow, Murray Arnold, and Kay Calhoun, Yvonne opened my package first. "A birdhouse." She lofted it for all to see. "How adorable." It was. Aaron's houses boasted delicate gingerbread roofs and copper trim. Each was lovingly hand-painted pale blue with white trim.

"It's handcrafted by a local woodworker named Aaron Maddley," I explained.

"What else would you expect from her?" Derek said with a gleam in his eye. "Not to mention, she was once madly in love with the guy." Derek has blue eyes, brown hair, stands over six feet tall, and is *keep your hands off him, he's mine* handsome.

I blushed and set my camera and binoculars on the picnic table. "You know that's not true. We went on one date. And that wasn't a real date."

"Yeah. Besides, now Aaron is seeing Tiffany," Kim said, being absolutely no help at all. Tiffany is a waitress at Ruby's Diner. A buxom, green-eyed blonde, she has set so many hearts on fire since her divorce that the fire department ought to follow her around to protect the town.

Kim's package was next. She had sealed it with enough sticky tape to bind every carton under a Christmas tree and still have some left over for taping holiday cards to her front door.

After cutting through all that tape, with the assistance of a steak knife, Yvonne lifted the cover of the box and pulled out an eight-inch-tall statue dressed in a red suit and matching top hat. The little man with the twisted, skeletal face seemed to be sneering at me.

I shivered.

He was someone whom I knew all too well. I threw Kim a look. Yvonne set the doll carefully on the picnic table and extracted a folded white card.

Dan whistled and leaned back.

"What is it?" several of the others asked at once.

"Yes, what the devil is it?" A man I'd been introduced to as Murray leaned in for a closer look.

Devil was right, I couldn't help thinking.

Yvonne unfolded the card and began reading. "Baron Sam—" She stumbled over the words and frowned.

"Samedi," pronounced Kim.

"Samedi," Yvonne nodded and continued reading from the enclosed card. "Baron Samedi is…"

As Yvonne read, I whispered in Kim's ear. "The Lord of Death? Really, Kim? I can't believe you brought the Lord of Death as a housewarming gift."

2

Baron Samedi, also known as the Lord of Death in the voodoo religion, was an outlandish spirit known for his scandalous and filthy behavior. The baron is said to spend most of his time in the invisible realm of voodoo spirits. He ought to make it one hundred percent of his time, if you ask me.

While married to another voodoo spirit, he was known to swear continuously, make filthy jokes, and chase the skirts of mortal women when given the chance—and he was always looking for chances.

Kim took a self-satisfied sip from her glass. "At least we're rid of it," she mumbled for only me to hear.

I was about to protest when I realized she was right. The Lord of Death had meant nothing but trouble for us ever since the day I had unintentionally purchased it from a fortune-teller whom I had suspected of murdering her husband. She had foisted the doll on me before I had even known what was happening.

I later foisted the devil doll on Kim. Since then, it had become an ongoing battle between the two of us.

I had read that Baron Samedi stood at the crossroads between the dead and the living. Personally, I didn't care where he stood as long as it was nowhere near me. Kim and I had been shuffling him back and forth and beyond, trying to get rid of him. Somehow, he always returned. This time, we might just be rid of him for good.

Maybe he would bring better luck to Yvonne.

Maybe I could talk Yvonne into carrying the little guy back to Hawaii with her on her next visit home and dumping him there.

Preferably in the center of a volcano.

The center of an active volcano.

Come to think of it, maybe she could take Craig Bigelow, my long-time, long-gone ex-boyfriend along for the ride. He'd look pretty good at the bottom of a volcano himself.

No, I don't have ex issues. Notice I didn't say *active* volcano in this instance.

"Truce," I whispered, raising my glass in a toast. Kim smiled, and we clinked our glasses in comradely fashion.

We got down to the business of eating. I was a little uneasy with Baron Samedi watching me eat from his perch beside our host, like a keen-eyed eastern screech owl waiting for his warm, fat dinner—in this case, me—to come trundling innocently along. But after my second glass of wine, I barely noticed him at all.

The yellow cardinal made a brief appearance near dusk. I managed to get a couple of decent shots, despite the lack of proper lighting.

None of the others shared my excitement over the sighting, with Murray Arnold proclaiming that it was "just a bird." Derek expressed some interest, but I knew that was just to make me happy.

Like I said, it was for the best that nobody made a big fuss about the yellow cardinal anyway.

"You've chosen a lovely spot to live," Madeline Bell remarked. She was a mature woman in her late fifties or early sixties, by my guess. Her frizzy blond hair held a trace of gray. A tightly knit braid hung to the middle of her back. "I know I have enjoyed it immensely."

"It can get quite lonely," said the woman at the far end of the bench from me. This was Kay Calhoun. So far, she had said few words. She was of average height with short dark hair and equally dark eyes. She wore a pale blue sweater open over her shoulders. The chest and sleeves were pilled, and the collar and cuffs were frayed. Underneath the sweater, she had on a shapeless dress—pink and lavender geraniums on a black background. She kept her shoulders pulled in tight as if trying to draw into herself.

"Thanks, Madeline," answered Yvonne. "I think so, too. And I am not worried about getting lonely, Kay. I intend to stay busy."

"If you don't mind my asking," said Dan, "what's your occupation, Yvonne?"

"For now, this place." Yvonne tossed her hand in the air. "I'm planning on returning everything back to as natural a state as possible."

"That sounds wonderful," I replied.

"By back to as natural as possible—what do you mean?" asked Dan. He scanned the trees as if counting them one by one.

"Yeah." Derek swiveled his head across the backyard. "This place is about as natural as you can get already."

"Add solar for power, for one thing. I plan to install a turbine for wind power, too. Get some bees, maybe a hive or two. I want to make the yard more wildlife friendly also."

"And bird friendly?" I asked with a smile.

Yvonne lifted her glass and sipped. "Bird and bee and every other living creature friendly."

"Except mosquitos and no-see-ums, I hope." Derek slapped the back of his neck.

Yvonne drank again and set her glass on the table. "I'm going to let the lawn around the house return to nature with grasses that don't require mowing or nasty chemicals."

"I like the sound of that." Dan chuckled. Dan is solidly built, with big brown eyes and black hair.

"I can attest to that," Kim said. "On his time off, Dan prefers working on his old cars to mowing the lawn." She gave him a friendly elbow in the ribs.

"Guilty as charged," he confessed.

"I am going to tear down the old stables and build a green-certified home for myself there."

"What about this house?" Kim was in her midthirties like me, but with long legs, blond hair, and to-die-for blue eyes. My eyes are blue, too, but no one had yet threatened to murder me for them. And my hair is the color of a chestnut woodpecker. Yes, it is my natural color. Those bottles of hair color in the bathroom belong to my mother.

"It will still be here," answered Yvonne.

"Sounds like a lot of work to me," quipped Murray Arnold. I noticed for the first time that his nose looked like it had been carved by the wind into a sculpted sandstone formation.

"I don't mind," Yvonne replied. "I'm ready for it."

"You aren't planning on letting this place sit empty, are you?" asked Ross Barnswallow. "We don't need another eyesore."

"Not at all," Yvonne assured him and us. "I'll run my business from here."

"What business is that?" Madeline Bell wanted to know.

"This and that. My feather craft work. I'm planning on farming and selling my produce. Do some canning and jarring, have a real country store. I want to start an organic farm. No pesticides." She rubbed her hands with relish.

Ruby Lake's newest resident had big plans.

"No, just a lot of pests blathering about toxins and saving the world," muttered Madeline Bell to my surprise. She twisted her napkin and dropped it on her empty plate. "Let nature take its course, that's what they say, but then where will we be?"

No one seemed to feel up to responding to Madeline Bell's comment. There followed an awkward silence until Ross Barnswallow broke it.

"Feather craft?" Ross erupted suddenly as if he couldn't hold the words in any longer. His face turned a mottled purple. It seemed Yvonne had struck yet another of the man's nerves. "You mean bird feathers? That's illegal, I'll have you know."

"I'm afraid he's right," I said, sorry to have to take Ross Barnswallow's side in the matter. I had seen him around town once or twice, but we had never met. He didn't seem like the most pleasant person at the party. "According to the Migratory Bird Treaty Act, it's illegal to even own feathers from most bird species."

"Even when they're fake?" Yvonne smiled.

"Fake?" Kim asked.

"I make them out of embroidery floss and wire. Here, I'll show you." Yvonne rose. She went into the cabin via the rear door. Through the window, I watched as she crossed to an antique china cabinet. She pulled open a drawer and came back outside to the table carrying an intricately carved wooden box under her arm.

Lifting the lid of the box, she pulled out a beautiful turquoise feather. Inside were dozens more of various shapes, sizes, and colors. She handed the turquoise feather to me.

"It's exquisite," I said, running my fingers over the fine, soft threads. "You make these?"

"Yes. I learned the craft in Hawaii."

"I thought maybe you were Hawaiian."

"Through and through. I grew up in the suburbs of Honolulu. Manoa to be exact."

"Me, too," exclaimed Dan. "I'm Hawaiian on my dad's side."

"Seriously?" Yvonne was delighted. "What part?"

"Hilo."

"Ah, the Big Island."

"That's right. Dad's a macadamia nut farmer."

"Cool."

"It's only fifteen acres, but he and Mom love it."

"Do you ever get back?" Yvonne asked.

"Not as often as I would like. Maybe someday I can make it permanent."

I held back a look of surprise. If Dan and Kim were to get married, would I be losing my best friend?

I passed the faux feather around the table. Dan wiped his greasy fingers carefully before Kim placed it delicately in the palm of his hand. "It really is something," he said, before passing it on to Madeline Bell.

To my surprise, Madeline gushed over it.

"It is lovely." Kay Calhoun stroked it like she was petting a cat on the head. I was half-expecting to hear it purr with satisfaction.

And that gave me an idea.

"I'd be happy to sell these in Birds and Bees."

"Would you?" Yvonne returned to her seat, looking pleased. "I'd be honored."

"Sure. You wouldn't have to give me an exclusive. You can still sell them out here."

"Actually, I was planning on setting up an online store. You can be my in-town exclusive distributor," Yvonne said. "How about that?"

"Deal. I'm always looking for local products to add. Like Quiles's honey and Aaron's bluebird houses. Come down to the store whenever you're ready, and we'll discuss pricing."

"Thanks." Yvonne smiled around the table and hoisted her half-full glass of deep red wine. "I think I made the right choice when I moved here. Cheers, everybody!"

One by one, we raised our glasses and drank.

"To a wonderful new friend," I said.

"And her lovely new home," Kim added.

"And birds of a feather," Yvonne said with a wink in my direction.

"If I ever have a house in the country, I'd like to do the same," I added wistfully. "Remodel, go green. Who knows? Maybe one day I will have a little cabin in the woods myself."

"With a bird feeder on every corner," Derek quipped.

"Yeah," Kim added rather wickedly. "And Paul and Esther will be living in your attic."

"Spoilsport." I stuck my tongue out at her.

"You will need a license to operate a business here," Madeline Bell interjected as if determined to find fault with everything and everyone.

"She's right," Kay Calhoun chimed in. "This is a residential and farming area."

"I'll show you the ropes," I promised. "I've had experience dealing with zoning issues." That was putting it mildly. There were those in town who had tried to run me out of business in pursuit of their own financial interests. Fortunately, they had not succeeded.

"A pity to see the old stables go," said Murray, handing the feather carefully back to our host. His eyes were pink. He smiled broadly. "I used to go riding with Del Stenson. That was before my knees gave out. It was Stenson and his wife, Sylvia, who initially built this place," he reminisced. "Fine folk. I was sorry to see them go."

"Not me," Ross Barnswallow said from across the table. "I never saw the man without a rifle or a shotgun under his arm. Stenson shot at everything that moved. No wonder there are hardly any birds or deer left."

"There's nothing illegal about a man hunting on a man's own property," Dan said.

"Did they move away?" Kim inquired, looking to move the conversation to more pleasant ground.

Murray shook his head in the negative. "If you call heaven away. Sylvia passed some years ago. Stenson went nearly two years ago."

"He didn't die here in the house, did he?" Yvonne wanted to know. She appeared uneasy. I didn't blame her. I'd had a dead body in my house once—two dead bodies, actually—and the images of them still showed up in my nightmares on occasion.

"No, it was a hunting accident." I was surprised to hear the answer come from Dan.

"That's right," Ross Barnswallow said, sounding rather happy about it. "Shot dead in the woods by another hunter. Right through the heart." He stabbed his fork into the yellow lump of potato salad on his plate. "Karma, if you ask me."

"That's horrible," said Kim.

"A freak accident." Dan patted her thigh. "Those things happen." As a police officer, he'd seen his share of accidents and deaths.

"If you ask me, it wasn't a freak accident, it was a freak that shot him."

My jaw went slack as I looked at Kay Calhoun. That was more words in one sentence than she'd said all through dinner. And those words were a doozy. "You mean somebody shot Mr. Stenson on purpose?"

"No, Amy," Dan jumped in before Kay Calhoun could make a reply. "It was an accident, plain and simple. I was here, and I remember the investigation."

"So there *was* an investigation?" I leaned closer to Dan.

"Relax, Amy. Don't start." Dan knew I had a slight tendency to poke my nose into any suspicious deaths. "There's always an investigation in an unattended death. Right, counselor?"

"I'm afraid Dan's correct," Derek said. "Besides, this is a housewarming party, not the convening of a grand jury. How about we change the subject?"

Why was he looking only at me when he said that?

Murray Arnold nodded sagely. "Not a soul walked this earth who would've wanted Stenson dead." With that he brought his glass to his lips and drank. Murray was a gangly fellow who towered over me when he had shaken my hand earlier. He kept his fingernails short, and wisps of light brown hair covered only the sides of his head. His nose was long and bent.

Not wanting to ruin the evening by bringing up the possibility of foul play in Stenson's demise, I changed the subject. "Are there any horses still?" I asked.

"No," answered Yvonne. "And I don't plan on purchasing any."

"A man the next county over bought the whole lot of them after the Stensons passed on," Ross Barnswallow noted.

"I did look into it. Horses are a hobby I can't afford." Yvonne offered Derek a second helping of potato salad, which he refused. "The cost of feed alone would break my bank. Now I understand the expression 'eats like a horse.' Not to mention the vet bills."

"I don't believe keeping horses is that expensive, Yvonne," replied Madeline. "Perhaps you might consider it? In fact, you could stable horses for other owners in the area. Make a tidy little profit."

I was surprised by Madeline Bell's approval of Yvonne running a riding stable but not a small market, but I said nothing. The woman was a bundle of contradictions.

"And offer riding lessons," suggested Dan.

"Sylvia loved her horses," reminisced Murray.

Yvonne frowned in consideration. "I suppose I could give it some thought. I've got a contractor coming out tomorrow. I'll see what he says."

"Who is it?" I asked.

"CC Construction."

"That's Cash Calderon. You'll adore him," I said.

"I take it you know him?"

"He's done a lot of renovations for me and my mother over the years." I explained some of the work he had completed restoring my house, as well as the projects he had done on our family home previously.

"If you do decide that the stables need to go, say the word. I helped build them myself. I reckon I can disassemble about as well as I can assemble," Murray said.

"I'll be sure to do that," replied Yvonne.

"Save you a few dollars on demo costs," Murray said with an accompanying wink.

"I suppose us neighbors should stick together." Ross Barnswallow flapped his napkin in front of his face and gave each of his neighbors a stern look. "You can count on me."

"I wouldn't be in a hurry, Ms. Rice." Madeline Bell plucked the last bit of burger from her bun and dropped it on her tongue. She swallowed. "You know what they say: haste makes waste."

With that she hurled the rest of her burger bun toward a pine tree and licked her fingers. A pair of crows descended on it hungrily.

I opened my mouth to admonish her—bread isn't really good for birds—but one warning look from Kim and I held back. Though I reserved the right to have a quiet word with Madeline Bell about the practice another time.

"I must say, for as old as the stables are, they do have a certain charm," Yvonne said.

"Why tear them down then?" Dan wanted to know. "Just remodel. Add on."

"I had an engineer out," explained Yvonne. "He tells me the stables are unsafe and that it would cost a pretty penny to restore them. Besides, the little knoll they are sitting on is the best location for the wind tower and the solar panels."

"Can't you place the tower near the house here and stick the panels on the roof?" Kim asked.

"Too many trees."

"You could cut them down," Kay offered.

"Too expensive," replied Yvonne. "Besides, I'd feel bad doing that."

"As you rightly should," was Ross Barnswallow's reply.

I nodded. The cabin was on a fairly wooded section of the property. "You know, Yvonne…"

"Yes?"

"I was just thinking. Stop me if I'm being too forward, but from the way you talk—"

"Spit it out already, Amy," Kim said across the table. "Dessert is getting cold."

Yvonne had promised us warm homemade pie.

I resisted sticking my tongue out at my best friend a second time. If we had been alone, yes, but it just wasn't done at a dinner party.

"Audubon North Carolina has been working with property owners to restore their lands for birds. Species like the golden-winged warbler have been struck particularly hard by habitat loss."

"That's a wonderful idea!" Yvonne grinned broadly. "Do you think you can help?"

"I'd love to."

"What is this golden-winged warbler?" Ross Barnswallow wanted to know.

"It's a small silvery bird with splashes of gold on its head and wings."

"I believe I have seen them around," Murray Arnold said.

Ross Barnswallow said he thought he had too.

"They are about four inches long and don't weigh more than a third of an ounce—about the weight of two quarters," I added. "The golden-winged warblers breed primarily in open, scrubby areas of young forests."

I further explained how the birds typically lay three to six eggs in cup-shaped nests concealed in weeds on or near the ground.

"I read that approximately one thousand golden-winged warblers breed in western North Carolina. It is critically important that we work to protect warbler habitat to ensure their survival."

"Boring." Madeline slapped her palm lightly against her lips.

"What you describe doesn't sound like anything around here," replied Yvonne. "Though I haven't begun to explore the entire property yet."

"I agree," I said. "But with a little work, you could open up some of your land. Make it a suitable habitat for warbler populations."

"What about…" Yvonne hesitated. "…other birds?"

I got her drift. "Don't worry. You can keep plenty of appropriate habitat for all sorts of birds—gray, red, yellow, black, you name it."

"Then consider it done," Yvonne said firmly.

"I'll help, too," Kim agreed, to my amazement. She wasn't the world's biggest birder—or volunteer laborer, for that matter.

"Me, too," Dan said, no doubt feeling duty bound. "Just don't ask me to mow the lawn."

Derek said something to similar effect. He lives in an apartment above his in-town law office, conveniently absolving himself of lawn-mowing obligations. Cousin Riley mowed the tiny patch of grass in the front yard of Birds & Bees for me.

"Count me out," said Ross Barnswallow. "I don't like it."

"What's not to like?" Kim wanted to know.

"I believe nature should be left to take care of itself." He pointed his finger at each one of us in turn. "There's a balance to the world, and people shouldn't go around upsetting it."

"We're only trying to help," Yvonne countered.

"Yeah, what's wrong with that?" asked Murray.

"I felt a drop of rain," said Derek, looking up at the darkening sky.

I followed his gaze. The sky did look gray, but I had a feeling he'd invented the drop as a way of neutralizing the topic of conversation.

Yvonne glanced upward and bobbed her head. "Let's go inside, everybody." She rose, picking up her plate and utensils. "We'll have dessert by the fire." She tucked Baron Samedi under her arm.

Personally, I would have chucked him into the woods.

3

"You don't have to ask me twice." Derek stood and began clearing items from the picnic table.

I grabbed my purse, camera, and binoculars. The bluebird house would survive a little rain. It was built for the outdoors.

Prancing toward the house, Yvonne glanced over her shoulder. "Who's ready for apple-rhubarb pie?"

We made our way quickly to the cabin and crowded together inside near the door, shaking ourselves dry.

The interior of the home was in shadows. Yvonne went around turning on lamps. "Have a seat at the table, everyone." The sitting room was largish for the size of the cabin. The dining table wasn't far from the fireplace. A pair of wooden end tables flanked a sofa and chair.

Several dark paintings depicting hunting scenes hung on the walls. Various brighter, more modern pieces of art, including more embroidery floss feathers, were placed casually around the room on tables and shelving.

"I'm afraid I haven't done much redecorating," Yvonne said, as if reading our thoughts. "Almost all of the furnishings you see came with the house. One of these days, I'll replace or refinish things more to my taste."

"I think the place looks great." Dan pulled out a chair at the big round dining table for Kim and sat next to her.

Moving to the kitchen, Yvonne conveyed two golden-crusted pies to the table. "I hope you like it. I bought all the apples and rhubarb at your farmers market downtown."

"I've never met a pie I didn't like." Dan wet his lips.

"I'll get some plates," I said, rising and crossing to the glass-doored cupboard. Derek grabbed the forks and a stainless-steel pie knife.

"Thanks." Yvonne sliced up the pie, and I passed the plates around the table.

"This is awesome," commented Kim.

"How do you all know one another?" I asked as we devoured the sweet dessert. "I'm going to need the recipe for this. You could probably get Moire Leora to sell these at the diner." Moire Leora Breeder owned Ruby's Diner in town.

"To answer your question," Madeline Bell said as she cut a precise little sliver off her wedge and pushed it to the edge of her plate, "we all live nearby here at the pond."

"The pond?" Derek said.

He was a relative newcomer to Ruby Lake, having moved to our town to practice law with his dad. Derek's ex-wife and daughter, Maeve, also lived in town. His former wife's name is also Amy. I call her Amy-the-ex when I am feeling generous, and I call her things that I can't commit to paper when I am feeling less so.

Add to that the fact that she had the audacity to open a bridal store immediately next door to Derek's law office, and you could see why she and I weren't sipping cappuccinos over mani-pedis on Wednesdays, down at Spring Beauty, the salon where my cousin Rhonda, Riley's twin sister, wields her shears.

"It's a small community called Webber's Pond," Ross Barnswallow explained.

"There are a number of cabins nearby. I believe they were all built by the same developer back in the forties. Except for this property. I suppose the owner wouldn't sell." Yvonne passed around a pot of tea. "At least, that's what the real estate agent told me."

"That sounds about right," Kim said. She should know. She was a former real estate agent.

"Right after the Second World War, a developer named Webber purchased the property the pond was situated on and built a handful of small bungalows," Murray Arnold added.

"Sounds charming," I said.

We managed to keep the conversation light and easy. Dessert was too good to spoil with any unpleasantness.

Derek yawned and tilted back in his chair.

Kay Calhoun rose quietly. A small black ribbon atop her head stemmed the flow of her cascading bangs. "I should be going." She had left a chunk of flaky crust on her plate.

The sun had set. Through the mullioned windows, stars twinkled silently. The threatening rainstorm hadn't come. The foreboding silhouette of the Lord of Death sneered at me from the mantel of the fireplace. Yvonne had positioned him there in what she called a place of honor.

I felt a little bad for Yvonne ending up with the Baron, but to balance it out, I felt a little good for myself and Kim.

"You can't go yet," protested Yvonne. "We haven't played my favorite game."

Derek winced. He wasn't big on party games. I had forced him into a game of charades with friends one evening, and he hadn't forgiven me yet. Like it was my fault he couldn't figure out my miming *Gone with the Wind*.

"What game is that?" Kim carried her dirty plate to the kitchen. Dan followed suit.

"I'll show you." Sliding open the side table drawer, Yvonne reverently extracted a yellowed wooden board approximately a foot by a foot and a half in size. Its corners were cut sharp, making it technically an octagon.

"A Ouija board?" Derek peered at it as if it were some exotic specimen from a museum collection.

"Here's the planchette." Yvonne reached into a second drawer and drew out a heart-shaped wooden object with a window in the top of it and three slender supporting legs at the corners.

"Sorry," said Kay, taking one ugly look at the thing. "But I really must be going."

"Me, too." Ross rose and limped toward the door. I had noticed he favored his left leg.

"Please, stay," Yvonne urged.

Kim fingered the planchette. "This thing looks old."

"It is," replied Yvonne. "Early nineteen hundreds. It is an original William Fuld model." She ran her hand over the surface. "It's made of yellow pine."

Like all Ouija boards I had seen, this one had the letters of the alphabet stenciled across it in two arched rows. The numerals one through nine, plus zero, ran beneath the letters. The numbers and letters were faded and worn, some more than others.

An image of the sun sat in the upper-left-hand corner, and next to it was written the word *Yes*. An image of the moon occupied the upper-right corner with the word *No* written beside it.

I could see by Derek's expression that he was leaning heavily toward *No* himself. Fortunately, I also knew he was too much a gentleman to say so.

"Did you know Mr. Fuld died in a freak accident?" Yvonne reported. "He fell off the roof of his factory."

"Fell or was pushed by a disgruntled Ouija player who had received bad news from the spirit world?" Derek grumbled. I stifled any further response from him with a look.

Ross Barnswallow returned to his chair. "No offense, Yvonne, but this is stupid."

"I haven't played Ouija since I was a teenager," I said. "Remember, Kim?" Our board had been made of cardboard and the planchette of plastic.

Kim grinned. "We used to have slumber parties, watch old movies—mostly musicals because Amy was obsessed with them."

I raised my hand. "Guilty as charged."

"We played board games like Life and Monopoly. We were absolutely convinced that what happened in those games was going to foreshadow our futures," Kim went on. "The Ouija board promised us all we'd marry rich and have lots of children." She laughed. "I can't believe how silly we all were."

"That could still prove to be half true," Dan said, snaking an arm around her waist. "Just say the word."

"Cool your engines, stud." Kim pushed his arm away. "I'm game. For a game of Ouija, that is." She shot a smile Dan's way. "We can talk about the rest later. In private." She pressed her index finger to his lips, and he kissed it.

Murray folded his hands under his chin. "I suppose one game couldn't hurt. Come on, Kay. It is the neighborly thing to do."

"You are right." Kay Calhoun fell into her chair. "I've never played." She shoved her seat closer to the table. "What do we do?"

"First, let me dim the lights."

Lights out but for the glow of the fire, we settled around the table as Yvonne explained the workings of Ouija. Talking boards—or spirit boards, as they were sometimes called—have been around for a very long time and have been used in many cultures. The planchette represented the spirit hand and was used, supposedly, by the dead to communicate with the living. "It's really simple. We all place our fingers on the planchette."

"That's it?" Kay said in wonder.

"Shush," said Madeline Bell. "Let Yvonne talk."

"That's okay," Yvonne reached across the table and patted Kay's hand with affection. "We all concentrate as hard as we can."

"And then the spirits come and take us away," Ross Barnswallow sniped.

Kay gasped in a breath.

"Don't worry," Yvonne said soothingly. "Nobody is taking anybody away. The spirits will talk to us. Tell us things we want to know. If we open our minds and hearts to them." She looked at us one by one.

"You mean we can ask these spirits questions?" Murray asked.

"That's right."

"Can they tell me who's going to win the Super Bowl?" Dan said.

Kim poked him in the ribs.

"Ouch. Sorry."

"The spirits are not going to come at all if we aren't serious about this. Right, Yvonne?" Kim said.

"That's right, Kim."

"But how will they communicate with us?" Kay asked. "Do they talk?"

"No, they communicate through the spirit board." Yvonne spoke patiently. "When the spirits wish to tell us something, they move the planchette across the board." Her finger moved over the board. "From letter to letter. Spelling out their message."

"Wow." Dan scratched his head.

"I see." Kay was fascinated.

"Let's get started." I was anxious to see what the spirits had in store for us. Then again, I hoped none of the victims of murder whose cases I had found myself involved in appeared before us. I didn't need any spirit visitations from the likes of them. That would be too weird and way too uncomfortable.

All I wanted to do was to get on with my life. A life that included my best friend, my mother, and Derek—all of whom were living.

After what seemed an interminable length of time but was really only a matter of minutes, during which both Murray and Ross had to be admonished for making snide comments and rude noises, the planchette shuddered.

"It's moving!" cried Kim.

"It-it is." I knew it was nonsense, and I knew it was just our subconscious minds playing games while our nerves shook or something, but it still surprised me when the planchette began vibrating.

The cynic in me concluded Kim was the power behind our little heart-shaped spirit ship.

Yvonne cautioned us to remain calm and to keep our voices low. "Who has the first question?"

We looked at each other's shadowy faces. Finally, it was Madeline Bell who spoke up. "I would like to speak with Jonathan."

"Who's Jonathan?" Kim whispered.

"Madeline's deceased hubby," explained Murray Arnold. "Good luck getting him to talk. The man barely said two words when he was alive. I can only imagine how taciturn he'll be now."

And taciturn he was. Jonathan failed to appear despite Madeline Bell's prodding and cajoling. Although Ross Barnswallow cattily remarked that he probably was there but had chosen not to speak.

I had a feeling that nobody but the host was taking the game all that seriously.

"I wonder if Del or Sylvia might want to speak." Murray Arnold leaned closer to the board. Shadows moved slowly over his face.

Kay hissed.

"Del Stenson, Sylvia Stenson," intoned Yvonne, "will you speak with us this night?"

The planchette swung around to *Yes*.

"Who?"

I felt my skin crawl over my bones and bit down on my lip.

The planchette began moving slowly.

"S-Y-L-V-I-A." I read the letters as the window of the planchette stopped momentarily over each one.

Derek and I shared a look. His was skepticism. Mine was pique. I was convinced that Kim was up to her usual shenanigans, having fun with us, just like she'd done when we were in high school.

"Hello, Sylvia." Yvonne said gently, glancing upward as if the deceased woman were hovering above us. Kim and I couldn't resist following Yvonne's gaze.

If Sylvia Stenson was up there floating around, she was doing a good job remaining invisible.

"Oh, dear," I heard Madeline Bell say.

"Thank you for sharing your home with me," Yvonne said next.

I shivered. Was she really thanking a ghost for sharing her house?

"What news do you have for us, Sylvia?" Yvonne inquired.

Silence but for the sound of flames hungrily eating the wood in the hearth.

Around the table, we looked at one another in the flickering light. It was several moments before "Sylvia" answered.

"G-O-H-O-M-E," the planchette spelled out.

I cast a dirty glance Ross Barnswallow's way. He was the likely culprit.

"Go home?" asked Yvonne. "What do you mean, Sylvia?"

The planchette spelled B-Y-E, then abruptly stopped.

"She didn't stick around long," quipped Ross Barnswallow. "Maybe we should take her suggestion and go home."

I was sure now that he had been the driving force behind GO HOME.

"We are not done yet," complained Kay to my surprise.

"That's right," Yvonne said. "We can't stop until the spirits tell us to." She scooted her chair closer to the table. "We don't want to offend them."

Somebody snorted, but I wasn't sure who. One of the men probably.

We continued. Several others asked mundane questions, such as Kim asking if it would be a hot summer. Ho-hum.

"Isn't there someone you would like to speak with, Kay?" asked Yvonne. The table shuddered.

"No," Kay said quiet as a mouse.

Derek surprised me by asking to speak to a deceased uncle, who told him that Ben, Derek's widower father, would marry again.

I couldn't wait to tell my mother that bit of news. Mom and Ben were something of an item.

"Let's ask the spirits some yes/no questions," suggested Yvonne.

"Good idea," I replied. "Um—"

Dan cut me off. "Will the Panthers win the Super Bowl?"

"That again?" Kim asked.

The planchette moved slowly to YES.

Dan grunted in satisfaction. He participated in several sports-related pools with other town employees.

Ross Barnswallow cleared his throat. "Spirits, are there any secrets you can tell us?"

The planchette vibrated a moment then moved slowly toward NO.

Ross Barnswallow appeared disappointed. "Spirits, will I succeed?"

At what, I wondered.

The spirits did not seem to share my lack of comprehension. The planchette moved straight to YES.

Barnswallow appeared to relax.

Kay cleared her throat.

"Yes, Kay?" whispered Yvonne.

"I think I do have a question."

"Go ahead, Kay."

"Spirits," Kay Calhoun began, "spirits, can you hear me?"

YES.

We all watched and waited. Finally, Kay Calhoun asked, "Are you... are you waiting for me?"

We all looked at Kay. What sort of question was that?

The table jumped. I pressed my fingertips against the planchette as it trembled and shook. Moving all over the spirit board, side to side, round and round in big sweeping arcs.

It came to a stop on NO.

"That was weird." Dan said what we all had been thinking.

Kay, however, seemed satisfied with the answer.

Kim suddenly said, "SPIRITS, will anybody else at this table be hearing wedding bells?"

I jabbed her in the side.

The planchette darted to YES then spelled out the word SOON.

I looked around the table. I was torn between wondering whose idea of a joke it was—probably Kim's—or if, indeed, someone among us was on the brink of matrimony. If so, could it be me? Or Kim?

"Oh, mighty spirits," Murray Arnold began. I could almost hear his eyes rolling. "Are you real?"

The planchette jiggled and moved quickly toward NO but at the last second it darted to YES and remained there.

"This is the strangest game of Ouija I've ever played," Kim muttered to me out of the side of her mouth.

I nodded my agreement.

"Maybe this is a good time to stop. It is getting late," our host suggested. There were murmurs of approval.

"Spirits," intoned Yvonne, fingers lightly touching the planchette next to mine, "have you any final words for us?"

The fire flickered and sputtered, and, I swear, Baron Samedi coughed—okay, maybe it was just the log spitting, but it sounded like a Lord of Death cough to me.

"I think the spirits are gone," Kay Calhoun said.

The planchette jumped as if to refute her.

The heart-shaped device danced as if electrified, whisking from one letter to the next.

Finally, the planchette, dragging our fingers with it, zoomed to a stop at the word GOODBYE, which was stenciled along the bottom of the Ouija board.

"Who did that?" a couple of somebodies asked.

"What did it say?" Madeline Bell asked.

"It was too quick for me," I confessed.

"Nothing but a jumble of letters," said Murray Arnold.

"I told you this was stupid." Ross Barnswallow pushed the planchette off the board.

I caught it between my hands. It was warm to the touch.

"I don't get it," Kim complained.

"What about you, Dan?" inquired Derek.

Dan nodded. His face shadowed by the light of the fire. "I am murdered." He scratched his head.

"What?" Derek said.

"I am murdered," Dan repeated.

"Excuse me?" I said.

"Not me." Dan chuckled nervously. "That's what the Ouija board spelled out."

4

"Are you sure?" Kim was skeptical.

"I-A-M-M-U-R-D-E-R-E-D," pronounced Dan, one letter at a time.

"Those might have been the letters," admitted Madeline Bell, her chin bobbing like she'd caught a trout.

"Could it have spelled something else?" I asked.

"Like what?" Derek said.

"I don't know."

"Everybody think," Kim said.

Everybody did, but no one came up with an alternative to Dan's conclusion, weird as it was.

"I am murdered," I whispered, pulling my hands from the planchette like I'd been burned.

Yvonne rose and flicked on the lamp beside the sofa.

"Very funny," I whispered to Kim.

"Don't look at me," she protested loudly. "I didn't do anything."

Kim was always teasing me about my nosing around in murder investigations. I wouldn't have put it past her to have spelled out that ominous phrase. Her idea of a joke. Kim liked gags best when I was the butt of them.

But if it wasn't her...

"Derek?" I asked.

"Hey, don't look at me, either." He raised his hands. "I was just along for the ride. Speaking of which, shouldn't we be going?"

"Yes." Murray scraped his chair against the floor and rose. "Next time, maybe we should stick to Pictionary." He turned his gaze on Ross Barnswallow. "Or pin the tail on the jackass."

Barnswallow ignored the other man and buttoned up his coat.

Yvonne slid the Ouija board back in the drawer. She thanked us all for coming and promised to come by Birds & Bees soon to talk about selling her feather craftwork. "And I love your idea about making this property a habitat that's friendly to golden-winged warblers," she added.

"I'll do some more research and figure out our next step."

"Thank you all for coming." Yvonne waved goodbye from the doorstep.

* * * *

"What was with Dan?" I asked from behind the wheel of my Kia. The strident strains of "To Life," from *Fiddler on the Roof*, fluttered around the interior of the van.

"What do you mean?" Kim lifted her feet onto the seat and wrapped her arms around her legs. Not the safest way to be traveling in a moving vehicle if we crashed, but I knew better than to say anything. She'd only order me not to crash. "That whole *I am murdered* thing? You think he wrote it?"

"No. Not that. He seemed distracted is what I meant."

Kim agreed. "That's probably because he's got an old friend, an old roommate of his, actually—they went to the police academy together—coming to visit for a few days. He's a little uncomfortable with it."

"Why would he be uncomfortable about that?"

"You know Dan. He's sort of set in his ways."

"It couldn't be because his pal is further along in his career than Dan, could it?" Dan didn't seem like the type to care much about such things, but one never knew.

"You mean like Dan's an officer and maybe his buddy is chief of police?" Before I could answer, Kim continued. "No way. Dan wouldn't care about that. Not that he wouldn't mind being chief of police one day."

"How about tomorrow?" I joked. My relationship with our current chief of police was not the best. I still maintained that was because the one date we'd had in high school had ended badly. By badly, I mean he tried his hormone-induced teenage moves on me, and I responded with a few *touch me like that again and you'll die* moves of my own. Since then, our relationship had been icy. Like Arctic icy.

And if Dan got a promotion, maybe he would stop dreaming about returning to Hawaii and I wouldn't have to see my best friend possibly make that move with him.

As we drove the big curve leading up to Ruby Lake—not the town but the body of water from which our town gets its name and for which many tourists visit us—I slowed the van and eased onto the shoulder. The car behind me honked like I'd committed a major crime, then shot past.

"What's wrong?" demanded Kim, swiveling her head. "Why are we stopping?" She groaned. "Not another flat tire?"

"No. Not to worry. We're good." To save money, I'd been buying secondhand tires for the minivan. They were cheap but not long-lasting. We had had a flat or two as well, literally wearing through the rubber until the air escaped. Air has the unfortunate habit of always being on the lookout for places of lower pressure to occupy. Derek tells me that's the law of physics.

Physics sucks.

"I forgot my purse. I'm gonna have to go back."

Kim sighed. "Can't it wait, Amy?"

"The ring that holds my keys to the cash register and floor safe is in that purse. I have to open the store in the morning, and I need the cash that's inside the safe to stock the till. I won't have time to get to the bank."

"Tell them to pay with credit cards. That's what I do."

"Not helping."

"Borrow Barbara's keys."

"Mom keeps all her keys on one ring, and I happen to know she's taken her keys with her." I had already locked myself out of the house once and had to call Esther. I wasn't about to grovel a second time. "And Mom's on vacation, remember?"

"Right. How about Esther?"

I glanced at the clock on the dash. "You want to be the one to wake her?"

Kim frowned. "Definitely not."

"Then back we go. Besides," I added, "my camera is in the purse. I'd really like to see those shots I took of that yellow cardinal." I had told Kim all about the rare bird after she had promised not to breathe a word about its uniqueness to anyone except Dan. I'd already shared the tidbit with Derek.

"Can't you drop me off at home first?"

I grumbled.

"Come on, it's only a mile or two from here."

I started to protest that each mile for her was a mile each way for me but knew that if I did convince her to make the return trip, I would only have to listen to more of her squawking all the way to Yvonne's house and back again.

Kim wasn't done with me yet. "Besides, this is all your fault for not trusting me with the keys to the register and safe."

"That's because you can't be trusted with them."

"Excuse me?"

"You're always losing keys."

"That's why I keep a spare house key outside."

"Yeah, outside your kitchen door under a flowerpot, which, by the way, I think the whole town—and possibly half the tourists—are aware of. And your spare car key is duct-taped to the underside of your rear bumper. You do know they make little magnetic boxes exactly for that, don't you?"

"Amy Simms, you can be so mean." Kim crossed her arms.

"And you cheat at Ouija," I countered.

"Do not."

We kept up our friendly banter all the way to her Craftsman-style bungalow.

"Your porch light is still out," I noted as I dropped her off. No ugly yellow light surrounded by a cloud of the night's finest flying bugs to greet us.

"I know." Kim climbed out. "Dan keeps promising to fix it."

Wondering at my best friend's inability to change a lightbulb, I pulled my cell phone from my back pocket and dialed Yvonne's number. After several rings, she picked up. I explained to her that I had forgotten my purse and would be stopping by.

"No problem. I'll be waiting," Yvonne replied.

I rang off and dropped the phone in the cubby under the dashboard. I swung the minivan around on the narrow residential street and started for the cabin.

Yvonne's matte black pickup sat at an angle on the gravel drive, as it had earlier. Several cardboard boxes were stacked side by side in the flatbed. The wooden handles of a couple of tools jutted up over the tailgate.

Lights were on in the cabin, but the drapes were pulled across the windows. I pictured Yvonne sitting quietly by the fire, crafting her faux feathers from colorful embroidery floss. My customers at Birds & Bees were going to love them.

Yvonne Rice was fashioning quite a life for herself. Then again, since coming home to Ruby Lake, so was I.

The threatening storm had never arrived, but the stars overhead provided little light. Turning the engine off, but leaving the key in the ignition, I stepped up onto the wooden porch and knocked on the oak front door. It could have used a coat of varnish. The wood was drying out and showing signs of cracking. "Yvonne, it's me, Amy."

The sounds of silence split only by humming insects—was it my imagination or were they singing "Don't Cry for Me, Argentina"?—filled the earth as the Milky Way filled the sky.

A twig snapped nearby, and I jumped.

Probably a deer.

Hopefully not a bear or a coyote.

I was definitely going with deer. A cute little Bambi of a deer.

But just in case, and since I didn't feel like waiting around to become bear or coyote food, I scooted around to the back door and repeated the procedure: Knock. State name. Knock. Listen.

I huffed out a breath.

I really needed those keys. The only thing worse than facing down a bear or a coyote was facing down Esther the Pester.

I jiggled the door handle. "Locked." Not that I would have dared enter uninvited if it had been open. I barely knew the woman.

I turned and gazed at the dark woods surrounding me. Was Yvonne out there somewhere communing with nature?

I had called her from the van less than ten minutes ago to tell her I was on my way.

Bathroom?

I walked carefully through the flower beds lining the back of the house to the far corner. I'd used the bathroom myself, so I knew the cabin's only facility was on the right, with an exterior window. That window was dark.

The sound of a siren split the silence like a jagged knife. I furrowed my brow. What could be happening nearby to disturb this tranquil world?

The siren grew shriller. In fact, it sounded like it was coming straight for me. I ran to the front of the house just in the nick of time to see a black car pull up. The siren ceased, but the red and blue lights on the roof kept dancing in circles.

A uniformed officer jumped out, his right hand on the butt of the weapon attached to his hip.

"Dan?" I said. "What are you doing back here?"

"Dispatch got a nine-one-one call. Since I was still in the area, I said I would respond."

"Respond to what?" I turned my gaze to the cabin. "Is Yvonne all right? Is she hurt?"

Dan took my wrists. "Stay here." He moved toward the house. I couldn't help noticing that his hand was still on his weapon.

What the devil was going on?

"Wait. Didn't you take Derek home? Why were you still in the area?" There was no sign of Derek, and Dan lived miles from Yvonne.

Dan ignored my questions. "Wait for me in your car." He took up a position outside the front door. "And lock your van doors."

"But, Dan—"

He turned and banged on Yvonne's door. "Ms. Rice? This is Dan Sutton. Open the door, please."

I hesitated with my fingers on the door handle of my van. "She's not answering, Dan. I tried."

He looked at me. "You're supposed to be in your vehicle. With the doors locked and the windows rolled up."

I moved even closer until we were shoulder to shoulder. "I tried the back door, too. Besides, with all the commotion we're making between talking and your siren, if Yvonne could answer, don't you think she would?"

Dan blinked then jiggled the front doorknob. "Locked. You say the other door is locked too?"

"Yes."

Dan nodded. "Stand back."

I took a step backward and slipped off the porch. As I rose and dusted myself off, I heard the sound of splitting wood. Dan had kicked the door in.

"Wait outside." All business now, Dan drew his gun and stepped inside.

The doorjamb was splintered. The front door dangled on its hinges. I tiptoed closer and peered inside. The fire was nearly out.

Yvonne Rice sat in the easy chair closest to the fireplace. Spools of embroidery floss rested on the table beside her. An unfinished magenta and gold feather lay in her lap. Her chin sagged, and her eyes were slits.

And, oh yeah, there was a red wound in her chest that needed patching.

5

My hand flew to my mouth. "Is she—" I noticed her knit cap on the floor between the chair and table.

Dan whirled, lowering his weapon to his side. "Damn it, Amy. I told you to wait outside."

I was trembling. "Is she? Is she dead, Dan?"

Dan frowned and laid a finger on her neck. "Yeah." The radio on his shoulder squawked as he called in to report the incident.

"Did she—Did she take her own life?"

"No. There's no weapon in reach. If there was, we'd see it." He lifted the skirt of the chair with his toe, and we both studied the empty space. "Nothing. Besides, from the wound, I would say she was shot from several yards away."

"So it was definitely murder," I whispered.

"You had better wait on the porch, Amy. Anita says Chief Kennedy is on his way." Anita was the town dispatcher. "He will be here in a minute or two."

And we both knew what he would think about finding me on the scene of another murder. And we both knew it wouldn't be good.

I retreated to the porch, settling myself on the simple pine-plank bench beneath the front window. It suddenly felt twenty degrees colder outside. I hugged myself for warmth.

A minute or two later, a police car came skidding to a halt beside my minivan. Chief Jerry Kennedy was at the wheel. But not for long. He hopped out, hitched up his pants, and stomped toward me.

"What are you doing here?" he asked sourly.

He was so predictable.

Looking up at him from my seat on the bench was making me uncomfortable, so I stood. "I was here earlier for dinner. So was Dan. I forgot my purse."

"Is your wallet in your purse?"

"Yes." His question confused me. "And my camera and my store keys. That's why I came back. Why?"

Jerry Kennedy grinned an evil grin. "That means you've been driving without a license. I can write you a ticket for that."

"I was not driving without a license," I shot back. Jerry always brought out the worst in me, no matter how far down I tried to keep it bottled up. "I have a driver's license, as you full well know. I simply did not have that license on my person on my drive here."

I shot what I'd hope he'd pick up on as a meaningful look inside the house. "If you'll let me have my purse now, this whole issue—which we shouldn't even be talking about because you've got a young lady inside who has just been shot to death, and it is catching her killer you should be concerned with right this moment and not whether or not I had a driver's license physically on my person when I arrived—can be resolved."

I took several, long deep breaths to calm myself. And catch my breath. I was winded. Yelling at Jerry Kennedy takes a lot out of a woman. I didn't know how his wife and daughter managed without blood pressure meds.

"Easy, Amy."

I turned. Dan was watching from the doorway. The EMTs had arrived, along with Andrew Greeley, who had pulled up rather ceremoniously in his own vehicle, a hearse—Death's delivery service, as folks around town liked to joke. Painted black, of course, with a soft black leather interior—not that such finery mattered much to the bulk of his passengers, who traveled in the fully reclined position.

"Let's get to it, Greeley," barked Chief Kennedy.

"That's why I'm here," came Andrew Greeley's soft reply. There didn't seem to be much of anything that could rile him, although Jerry did his best to try.

Greeley is a gentle giant of a man who has been around about as long as the dinosaurs. He serves as Ruby Lake's coroner and operates his family's mortuary and cemetery. As far as the Town of Ruby Lake goes, he's got the dead covered—from head to toe to dirt.

One day, hopefully far, far away, he or one of his kids, when they took their turn running the mini-empire of death, would probably be seeing me without my clothes on. Not a pleasant thought, so I dropped it.

"Hello, Amy. This is a surprise." Andrew Greeley wore a frumpy black coat with a high collar and gray trousers with cuffs. Stringy white hair fluttered around his long face.

"It's been a night for surprises," I replied numbly.

"Enough chitchat," Jerry snapped. A stiff brown policeman's cap covered blond crew-cut hair. Jerry still looks pretty much like he did as far back as middle school, with a fleshy, boyish face, squat nose, freckles, and dark jade eyes. His gut hadn't gotten any bigger since the last time I had seen him, but it hadn't gotten any smaller either.

Jerry paused at the door, suited up, and slipped on a pair of crime-scene gloves with far less grace than I'd seen in the movies and cop shows. "Park it right there and wait, Simms. I'm gonna need your statement."

I bit my lip to keep from giving him a statement right then and threw myself down on the bench. But I didn't last long. I peered through the crack in the curtains, watching Jerry and Dan work their way around the cabin, opening and closing doors, poking into every nook and cranny.

I could not see from my vantage point, but he probably peeked in her underwear drawer too.

Andrew Greeley examined the body with slow deliberation while two EMTs waited with their hands folded behind their backs. A stretcher sat on the floor between them. Officer Reynolds had arrived and was photographing the scene from all angles.

Nervous, I rose and paced the length of the narrow porch. Back and forth. Up and down.

I was itching to go inside. I wanted to see what they were seeing—well, except for that underwear drawer. I wanted to hear what they were saying.

What *was* going on inside?

Why was Yvonne Rice dead?

Officer Albert Pratt arrived in uniform and carrying reinforcements in the form of trays of coffee from Truckee's Road Stop, a highway establishment popular with truckers and known for its accommodating, capacious parking lot, hot showers, decent food at reasonable prices, and, perhaps best of all, a no-frills, low-cost bar.

Pratt was an intimidatingly large black man with curly black hair. He had recently joined the Ruby Lake police force, having relocated from New Orleans.

"Ms. Simms." He tipped his head as he balanced the coffee. "I heard you were here. Discovered another dead body, did you?"

"Actually, just to be clear, it was Dan who discovered Yvonne dead inside."

"But you were here when he did."

I couldn't deny that, so I didn't even try. Pratt and I had some history, too. He had once handcuffed me, and, no, we had not been dating at the time.

"Have a coffee?" Officer Pratt asked.

He held out the tray, and I didn't wait to be asked twice.

"Thanks." I peeled back the plastic lid and inhaled. Truckee's brews great coffee.

Officer Pratt settled the two trays of coffees on the now-empty bench. "I'd best get inside."

He wiped his feet on the sisal mat at the door, not that Yvonne would be complaining about him tracking dirt in the house, and stepped inside. I decided it couldn't hurt to watch from the doorway. Sipping my coffee, I leaned against the door frame and watched in silence.

Yvonne Rice's body had been shrouded and placed on the stretcher that Chief Kennedy and Andrew Greeley now said was clear to be moved. I stepped aside to let the EMTs pass.

"What the hell?" I heard Officer Pratt exclaim.

"What is it, Al?" Chief Kennedy approached his underling.

"That thing."

Chief Kennedy quirked his eyes at Baron Samedi on the mantel. "Ugly, ain't it?"

"Hush. You shouldn't say that, Chief." Officer Pratt looked alarmed.

"Huh? What the devil's got into you?" Jerry Kennedy wanted to know.

"That there is the Lord of Death," Officer Pratt explained. He pointed a finger at the statuette. "You don't want to be speaking ill about him. He might put the juju on you."

"Juju?" Jerry laughed. "Next thing you'll be theorizing that he murdered this here young lady. What do you think, Dan? Shall we cuff him? Assuming you've got a pair small enough to wrap around those tiny wrists of his," he added with a second chuckle.

The man was a real card. That card being the joker.

Pratt was shaking his head unhappily. "You shouldn't be making jokes, Chief. I've seen things…heard things."

"That's right, Al," Dan remarked as he joined them. He seemed to be determined to be the lone voice of reason. "You're from Louisiana, aren't you?"

Pratt nodded. "Had me an aunt who kept hers in her cupboard in the living room. Hers was dressed all in black but for a blood-red vest." He turned and looked at the chair where Yvonne's body had been found. "Baron Samedi was looking right at her."

Dan visibly bristled.

Officer Pratt's fingers hovered an inch from the statuette as if he feared touching it. "They say the most potent ones are carved from ancient English yew trees. I bet this one's made of yew."

Officer Reynolds stepped between them and the fireplace and snapped a picture of the statuette.

I eyed Baron Samedi from a safe distance. The yew is known in mythology as the Tree of Death, probably owing to the toxic qualities of its leaves and seeds rather than its being the physical manifestation of voodoo deities.

Jerry cussed. "Cut that out! I've seen and heard enough. Our victim was shot once in the chest with a real bullet, not voodoo-cursed to death." He put a hand on Pratt's shoulder and forced him to turn around and face the crime scene. "Let's focus on that, shall we?"

"Yes, sir," Officer Pratt said reluctantly. He rubbed the back of his neck as if the Lord of Death's eyes were burning a hole in him.

"Do you know what sort of weapon it was?" I asked from the doorway. I could still smell the coffee and dessert we had enjoyed only a little while ago—albeit mixed with the smell of gunpowder and blood.

Jerry snapped his head around and glared at me. "Are you still here?"

"You told me to wait for you."

Jerry frowned. "Outside, I said."

I glanced at my feet, which were clearly on the front doormat. "I am outside."

"Follow me," he said, brushing past me. "Let's get this over with." Back on the porch, he lifted the trays of coffee and set them on the ground after helping himself to one. "Park it, Simms."

I did.

Although I was tempted to tell him that without my driver's license on my person I shouldn't legally be parking anything. It was a good retort, and I intended to save it for another time. One where a murder hadn't just occurred.

Jerry took a sip of coffee, cursed that it wasn't hot enough or sweet enough, took a second sip, then squeezed the cup between his thighs. Maybe it was a form of male birth control.

Finally, the questioning began. What time did I arrive? Which I had already pretty much answered. I've discovered that the police are big on redundancy.

"Did you see or hear anything?"

"No. Nothing. I mean, not really."

"No." Jerry snatched the cap from his head and waved it madly at the nocturnal insects buzzing around us. "I do not know what you mean by 'not really.' How about spelling it out?"

I tightened my fingers over my knee to control my anger. "I heard bugs, creatures of the night—"

"For crying out loud, Simms. Don't tell me you believe in all this Lord of Death business, too!"

"I'm talking deer and raccoons, Jerry. Not hobgoblins."

"So you didn't see anybody prowling around?"

"No. I'd have said so if I had."

"What about out on the main road?"

I thought a moment. "Just cars and trucks."

"No hitchhikers?"

I twisted to face him. "What's going on, Jerry?"

"A woman has been shot, and I'm trying to clue out who the killer is," Jerry said evasively. He twisted his cap back on his head and drank some more coffee. "This stuff's almost as bad as the stuff you make," he spat. "Did Ms. Rice seem scared? Anxious?"

"Do you mean earlier or when I called her to say I forgot my purse?"

"Take your pick. Both."

"Again, no. Both times. Yvonne sounded perfectly normal."

Jerry nodded. "Dan said as much. He said she appeared completely at ease over dinner. He said you played some silly game of Ouija."

"That's right. What about fingerprints, footprints, tire tracks?"

"Who are you, Mrs. Columbo? Be quiet and let me think." Jerry banged his fist against his temple.

I balled my free hand into a fist, tempted to help him with a few well-placed jabs to jump-start his brain cells.

"We know our jobs, Amy. We'll check everything out. It's all part of the routine. I don't expect much good will come of it," he said with an accompanying sigh. "Ms. Rice had just hosted a housewarming party. The doorknobs are bound to be covered in fingerprints, including yours. Not to mention footprints of every person and every critter that was out and about tonight."

He stood and flicked a freeloading moth from his trousers.

I followed him to the busted front door.

"You say both doors were locked from the outside when you arrived, Dan?" he hollered.

"Yes, sir. Amy can confirm it. And all the windows are locked."

"There's no dead bolt. Only a simple lock," I noted. "The killer could have turned the lock on their way out."

"Who would do that?" snapped Jerry. "Why bother?"

"To throw the police off the track. And that's just what they've done."

Jerry huffed and started pacing. "I don't believe it."

"There's more, Jerry."

He turned and glared. "With you, there's always more, Simms."

"Do you want to hear it?"

Jerry worked his jawbones from side to side before answering. "Tell me."

"Where's her cell phone?"

Jerry turned to Dan and Larry. "You guys turn up a cell phone?"

Both shook their heads in the negative.

"What about inside her truck?" Jerry asked.

That was a good question. I hadn't thought of that.

"I'll check it out." Larry Reynolds methodically searched Yvonne's truck. "No phone there either, Chief." He placed his hand down on the hood. "Plus, this vehicle hasn't been driven for hours. The engine is cold."

Larry's a good guy. A bit on the quiet side. He is a shade above six feet tall, with thinning blond hair and a pinkish complexion. He's in his midforties and never been married. Other than that, I didn't know much about his personal life.

Somehow, Larry's brown uniform always looked far more rumpled than those of his comrades.

"So her cell phone is gone, and there is no landline," I said. "Not that I've seen."

"In the bedroom maybe," Jerry said, sounding none too impressed with my observational skills.

Dan poked his head in Yvonne's bedroom. "Nothing. No phone there, sir."

"What's her number?" growled Jerry, aiming his anger at me.

I pulled out my phone and read the numbers.

"Dial it," Jerry ordered.

I held my tongue and did so. I put it on speaker. We held our breaths and listened. The call rang twice, then went to voice mail.

Dan stepped to the front porch and waved his flashlight around. "I don't hear anything."

I ended the call. "So that begs the question," I said to my now keen audience. "Where is her cell phone? She answered my call not ten minutes before I arrived." And sometime between that call and my arrival, she had been shot to death.

"That's easy," the chief said after thinking a moment. "The killer took it. And that killer is Alan Spenner."

"Alan Spenner?" How had he pulled that name out of the hat? "Who is Alan Spenner?"

"A nasty customer," Dan interrupted. "He escaped from Craggy Mount CC."

"CC?"

"Correctional Center," Larry said. "He went missing the day before yesterday."

"And he's been rumored to have been seen in this vicinity," said Jerry, taking back center stage. "If I were you, I'd keep my doors and windows locked, Simms."

I raised an eyebrow in the direction the shroud-covered corpse had gone. "That doesn't seem to have done Yvonne much good."

"The young lady lived alone in the woods and had a two-bit lock."

"You say that as if getting killed was her own fault," I said angrily. "She's the victim, Jerry. Not a criminal."

"Yeah, yeah. I know that. Don't get your shorts in a knot, Simms. It always makes you walk funny."

"You're hilarious, Jerry. Your sense of humor hasn't changed since high school."

Officer Larry Reynolds chuckled. Dan Sutton and Al Pratt knew better, so it was Larry whom Jerry ordered to go trundling through the dense woods and rouse the neighbors to see if anyone had seen or heard anything unusual.

Me he ordered home.

6

The next morning, I was downstairs early. With my mother gone, the apartment was too quiet. And I did not feel like being alone.

I dressed for work and made a much-dreaded stop on the second floor at the door to Esther's apartment.

Paul Anderson and his recently adopted dog, Princess, were just stepping out of the apartment next door. "She's not home, Amy." His hair was damp, and he smelled of lime. The man, not the dog.

My hand hovered over Esther's door. "Are you sure?"

"Yeah. We had coffee together. Me, her, and Floyd."

Floyd was Floyd Withers, a fellow retiree whom Esther seemed to be growing fond of. Floyd was definitely fond of her.

"Rats. I need my register and safe keys."

"What happened to yours? Lose them?" Paul was about my age, with wavy brown hair and brown eyes. Princess was a black and tan hound dog. Like her master, Princess was easygoing. The dog had once belonged to the same fortune-teller who had sold me the Baron Samedi statuette, but, fortunately, she carried none of the baron's Lord of Death baggage.

Long story.

"No." I explained about the murder of Yvonne Rice and how Chief Kennedy was holding onto my purse. "He promised I would get it back today." I wasn't sure how I felt about posting the pictures of the yellow cardinal in light of Yvonne's murder, but I was dying to see them.

Ouch, poor choice of words.

"Wow." Princess tugged at her leash. "If you want, I can let you borrow mine." Paul changed his grip on the leash to his left hand and dug into the pocket of his black jeans with his right hand.

"You have a copy of the key to my cash register?" I watched in amazement.

"Yeah, the safe, too." He dropped the key ring in my open palm.

"Where did you get these?"

"Esther made me copies. She said it was important to have backup."

Princess yipped as if concurring.

"Gotta go." Paul wiggled his fingers at the keys in my hand. "You can give those back to me whenever it's convenient."

He patted my shoulder affectionately. Dog and biergarten owner bounced down the stairs and out the back door.

It was only the shortest of commutes to his business, Brewer's Biergarten next door, where dog and owner would spend the day smiling and greeting the customers and accepting belly rubs from the gushing ladies. There was no telling whether it was man or beast that got the most attention or belly rubs.

I had a feeling the competition was close.

I had just turned the sign in the window to OPEN and unlocked the front door when Kim came strolling up the sidewalk.

Kim stamped her feet at the door and then rushed inside and wrapped me in her arms. Her wool scarf scratched my chin. "Are you all right?"

"Yeah," I answered. Although it had been a sleepless night. "You heard about Yvonne then."

"Dan told me." Kim unwound the eggplant-colored scarf from around her neck and hung it on the coatrack at the door. She draped her fleece jacket atop it.

I grabbed her arm and pulled her to the kitchenette in the far corner of the store, where I already had a pot of coffee and a second pot of hot water for tea and cocoa brewing.

"Tell me what you've heard." I had a package of Belgian speculoos cookies and a box of mixed dark chocolates open on the counter. Both had come from Otelia's Chocolates across the street. The lovely owner, Otelia Newsome, had taken to experimenting with adding specialty cookies to her repertoire. It was bad enough that her chocolates kept me from losing weight no matter how many birding walks I took. Now I had cookies to contend with.

"Dan wouldn't tell me much," Kim said, taking a cup of coffee from me and adding two spoonfuls of raw sugar and a splash of low-fat milk.

I threw plenty of sugar in my cup and then plopped what I was pretty sure was a dark chocolate truffle in as well. It sank like a stone to the bottom, where it would dissolve slowly into a cloud of gooey heaven.

It was too early in the morning to be eating chocolates, but adding it to my coffee made it a flavored coffee drink, not a sinful dessert. That was my theory, and I was sticking to it.

I joined Kim, taking a seat at the second rocking chair in the nook that served as both a spot to relax and read from our small lending library of bird-related reading material and a place to get caffeinated and indulge in some sweets.

"Only that Yvonne had been shot." Kim blew across the top of her cup then sipped. "The poor guy was up all night."

"Is he still out at Yvonne's house?"

"No. He's home napping. I'll go check in on him later."

"Let me know if you learn anything new when you do."

Kim smiled. "Of course. You have no idea what happened?" She knew that I was dying to know what was going on with the investigation.

"Not a clue." I explained, as I had to the police, that I had not seen or heard anything unusual. "I listened to the radio this morning while I ate, and Violet didn't have much to say that I didn't already know." Violet Wilcox ran AM Ruby and was a one-woman news and entertainment machine. "Did Dan say anything to you about a man named Alan Spenner?"

"No. Who is he?"

"An escaped convict. He has apparently been seen in the general area. Violet did mention his name on the air."

"That's going to have people nervous." Kim ran a hand along her leg. "I wonder why Dan didn't tell me. Do the police think he's responsible for Yvonne's death?"

I shrugged. "Jerry seems to think so. Speaking of whom, he promised me that he would return my purse today."

"What is he doing with your purse?" Kim's eyes twinkled mischievously. "Did it match the outfit he was wearing?"

We laughed at Jerry's expense.

Hey, somebody had to pay.

"He claimed that, because it was in Yvonne's cabin, it was evidence."

"That's silly."

"Tell him that." I finished my coffee and rinsed my cup in the sink. "Did you notice anything odd last night at Yvonne's house?"

"No, not really. I mean, the Ouija board. That was odd, I guess."

"Derek certainly thought so," I noted.

"Does he know about the murder yet?"

"I called him this morning and broke the news. I didn't want him hearing about it from a stranger and worrying about me."

"Or worse," Kim said.

"What could be worse?"

"Him hearing about it from Amy-the-ex."

"You're right. That woman has it in for me."

Kim grunted an agreement. "I probably shouldn't be saying this..." Kim's fingernails tapped out a beat on the side of her cup.

"But you are going to." I planted my hands on my hips. "So spill." I wriggled my fingers in come-hither fashion.

"Well," Kim scooted to the edge of her seat, "Liz happened to mention that Amy, Derek's Amy, that is, I mean—"

"I know what you mean," I said impatiently. "Get to the point."

"Liz said that Amy-the-ex is concerned that you are a bad influence on Maeve."

"What?" I gaped at my best friend. "That's crazy! How am I a bad influence on that sweet, little thing?" Maeve was Amy and Derek's child, a bright eleven-year-old. I adored her. Liz was Liz Ertigun, Kim's friend and Amy Harlan's business partner in Dream Gowns, a boutique she just happened to *coincidentally* open next to Derek's and his dad's law office.

I believed the move was about as happenstance as the moon circling the earth last night. Everything, and I mean everything, that woman did was well-plotted. And her goal seemed to be reunification. She hadn't dated a single man since her arrival in Ruby Lake. What was that all about if not a sign that there was only one man that held her interest?

"It seems Amy-the-ex believes you attract unsavory and dangerous sorts. She's concerned for Maeve."

I sputtered, searching for words. "Kimberly Christy, that is so not true." Or was it?

"Has Derek ever mentioned anything like that to you?"

"No, never!"

"Well, don't get upset with me. I'm only repeating what Liz told me."

I groaned. "If Liz is talking, the whole town is probably talking."

"I wish I could say you were wrong, but I can't," Kim said in a really, really unhelpful way.

I blew out a breath. Anger and indignation boiled up under my skin, looking for an escape route. Unfortunately, there was none, and I was on the brink of bursting. "I would never do anything that would even remotely cause Maeve any harm."

"I know that." Kim flashed a grin. "Amy-the-ex is an idiot. Hey, that's what we should start calling her: Amy-the-idiot."

I couldn't resist laughing. "I needed that." I fixed my eyes on my best friend. "Fess up. That was you claiming to be the ghost of Sylvia, wasn't it?"

"Of course not!"

"And writing that whole *I am murdered* line." I shook my head. "You should be ashamed of yourself."

"I did no such thing. Maybe *you* were the one whisking that planchette all around the board. Maybe," said Kim, refilling her own cup and haphazardly adding more milk and sugar, "Yvonne did the guiding herself."

"Yvonne? Why would she do that?"

"Why not? She was the one who suggested playing. And it was her game." Kim's cup jostled in her hands. Coffee hit the floor. "If anybody could move that planchette around the board without causing suspicion, wouldn't it be her?"

I soaked Kim's spill up with a paper towel. I balled up the damp towel and tossed it in the trash can. "And she was murdered."

Kim paled. "Do you think it was a premonition?"

"Maybe." It was certainly worth thinking about. "Maybe she had an idea that she was in danger and it was her way of telling us."

"If Yvonne thought she was in some sort of danger, why not just say so outright? If I was in danger of being murdered, I'd make sure everybody knew. I wouldn't beat around the bush announcing it through a Ouija board."

In such a case, I might just lock myself in one of Ruby Lake's jail cells, surrounded by armed police officers.

I stared out the side window at a yellow-rumped warbler, a species affectionately named butter-butts, diligently plucking sunflower seeds from the bird feeder at the side of the house. A second warbler perched on the bare branch of a nearby hickory edging the street.

"What are you thinking, Amy?" Kim asked in response to my extended silence.

"I'm thinking that we hardly knew Yvonne Rice."

"And now she's dead." Kim rested a hand on my shoulder. "Such a pity. So young. Plus, she had all those big plans."

"And I was wondering whether Yvonne's killer knew her too, or if it really was an intruder who's responsible."

"Like Alan Spenner."

"Like Alan Spenner," I said. "According to Violet, there's a nationwide alert out for him."

"They'll catch the guy."

"If he isn't long gone."

"True. If I were Spenner, I'd be halfway to Mexico by now."

"Let's hope he thinks like you." It wasn't that I didn't want the man caught, I just wanted him as far from Ruby Lake as possible. I was grateful that Aunt Betty and my mom were in Louisiana, far from escaped convicts and killers—possibly one and the same. "I suggest we keep our doors and windows locked at night."

I hated myself for repeating Jerry Kennedy's advice.

"Dan's always telling me the same thing." Kim pulled her hand away as the front door chimed. "Shoppers." She smoothed her store apron and moved toward them.

"You take care of the customers. I'll scoop out the peanut bins."

"You are scooping peanuts *out* of the bins?" Amy said in wonder. "What's that all about? Bug problem?"

"Vermin," I said, without stopping.

"Mice?" Kim looked anxiously at her feet.

"Rats. A two-legged brown rat."

Kim thought a moment, then laughed. "Oh, I get it. Jerry's coming to return your purse, and you're making a preemptive strike."

It was a well-known fact among us that Chief Jerry Kennedy often stopped into Birds & Bees, treating our store as his private snack bar. His specialty was coming just as the coffee was fresh-brewed (how did he know?) and we had cupcakes from C Is For Cupcakes, the bakery downtown near the square. Maybe he had a spy in town.

I did a mental double take. Could that spy be Esther?

No, she had no more affection for Jerry Kennedy than I did. Though for reasons I didn't want to think about just then, I couldn't discount Esther's potential as a spy, even if it wasn't in the employ of our chief of police.

She recently had alluded to a very peculiar past. I still wasn't sure what to make of her claims. After all, the woman still claimed not to have a cat. If that was the case, why was she always covered in fur of the feline variety?

Jerry's biggest weakness was the peanuts. There are two long rows of plastic bins holding various seeds and mixes to the left of the front door. Jerry always goes straight for the peanuts, popping them in his mouth like candy. After he's had his fill, he stuffs his pockets like a squirrel preparing for the long winter months ahead.

Sure enough, Jerry Kennedy waltzed into the store as I was madly emptying the peanut bin.

At his approach, I caught the stomach-turning scent of gunpowder and musk. "Been to the shooting range? Or have you discovered a new cologne?"

Chief Kennedy ignored my barbed question. "Here's your purse, Simms. I don't mind saying, that's a heck of a lot of makeup you haul around." He jiggled my purse by its leather strap.

I snatched it from him. "Thanks. My camera was in there, for your information." I grabbed it to make sure he hadn't damaged it.

"I know. Nothing but pictures of birds."

"You looked at my photos?" I boiled. "That's invasion of privacy."

"No, it's not. It's searching for clues."

"You wouldn't know a clue if it bit you in the butt."

"Are you suggesting we try?" He wiggled his rear end at me.

"Grow up, Jerry. Or is that even possible?"

"Yeah, yeah. Where's Kim?" Chief Kennedy snatched the plastic scooper from me. "Here. To show you what a nice guy I am, I'll finish this up for you."

Jerry began quickly shoveling peanuts from the box I had been dumping them in back into the almost empty bin. He refilled the bin quickly and plucked a handful of peanuts out for his trouble.

Jerry threw the scooper into the plastic-lined box that the peanuts had come shipped inside. These were Georgia peanuts, roasted, shelled, and unsalted—his favorite.

"And I would appreciate it if you wouldn't snoop at my personal effects." I peered inside my purse to survey the damage. Actually, the whole kit and kaboodle seemed as tousled and messy as ever. A handful of strangers could have rummaged around in there and I wouldn't have known.

"Official police business," Jerry said with a guilt-free shrug. "You never said where Kim was." He hitched up his trousers with his free hand.

I watched with a frown as he ate my profits.

"She's helping customers. Why?"

Jerry, although married, has a bit of a roving eye.

"No reason," Jerry said, meaning he was about to tell me the reason. "I was just wondering if she's seen Paula."

"Who is Paula?"

"Paula d'Abbo, Sutton's friend from Scottsdale."

"Dan's friend?"

"Yeah." Jerry was smirking like a six-year-old. "His *houseguest.*" He wrapped the word in finger quotes. "Dan brought her around to the station to meet everybody."

"Right. Kim mentioned that a friend of Dan's was going to be visiting from out of town." I snapped the lid on the peanut bin, catching his fingers as he went in for seconds.

"Ouch! Hey! Careful, there." Chief Kennedy sucked on his fingers, then shook out his hand.

What a sissy.

"An old classmate, right?" I brushed a lock of hair from my eye.

"She ain't all that old. About our age."

"You know what I mean." Since it was too late to stop Jerry from pilfering the peanuts, I went about refilling the rest of the bins. Jerry sometimes ate the safflower seeds but always ignored any mixes that contained millet. He claimed the bits got stuck in his teeth. The man was as fussy as a finch.

One of these days, I'd fill each and every bin with nothing but millet. That would get his goat.

Jerry swung his eyes across the store. Kim's head and the heads of the older couple she was helping showed above the shelves. "Kim hasn't met her yet?"

"I don't think so." I was getting tired of this conversation and of Jerry's presence. "Why?" Jerry's middle name should have been Exasperating, not Jasper.

"No reason." Jerry threw back the lid of the bin and thrust his fingers in deep. He shoveled another handful into his mouth and chewed.

"I'll say this, though," he began, as chewed-up bits of peanut fell like rain on his shoes and my once-clean hardwood floors. "Paula could give Kim a run for her money. Heck, she could give Tiffany over at the diner a run for her money." He cast his eyes on Ruby's Diner across the street.

"I get it." I folded my arms over my chest. "You're saying she's pretty. So what?"

"I'm saying she's drop dead gorgeous. Younger, too."

"Oh? Shall I mention that to Sharon? You know, your wife?"

Jerry reddened and sputtered as he wiped damp peanut crumbs from his official *Hey look at me, I'm a police officer* trousers. I could only imagine what debris and germs those cuffs contained. "You remember anything else about last night that might be useful?" His tone had turned all official.

I didn't let his bluster bother me. Not now, not ever. "No." And I'd given it a lot of thought, too, tossing and turning in bed throughout the night. "I tried calling Yvonne's mobile phone again this morning."

"And?"

"It went straight to voice mail."

"Are you sure it was Yvonne Rice that you talked to last night?"

"Of course. I recognized her immediately."

"It couldn't have been a man pretending to be her?"

"You mean like Alan Spenner?"

Jerry shrugged his reply.

"It was a woman's voice."

"Are you sure?"

"Absolutely. What about the 911 call?"

"That was a woman's voice, too. Anita swears to it."

I knew Anita, the dispatcher, well. She was a friend of my mom's. The woman was beyond reproach. "Excuse me a minute." One of my regulars, Francoise Early, had come into the store.

"Hello, Francoise." She is a silvery-haired widow who owns a small nursery on the outskirts of Ruby Lake.

"Hello, dear. I only stopped in for a bag of seeds and to tell you that you can expect some wonderful blooms this year."

"That's good news." I purchase a supply of bird- and bee-friendly flowering plants from her, which we display and sell in the store's front garden from spring through fall.

"I'm experimenting with milkweed this year, also," she said rather proudly.

"The monarch butterflies will love you for that. Be sure to bring me some plantings."

She promised she would on her next trip into town.

"Would you like some coffee, Francoise? I have chocolates and cookies, too."

I noticed Jerry's face brighten at the announcement. I wished I'd kept my mouth shut until after he had departed.

"No, thank you. I must get back. The bus will be by again in ten minutes." Francoise studied the shelves a moment, looking down her nose through the thick lenses of her reading glasses. She selected a prepackaged three-pound bag of my Bird Lover's Blend. I rang her up at the sales counter.

Taking great pains, Francoise wrote out a bank check and signed it. She turned to Chief Kennedy as I slipped the check into the cash drawer. "I heard about this man running around town murdering women, Sheriff."

Francoise pulled the sides of her navy coat together. "What are you doing about it? Something, I hope." She tugged again and carefully placed her checkbook back in the side pocket of her voluminous purse. I'd seen her carry her Brussels Griffon in that very same purse.

"We are doing everything we can," Jerry said, mustering all his authority and tipping his hat to her. "And that's 'Chief,' ma'am."

She frowned at him. "I do not care what you call yourself, young man. Make yourself a general, if you so choose." She waved her ballpoint pen at him. "See that you catch him, that's all."

"Yes, ma'am," Jerry's cheeks were rosy red, and he suddenly found his shoes very interesting as Francoise worked her way out the door. I waved goodbye to her and watched as she moved slowly to the empty bench at the bus stop.

I loved that woman.

7

When I turned around, Jerry had disappeared. As expected—and feared—I found him in the kitchenette munching on my cookies.

"These ain't half bad." Jerry held a golden cookie up to the light and examined it before snapping it in two with his front teeth like some cartoon chipmunk. He deposited both halves in his big mouth.

"If you like them so much, you can buy them at Otelia's." I counted three newly missing cookies. "That's what I do."

Jerry shrugged. It was his answer to just about everything.

"How about buying something from me for a change?" The man had been in my store on more occasions than I could count but never left with a receipt for a single item in his hand.

"Like what?" He truly looked baffled. "All you've got is stuff for birds."

"How about a feeder or a nesting box?"

Jerry looked at me like I'd just tried to sell him a seat on the next lightship to Arcturus.

"Never mind," I said. Time to shift gears. "Was anything taken from Yvonne's cabin, Jerry?"

"That's Chief Kennedy."

"Okay, *Sheriff*," I sniped, taking the tray of cookies from him. "Was anything stolen?"

"Not so's we could tell."

"Don't you think that's odd? If it was Alan Spenner or even some other thief, wouldn't they have taken something?"

"Did you notice anything particular of value there?"

I couldn't say that I had and admitted so. "But still…" I thought some more. "What about cash?"

"She had fifty-three dollars in her purse."

"That the killer didn't take."

"That the killer didn't take," repeated Jerry. He filled a to-go cup with hot water and stirred in a packet of cocoa. "Where are the lids?" He held up his cup.

I frowned and pulled out a sleeve of lids from one of the upper cabinets and handed him one. "So it was Yvonne Rice who called 911." I creased my brow in thought.

"You talked to Ms. Rice. A few minutes later she called 911—"

"And a few minutes after that she was shot dead."

Jerry frowned. I noticed for the first time that he had a mouth shaped like a mail slot when he wasn't frowning or grinning. "Are you sure you didn't see or hear anything when you arrived? Or on the way?"

"We've been over this, Jerry." I motioned for him to follow me up to the front of the store, and thankfully, he did. "There was nothing, nobody.

"I passed a car or two, a motorcycle, a truck, maybe. But no one near the house. And I did not see anybody speeding away from her house. Could the killer have come from the woods?"

"It's a possibility. We're tracking with dogs. That's a big property, surrounded by a lot of other properties and a conservation area. There's state and national forests beyond that. That's a lot of ground to cover."

"I don't suppose any of the neighbors saw or heard anything?"

Jerry shook his head no in frustration. "Too far away." He reached into the pocket of his brown leather bomber jacket and unrolled a sheet of paper that he pushed on me.

"What's this? Oh, Alan Spenner." I got a chill as I read the name in big block letters at the top of the page. I studied the picture. A shaved-head man with a chipped lower incisor and dull blue eyes faced the camera head-on. He was slack-jawed and glared defiantly at the camera.

"Yeah, Mr. Spenner. Though I doubt he's going around calling himself that now. I'm handing out copies around town. If you see him, you let me know. *Before* you try anything stupid," he added on his way out the front door.

I stood in the sunlight slanting in through the window, studying the printed photo. Spenner looked mean and brutish. Would Yvonne Rice really have willingly let this man into her house?

I would not have.

"What have you got?"

I jumped and snapped my head around, cracking foreheads with Kim, who was peering over my shoulder.

"Ouch!" we cried together.

"Don't do that," I said. I had heard the sounds of a cash register in the background and out of the corner of my eye noticed our customers walking out with bags under their arms. I had assumed Kim was still at the register.

"Do what?"

"Sneak up on a person." I was seeing stars. Nice at night—calm and romantic, even—but not a good thing in the middle of the day.

Kim's pupils moved back to the paper now wrinkled in my hand. "Is that who I think it is?"

I nodded. "Our escaped convict, Alan Spenner."

Kim snatched the sheet from me. "It says here that he almost beat a man to death with an aluminum baseball bat."

"Wow."

"Twice." Kim held up two fingers.

"Double wow." I stood at the door and looked up and down the street. Francoise was long gone. Ruby Lake is a lovely little town with an unspoiled lake and friendly people, for the most part.

Was there a killer wandering among us now?

"Do me a favor and tape that photo in the window, would you?"

"Sure," Kim agreed. "And I'll write on the side here that if people see Spenner, they should call the police first and you second."

"Not funny." That comment of Liz's, repeated to me by Kim and attributed to Amy-the-idiot (yes, I liked the new moniker very much, thank you), still stung.

Kim went to fetch the tape dispenser. "Did Jerry say if there was anything new on Yvonne's death?"

"No. Too early, I guess. Have you met Dan's friend yet?"

"You mean Paul?"

"Paul?" Somebody had their signals crossed.

Kim knitted her brows. "I think Dan said Paul. Something like that."

I watched as Kim affixed the brute's face to the corner of the window nearest the front door. Did she not know that Paul was Paula? Had Dan not told her? Maybe he had told her and she had gotten it wrong, misheard him.

Paul was definitely Paula. Jerry makes a lot of mistakes, but he wouldn't have made that one. "Maybe you should go check on Dan when you're finished with that. See how he's doing."

"This early?" Kim glanced at her watch. "I've barely started my shift."

"Things are a little slow." Tuesdays generally were. "And I can always call Esther if I need to."

"Are you sure?"

"I'm sure."

Kim wasted no time bustling out the door. She had forgotten her scarf, but it was warming up, and she wasn't going to need it.

Hopefully, Dan would have some inside scoop to offer up. Plus, it wouldn't hurt for Paula to know that there was a Kim and vice versa.

* * * *

The next day, the town was abuzz with gossip about Yvonne Rice's unexplained murder and the possible presence of Alan Spenner in our area.

Kim hadn't been back into Birds & Bees, but that didn't surprise me any. Give her an hour off and she stretches it to three days.

I checked in with my aunt and mother. They were safely ensconced in southern Louisiana, busy touring antebellum plantations, swamps, and cemeteries and drinking mint juleps.

"Kim's late for her shift." Esther was with me in the store, running a feather duster over anything that wasn't moving.

"A little," I admitted in my friend's defense.

"A little?" Esther eyed the clock on the wall above the door. The clock face featured birds rather than numerals. The big hand was on the owl and the little hand on the sparrow. That meant twelve thirty in people time. "You ever consider getting a time clock?"

It wasn't a bad idea, but I didn't want to encourage Esther. She was impossible enough at the best of times. "Don't you think that's a little corporate?"

Esther grumbled. "I hope she gets here soon. I have plans for dinner."

Esther is a small, narrow-shouldered, elflike septuagenarian with a hawkish nose, sagging eyelids, and silvery hair normally pulled tightly to the back of her head in a four-inch ponytail. Lately, she had taken to wearing rouge and some perfume from the bargain store out by the freeway that seemed to be putting me off as much as it was repelling the birds.

I cracked a grin. "Would that dinner be with Floyd?" Esther would never admit to it, but I had a hunch the makeup and perfume were on account of Floyd.

"Do I ask you who you eat with?" Esther thrust the long handle of her duster into the apron strings wrapped tightly around her waist.

"Yes, you do. Frequently."

It was Esther's turn to smile. "So when's that lawyer of yours going to ask you to marry him?"

I colored. "Marry him? We've only dated a little while, Esther."

"It has been a lot more than a little while. You aren't getting any younger, you know."

"I'm not that old," I said stiffly.

Esther waggled her finger in my face. "You wait too long and nobody will want you."

"We haven't even discussed the idea of marriage."

Esther knitted her brows together. "Why not?"

I frowned. "I-I'm not sure. The subject has just never come up."

"Huh." Esther scratched the top of her head.

The whole conversation with Esther was making me uncomfortable—on more levels than I cared to count, so it was a relief when the store telephone rang and she bustled behind the counter to answer it. "Birds and Bees!" Esther shouted into the phone.

"I'm going for a short walk," I announced to Esther, who was still engaged in conversation on the phone. I moved quickly to the door. "I'm sure Kim will be along any minute."

But she wasn't.

I took a walk downtown, rewarding myself with an espresso and key-lime cupcake at C Is For Cupcakes, the quaint little bakery on Lake Shore Drive.

I could see the offices of Harlan and Harlan from my seat at the window of the bakery. That meant I could also see Dream Gowns, Amy-the-ex's boutique next door to the offices.

I wasn't spying, but I was keeping my eyes open.

8

Later that afternoon, I was surprised to see two familiar faces in Birds & Bees. Rather, I wasn't surprised to see them, but I was surprised to see the two of them together. Together with friendly—albeit inquisitive—smiling faces rather than locked together in hand-to-hand combat as usual.

"Hello, Lance. Hello, Violet." I untied my apron and threw it onto the open shelf under the sales counter. "I was just closing up for the day." Esther had left to get ready for her dinner date. "Whatever you want, we'll have to make it quick." I myself had dinner plans later with Derek and wanted to give myself plenty of time to get ready.

And soak in the tub for an hour. A bubble bath and a glass of bubbly were part of that well-considered plan.

"I didn't realize the two of you were into birds." I grinned from one to the other. "I didn't realize you were a couple." My finger moved from one to the other.

Lance blanched.

"Yuck!" Violet screeched a squeaky reply. It was an obnoxious sound for a human, but not bad if taken as an imitation of the brown-headed nuthatch.

She was a bit of a nutjob herself. Pun intended.

Lance Jennings was a fairly innocuous reporter for the *Ruby Lake Weekender*, our town's local newspaper. He was about forty years old and forty pounds overweight for his under-six-foot frame. He had a thick nose and wavy black hair, although those waves were slowly but surely receding.

His father, Montgomery, Monty to his friends, owned the newspaper. Monty had plenty of friends. Nobody wanted to get on the wrong side of the man who owned the only newspaper in town.

Monty liked to keep the *Weekender* running with a ratio of about sixty-forty—advertisements to news, that is. Lance was eternally fighting for more news space. So far, Daddy was winning.

Profits over information seemed to be his unwritten motto.

Violet was a platinum blonde with a milky complexion. Whether that was by choice or due to the nature of the long hours she spent inside a windowless radio studio, I didn't know. Her hourglass figure seemed to have rounded a bit since I'd last laid eyes on her.

"We're here to talk to you about Yvonne Rice." Lance whipped out his ever-present spiral notebook and an ink pen bearing the name RUBY LAKE MOTOR INN on its barrel. He had switched to an electronic tablet for a time, but when he lost the expensive instrument, Daddy handed him back his old-school notebook.

To be fair to Lance, he hadn't actually lost his tablet. He, and practically everybody else but Daddy, knew exactly where it was or at least approximately. Lance had had the misfortune of using his electronic tablet to take a photo from the bow of a moving boat. He'd been doing a story on a local tour boat operator.

Oops.

The twenty-two-foot skiff he had been standing in hit the wake of a larger craft. That tablet, property of the *Ruby Lake Weekender*, was now buried in the muck at the bottom of Ruby Lake.

Violet pulled out her mobile phone and pressed the big red RECORD button. She thrust the phone in my face. "Give us your firsthand impressions, Amy."

"Whoa, whoa." I waved my hands in the air and took a step back. "I have nothing to say to you." I looked at them both. "To either of you."

"Come on, Amy," whined Lance. "You know I can't go back to the office without a story. Dad will kill me." He was wearing his blue suit. The one with the wide lapels that looked like it might have been popular in the seventies. He reminded me of a great blue heron, a rather plump one at that. His button-down dress shirt was the palest of pinks.

Violet rolled her sharp blue eyes for my benefit. "Our listeners want to hear from you, Amy." She sported a snug canary-yellow dress and a black sweater. Her heels were higher than a stork's legs.

"And readers," Lance interjected, elbowing Violet to one side.

Violet ignored him. She was used to getting her own way. "You were there minutes after the murder. Describe the scene at the cabin. Tell us what you saw."

I pushed her phone away from my lips. "I'm gonna chip a tooth on that thing if you aren't careful."

"Did you get a glimpse of the killer?" Lance demanded.

"No, I—"

He didn't wait for me to answer. "Did you have any premonition that something might be wrong? Is that why you went back? We heard you were having dinner with her earlier."

"No," I said. "I went back because I forgot my purse and—"

"Did you see any signs of a struggle?" Violet's eyes pierced mine.

"What?" I swiveled my attention from Lance to Violet. "No. I mean, I could see she had been shot, but—"

"And you didn't hear the shots?"

I wasn't sure who had even asked the question, maybe both of them, but I answered no because no was the answer. "And there was only one shot."

"Are you sure?" Lance squinted at me. His pen flew across the paper. Purple ink—what was that all about?

"No." I waved my hand for him to stop writing. "Don't quote me on that."

"So you only heard one shot?" Violet twisted her phone sideways, and I watched the green squiggles as they shimmied.

"No. Like I said, I didn't hear any shots."

"Did the killer use a silencer?" That surprising question came from Lance.

"I don't think so." I was sinking. "But you'd have to ask the police that question. Can they determine such a thing?" I scratched my cheek. "I don't know..." Maybe I would ask Dan myself.

"Could it have been a sniper?" Lance hammered.

"A sniper? Really?"

"Have you talked to Lani yet?" Violet wanted to know.

"Who or what is Lani?" I demanded. I felt like I was involved in a swordfight and it was two swordsmen against one.

"Yvonne's brother. He flew in from California." Violet wiped her mobile phone against her blouse to remove my spittle from its screen.

"Test, test." Green squiggly lines on whatever program she was using danced merrily. Violet nodded, satisfied, and jammed the device back up under my chin.

"Boy, he sure doesn't like you," Lance said.

"What? Who?" I could barely think straight with the two of them on the attack at once.

"Lani." Lance flipped through his notepad. "He blames you for the death of his sister."

"He blames me?" I spluttered. Violet was forced to wipe the spittle from her phone again. Hey, it wasn't my fault. She shouldn't have been trying to shove the darn thing down my throat.

"I've got to get back to the paper and write this up." Lance flipped his notebook shut and tapped the cover with his pen, which he then buried in his shirt pocket.

"Me, too." Violet dropped her phone in her pocket. "I need to get back to the station. Before Joey manages to burn it to the ground." Joey was a pimply-faced first-year community college student who had dropped out of school to become Violet's gofer and doormat.

"What? Write what up?" I hadn't told them anything, had I?

"Come see me if you think of anything else, Amy." Lance slipped me his business card. As if I didn't know who he was and where he worked.

Violet tugged my sleeve. "Let's set up a radio interview." She suddenly beamed. "Hey, we can make it a live call-in show."

"Talking about what?" The door tinkled as Lance showed us his backside. One down, one to go.

"Listeners can call in and ask you about the murder."

"Yvonne Rice's death is an ongoing official investigation," I snapped. "The police are not going to want me talking about it. I'm sure you can understand that, Violet."

She shrugged off my concern about such things as points of law. "We can even talk about some of your old cases."

"Old cases?"

"Yeah, you've assisted the police on more than one occasion, and that's just what I'm aware of since I moved to town and took over the station." She was practically licking her lips in anticipation. "I'll bet you've got dozens of stories to tell."

A sudden vision of dozens of murder victims, stacked up like so many buttermilk pancakes, made me woozy. "I think not."

I gave her a gentle nudge toward the door.

She dug her feet in. "If you change your mind, you know where to find me."

I opened the door. "If I change my mind, I'll make an appointment to have my head examined."

I got the impression my words just bounced off her like pebbles off a brick wall. Violet slung her purse over her chest. "If you find Alan Spenner, I'd love to get an exclusive. Before the police get to him."

I planted my hands at my waist and yelled to be heard as she moved with way too much hip action down the path leading to the sidewalk. "I have no intention of finding Spenner!"

And I hoped he never found me.

Violet's black van, the AM RUBY name and logo emblazoned on its side in couldn't-miss-it-from-the-moon bright red and yellow lettering, stood at the curb. Idling, no less. Didn't the woman believe in air pollution? Her station sure put out enough of it.

Gizmos and gadgets, antennae, and satellite dishes covered practically every inch of the van's roof.

I moved halfway down the sidewalk. I needed to blow off some steam, and Violet was as good a target to direct that steam at as anything or anyone. Besides, there was no one else around, with the exception of some sparrows and robins, neither of which I had the heart to verbally assault.

"If Spenner has any brains at all, he's probably halfway to Bolivia!" I hollered, thinking about Butch Cassidy and the Sundance Kid. "In fact, I'll bet he was never anywhere near Ruby Lake. Chief Kennedy just figures an escaped con makes the perfect scapegoat for the latest murder. If somebody gets killed within a hundred miles of here, Spenner's name will probably be at the top of the suspect list."

Violet slipped behind the wheel of her station's van and rolled down the passenger-side window. "I'm surprised you didn't know, Amy."

"Know what?"

"Alan Spenner's fingerprints were found on the handle of a shed at Ms. Rice's property."

I opened my mouth, but no words came out.

"Call me! Toodles!" Violet wriggled her fingers, rolled up the window, and hit the gas.

As she peeled away from the curb, I noticed she had never changed her Texas license plate to a Carolina one and that it was six months expired.

9

Derek called, and it was bad news. Dinner was canceled.

After listening to his apology and promising that I understood completely, I hung up the phone in the kitchen and pouted.

Maeve was running a high fever, and his ex had called to say that his daughter was asking for him.

What could he do but go?

I couldn't blame him. I couldn't blame Amy-the-idiot. And I certainly couldn't blame Maeve.

That was what was so annoying.

I consoled myself with a frozen mac and cheese dinner and half a bottle of red wine. Next, I went downstairs and retrieved the box of chocolates from the kitchenette. I ate half the box before realizing it and pushed what was left under the sofa. Out of sight, out of mind. Or so I hoped.

I watched a little TV, then dragged my laptop to the kitchen table and fired it up. An internet search on Alan Spenner was just full of lovely words about him and his nefarious exploits. The man had a temper. Of course, there were also plenty of news articles about his recent escape.

Sadly, there were no late-breaking stories detailing his recent recapture— meaning it hadn't happened.

I had locked my apartment door and all the windows. Sure, I was on the third floor, but I was taking no chances.

With my dinner date kaput, I had traded my sexy little black number for a pair of gray sweats and a top from the bargain store. The way they itched, the set had been no bargain. The whole outfit had cost only ten dollars, but I still expected fleece to feel like fleece and not steel wool rubbing against my chest and thighs.

I fell asleep on the sofa watching my DVD of *Dreamgirls*. Ironically, I slept through all the lively songs, and it was the ringing of the phone in the kitchen that woke me up in time to see the film's credits roll by.

I yawned, tumbled to my feet in a haze because my legs were numb and tingling. I glanced at the analog clock on the stove as I hurried to the telephone.

Midnight. It had to be either Derek calling to say good night or my mom, although it was quite late for her to be calling for any reason other than an emergency.

I'd have been happy to hear from either one. At that point, I'd have been happy to get a wrong number as long as it wasn't some stranger asking for money.

"Hello?"

"Amy?" It was a man's voice, but it didn't sound quite like Derek. The fuzz of sleep filled my head as if somebody had filled my ear canals with cotton balls. Still, optimistic, I said, "Derek."

"No, this is Paul."

"Paul?" I looked at the clock on the rear of the stove once more to see if I was seeing straight. I was. "It's midnight. What are you calling about?"

"It's not a what," he answered cryptically. "It's a who."

I yawned and leaned against the counter. "Okay," I said. "It's a who. It's also late, and I'm very tired. Tell me *who* you are calling about, and let me get back to sleep."

"I'll tell you," Paul said in that way he has of sounding annoyingly chipper and teasing, all wrapped in a bundle of masculinity. "When I do, you won't want to get back to bed."

I yawned again and tried to stuff my fist in my mouth. It wouldn't quite fit. "Out with it, Paul."

"It's Kim."

My brow went up. "What about Kim?"

"She's here."

"Here where?" I pictured Kim directly below me in Paul's apartment on the second floor. But why?

"At the biergarten."

"Oh," I said with relief. "So why are you calling me?"

"Because she's been draped over the bar for hours and won't leave."

Silence filled the space between us as I swirled Paul's words around inside my brain. Whatever was going on, it was too late at night, and I was too befuddled to make sense of it.

"Did you hear me, Amy? I said she won't leave."

"What do you want me to do about it?"

"Come get her."

"Is she alone?"

"Yes. Completely. And she's been drinking."

I heard morose singing in the background and pressed my ear to the phone. "Is that—"

"To answer your question, yes, that is Kim. Her idea of karaoke, I guess."

I recognized the a cappella warbling of Queen's "Fat Bottomed Girls."

"She's not that bad."

"This is *not* a karaoke bar, Amy. We don't have a karaoke machine. You know that."

More screeching ensued. Was there a kookaburra loose in the bar?

"You hear that, Amy? Come get her before I am forced to resort to drastic measures."

I had never heard Paul so angry, and that included the time he'd lost a bet to me and had to wear a god-awful dress that belonged to my plus-sized cousin. "I'll be right there."

Hanging up, I grabbed my denim jacket from the hall closet and my keys from the glass dish, a Gatlinburg souvenir featuring a primitive painting of a black bear mommy and her two cubs, which we kept on the table beside the door for safeguarding just such things.

Brewer's Biergarten was mere steps away. An open-air patio stood between Birds & Bees and the main entrance. Despite the portable propane heaters the biergarten employed, the patio was deserted. Maybe it was the lateness of the hour rather than the cold keeping the customers indoors.

I wasn't two steps inside the biergarten when Paul grabbed me firmly by the elbow and guided me to the bar. Large beer-brewing vats connected by a tangle of plumbing were visible through the tall glass viewing windows.

Paul sat me down on a bar stool beside Kim. "Good luck, Amy."

I watched him disappear.

Kim slowly turned. "Amy?" A smile lit up her face. "Amy!" Her eyes were lit up, too. I didn't know if the red had been caused by tears or drinking.

I had a feeling it was both.

I laid a hand over her shoulder.

"What are you doing here?" Kim hiccoughed. "'Scuse me."

"The question is what are *you* doing here?" There was an empty beer mug in front of her. Her fingers were wrapped around its glass handle.

"Paula's gorgeous."

"Ah." I nodded.

"I mean, really Victoria Secret model gorgeous." Kim shook her head slowly side to side. "Can you believe my luck?"

Kim was wearing dark jeans and low black heels and a white blouse with silver sequin trim. A black leather jacket was draped over the bar. "Why did she have to be a cop? Why isn't she out strutting the runway?"

"Yeah, how dare she risk her life to keep us safe when she could be pouting and walking the runways of New York?"

Kim's eyelids drooped. "You're not helping, Amy." She waved to the woman behind the bar for another drink, but I waved even more emphatically for the woman to ignore the request.

"Sorry." I slid my hand from around Kim's back and patted her arm. "How about if we get out of here? We can talk at my place. Better yet, you can spend the night. Mom's away." Kim definitely shouldn't be driving. We had no regular taxi service in town, and the bus would have stopped running by now. It was either Amy's taxi service or Amy's house. "You can sleep in her bed."

"She was giving him a massage when I got to his house." Kim stared at the wall of liquor bottles behind the bar.

"Were they, ah…" I wasn't sure how to phrase the question so I spat it out: "dressed?"

"What?" Kim jolted. "Of course they were dressed! Completely! Sheesh, Amy. What kind of question is that?" She burped. "Were they dressed." She fondled her empty mug and frowned. "Of course they were dressed."

"Sorry," I mumbled. I wasn't quite sorry that I had answered the ringing telephone at midnight, but I was edging that way. Who answers a telephone at midnight? Nobody, that's who. Only people looking for trouble.

And I was looking *at* trouble. Drunken, best-friend trouble.

I sighed. Such things were the price of friendship.

Kim leveled her eyes on me. "They were at the kitchen table. In the kitchen."

"Paula and Dan. Kitchen table. Got it." As if the kitchen table might be someplace else? I kept that quip to myself.

"Dan was sitting in a kitchen chair. Paula was rubbing his neck."

"That doesn't sound so bad." It had been the middle of the day, and they weren't naked, thank goodness. What was the problem?

"Do you think I'm pretty?"

I couldn't help but smile. "I think you are beautiful. Dan thinks so too."

"You think so?"

"I know so. Don't tell me he's never told you how beautiful you are."

Kim shrugged. Tears formed in the corners of her eyes. "I guess so." She sniffed. "So you think I'm making a big deal out of nothing?"

"Of that I am positive." I grabbed her coat and tossed it over her shoulders. "Here, put this on. We'll go home, brew up some decaf or a pot of nice chamomile tea. We can talk some more in private there."

Paul was hovering nearby, pretending to dust beer bottles. Please. Could the man be any more obvious?

Kim complied. She slid off her stool and thrust her arms in her jacket.

Paul mouthed a thank-you.

I nodded.

Kim took a step, stumbled, and glommed onto my left arm for support. "I am acting like a bit of an idiot. I mean, I'm sure if you walked in on Amy—the other Amy, that is—massaging Derek's neck, you wouldn't mind at all."

I flinched but forced my legs to keep moving toward the exit. "Of course," I said rather more tersely than I had intended.

"It wouldn't bother you one bit." Kim's weight dragged on me as we walked.

"Not one bit." Truth be told, I might wrap my own two hands around Amy-the-ex's throat and return the favor, rather forcefully, but I couldn't tell Kim that. Not in her current, fragile condition.

Kim stopped at the door, which was being patiently propped open by the hostess. "Has Derek ever told you that he loves you?"

"Well...not in so many words, exactly." Cold wind shot through the door, buffeting us. We scooted outdoors and began moving toward Birds & Bees. "What about Dan? Has he ever said the L word?"

"Not a peep. Not even a hint."

Our heels clattered against the sidewalk. The streets were nearly deserted. Except for the biergarten and the diner, there wasn't much foot or vehicle traffic in this part of town at this late hour.

"Dan's never even brought up us being exclusive. You know, like you and Derek. You're so lucky, Amy."

I turned the key in the front lock of the store. I'd left the interior lights on. I thought about my relationship with Derek as we made our way up the stairs to my apartment. Kim was having a hard time of it. I figured the exertion would do her good. Help sweat out the alcohol.

Were Derek and I exclusive? I certainly was, and I thought he was too. But it was never something that we had talked about.

Maybe we should.

Inside the apartment, I boiled water for tea and settled next to Kim on the sofa. But by the time I had gotten to my seat, Kim was sound asleep. I plopped a chamomile tea bag in my cup and added a spoonful of honey.

I shut my eyes and took a sip. If the telephone rang again, I was not answering it.

* * * *

I hadn't had the heart to wake Kim, so she had spent the night on the sofa. I had tossed a comforter over her torso and taken off her boots.

The smell of coffee forced her head off her chest. "Ow!" She pressed the palm of her hand into her forehead and groaned loudly. "I feel like I ran head-on into a semi."

"Have a bit of a hangover, have we?"

"I have the mother of all hangovers, thank you very much."

"Don't go thanking me. You have only yourself to thank."

Kim took the coffee. I had made it hot, and I had made it black. She took a comforting sip.

I moved to the kitchen and filled a cup with coffee for myself. I dropped a couple slices of sourdough bread in the toaster.

Kim ran her free hand through her tangled hair and took another sip. A loud yawn followed.

"Where did you leave it with Dan yesterday?"

Kim reddened. "I sort of stormed out." She clutched her head in her hands. "I made a fool of myself in front of Paula. How embarrassing."

I couldn't argue otherwise so didn't bother to try. "Why don't you take them some cupcakes and some coffee? A peace offering," I suggested. "I'm sure there are no hard feelings."

"But I'm so embarrassed," whined Kim.

"Suck it up, girl. You don't want Dan to see you behaving all crazy. Save the lunacy for me."

"Ha-ha."

"Seriously, you don't want to drive him off or scare him away, do you?"

"Of course not." Kim pouted.

"Then off you go." I pushed her toward the door. "Man up, woman!"

"But I haven't had breakfast yet." Kim dragged her heels. Between being hung over and stiff from sleeping on the sofa, she was no match for me. "That's what cupcakes are for."

Kim excused herself to go wash up. Some minutes later, she exited the bathroom, looking almost human.

"How do I look?" Kim fluffed her hair, which still looked like a squirrel had built a nest in it. Sleeping off a bender on a couch was definitely not the equivalent of a beauty rest.

"Perfect." I gave her a big A-OK sign.

"Okay. I can do this." Kim took a deep breath and shrugged into her coat.

I watched as Kim tumbled unsteadily down the stairs to make sure she didn't hurt herself. Seeing she was safely underway, I returned to the kitchen to appease my grumbling stomach.

Stuck with two pieces of sourdough toast, I was forced to slather an inch-thick layer of Nutella between them and eat the entire thing for breakfast.

My life is full of sacrifices.

Downstairs, I greeted Esther. I noticed she already had the lights on and the store open. "I have some errands to run." I smelled coffee brewing in the alcove. "Would you mind handling the store for a while?"

Esther harrumphed to let me know she was being put upon when we both knew perfectly well that she always preferred it when I wasn't there.

She said the store ran better that way. She liked things done her way. I liked things done my way.

Life is a constant battle between pester and pestee.

"How long will you be?" Esther adjusted the ASSISTANT MANAGER badge on her sweater. Every time I saw the badge, I was surprised that she hadn't swapped it for a new one that said CO-OWNER, which she now was due to her investment in the business.

Which was due to my home and business's many needs and my major lack of sufficient funds to handle those needs.

To my amazement, Esther had invested in the business. I had no idea she had any money, let alone enough to invest in my fledgling operation.

Then again, there was lots I didn't know about Esther. Some of which she said she'd have to kill me if she told me. After some of the things that had happened lately, I believed her.

As for the badge and her title, I wasn't saying a word because the minute I did, she'd order herself a new badge. At store expense.

I grabbed my hat and coat and retrieved my van from the back parking area. The interior of the van was cold. I cranked up the heater and the Broadway show tunes.

Music couldn't stop a bullet, but it could soothe the soul.

I had been in such a hurry to get Kim on her way that I had forgotten to ask her if she'd learned anything new about the Yvonne Rice murder investigation from Dan.

Then again, I rather doubted it. She'd had other things on her mind. Plus, from what she had described of the scene yesterday, the subject of murder hadn't come up.

Well, it might have come up in Kim's mind, but the victim she'd have had in mind would have been one Paula d'Abbo, not Yvonne Rice.

I made a personal vow to help Kim with her personal issues later. Right now, Yvonne Rice's murder was weighing heavily on me. I'd learned that the only way to lift that weight was to push back.

10

Wanting to pay my condolences and set Yvonne's brother straight, I drove to Yvonne's cabin, or at least tried to. Construction vehicles and barricades blocked my intended route. A man in an orange vest lethargically waving a yellow flag explained that work was being done on a bridge over one of our many streams. I was forced to make a circuitous detour.

Coming along the snaking road from the other direction, I spotted a small wooden sign half-buried in some tall grasses: WEBBER'S POND. This was the community where Yvonne's dinner guests dwelled.

I slowed. There was a compact log cabin, not dissimilar to Yvonne's, located near the road. The property was narrower along the road front, maybe a hundred yards or so, with the bulk of the property spreading behind in a wedge shape.

I counted five more cabins spread throughout the glen. A rutted, hard-packed trail the width of a set of car tracks went around the outside of the other five cabins, as if stringing them all together like rough stones on a primitive necklace. The other side of the road contained nothing but woodland.

At the first cabin, a woman was bent over in a garden bordered by a weathered split-rail fence. Wind gave life to her light-colored hair. She turned her head and brought her hand up to shield her eyes from the sun.

It was Madeline Bell.

I waved and eased to a stop in her gravel drive. My feet crunched over the loose stones as I approached her. Madeline Bell stood, hands on hips, waiting and watching. She wore a billowy white apron showing signs of dirt and wear. Wrinkled, baggy khakis protected her legs, and a red-and-black-checked flannel shirt kept her warm.

"Good morning, Mrs. Bell." I opened the garden gate and stepped carefully between rows of neatly planted vegetables.

"A good morning for you maybe." Madeline Bell toed the ground with a pair of dusty brown lace-up boots. "Not for me."

"Oh?"

"Somebody has been vandalizing the garden again."

"Vandals? Out here?" I did a turn. Madeline Bell's house was nearest the road. There was a broad meadow with Webber's Pond near the middle of it. A big, wet, tear-drop-shaped stain surrounded by cattails.

"They've tramped over everything. Nasty kids. They've dug up carrots, kale, and my broccoli."

What kids would drive all the way out here to ransack her vegetable garden? And for kale and broccoli, no less. Sure, plenty of kids hate broccoli, but would they spend precious gas money scouring the countryside to rid the world of the green plague?

I kept these thoughts to myself. "I'm sorry. Can I help?"

"No, thank you." Madeline Bell grabbed a hand trowel and eased to her knees in the soil, then pulled her apron down over her thighs. "I have half a mind to sit out here all night if that's what it takes. A backside full of buckshot, that is what they need."

I followed the line of footprints in the soft earth nearest the garden. "I only see one set of prints, and they appear to go into the woods there." I pointed.

A scowl was my thanks. "That's where they go to drink and smoke their pot. They've got a hangout."

A hideout where they gathered to eat kale, get drunk, and smoke grass? Hard to imagine. "Are you sure?"

"What brings you here, Ms. Simms?"

"Call me Amy, please." I wasn't invited to do the same for her.

Madeline Bell nodded as she salvaged some baby carrots scattered in the path and replanted them. "Who knows if these will grow anymore."

"I'm sure they'll do fine, Mrs. Bell."

She grunted. "You did not answer my question. What are you doing here?"

"I heard Yvonne's brother had come to town. I came to pay my condolences."

Madeline extended her hand, and I helped her climb to her feet. "Lani." She wiped her face with the edge of her apron, leaving lines of dirt in the creases of her forehead. "He's as bad as she was."

"Yvonne? I thought you were friends?"

"We were neighbors. That does not make us friends." She waved her hand truculently. "You think just because I've lived surrounded by these folks all these years that we all sit around chumming it up?"

I cleared my throat, unsure what to answer. "Why did you come to the housewarming?"

"I was invited," Madeline Bell said as if no other answer was possible.

"Tell me," I said, following her to the side of the cabin, where she drew water from a barrel attached to the drainpipe extending from her roof, "did you hear anything unusual that night?"

Her fingers twisted the tap shut. She hefted the steel watering can. "All that spirit mumbo jumbo. I don't believe in ghosts."

"Neither do I," I was quick to agree. "I meant afterward."

Mrs. Bell twisted her face my way as she watered a clump of half-dead flowers beneath her kitchen window. "You mean did I hear any arguments or gunfire?" She shook her head in the negative. "I heard nothing." She set the can between her feet. "I saw nothing. And that's what I told the police." She sneered. "I don't think that Chief Kennedy knows his butt from a bullet. And you can tell him I said so."

That was one thing Madeline Bell and I could agree on. It might have been catty of me, but I couldn't wait to tell Jerry what she thought of him.

"You didn't notice any strangers around? Any strange cars in the neighborhood? Maybe you—"

Madeline Bell tapped my shoulder with a firm finger. "If a person wants to stay alive, it's best if they keep themselves to themselves, Ms. Simms."

"As for Lani Rice, he's loud and obnoxious. I hope he clears out soon." She angled her eyes in the direction of Yvonne's place, though it was invisible from here because of a dense wood between the two cabins. "This is no place for outsiders."

I wondered if she was talking about me, Yvonne, or maybe both of us. "Yvonne was shot sometime shortly after we left." I explained how I had returned to her cabin to get my camera and purse. "What time did you get home that night?"

"I really couldn't say. Ask Murray, if you really must know. He was the one driving." She picked up her watering can and placed it beside the rain barrel.

"Murray said that he drove you all to his cabin. You all stayed for a nightcap, except for Ross, who declined and went straight home."

"There you have it. I have nothing to add." She wiped her hands on her apron. "Why are you bothering me?"

"I'm sorry. I only want to find out who killed Yvonne."

"Sometimes killers can't be found," Madeline Bell said. "Sometimes maybe they shouldn't be found."

"I'm not sure I understand."

"If you don't mind, I have some baking to do." She hurried to the back porch, kicked her toes against the step, and climbed. She opened the door and closed it behind her without so much as a goodbye.

I was about to head back to the van and continue on my way when I noticed a man in a wheelchair seated out on a narrow dock at the cabin farther along the pond. He appeared to be waving to me, although I could not imagine why.

I stopped and pointed to my chest. He waved again.

Leaving the van near the road, I walked across the field to him.

"Good morning," I called when I was within thirty feet or so. He was an elderly man with a tanned, unshaved face. His wheelchair was ancient. He wore a torn black parka. A tweed cap sat atop his head. A twisted pipe jutted from between his lips.

Several of the cabins had docks. Whether they belonged to the owners of the cabins individually or were communally owned, I didn't know. There was a small pale green skiff tied to the piling of the one across the water.

This particular dock was bare but for a slender fishing rod and a pail of bait containing chopped fish. What kind of fish I didn't know, and I didn't care to look close enough to figure that out.

Several crows hung near the edge of the dock, no doubt hoping for a chance at the bait. They moved aside as I stepped onto the dock.

"Hello, young lady." His voice was scratchy with age.

I liked him already.

"Hello." I studied him carefully. Rheumy brown eyes looked right back at me. I was pretty sure I had never seen him before. Silvery, shaggy hair jutted over the tops of his ears. "I'm sorry, do I know you?" There was a vague sadness to his face.

"Gar Samuelson. Call me Gar. Everybody else does. If they're not calling me something worse." He chuckled as he removed the pipe from his lips. He studied it for a moment before placing it back in the corner of his mouth, then taking it back out again and pointing it at me. "You, young lady, are Amy Simms."

My brow rose.

"Am I right? I am right, aren't I?"

I smiled. "Yes, you are. How did you know? Are you sure we haven't met?"

"Nope. Never. I don't travel much or far in this." He bounced his elbows against the armrests of his wheelchair. "I don't get into town much neither." The pipe went back into his mouth, and he puffed merrily, like a steam locomotive out for an afternoon jaunt. "But I have heard of you." He leaned over the side of his wheelchair toward me. "You've got a reputation."

"Excuse me?" I felt my cheeks glow.

"You have got your finger on the pulse of what is going on in this town."

"What do you mean?"

"I mean murder."

I shivered as a cold breeze rolled across the dock.

Gar whistled sharply. An Irish setter appeared out of nowhere. The dog brushed between my legs and hurried to his master's side, where he was greeted with a vigorous scratching of his chin. Tail wagging, the dog followed his nose to the bait bucket. At a word from Gar, the dog retreated obediently and settled for chasing the crows around the edge of the water.

"Pep's a good boy." Gar followed his energetic dog with love in his eyes. "Keeps me good company. All the company I need anyway."

I stuffed my hands in the pockets of my coat to take the chill off. "Why weren't you at Yvonne Rice's housewarming party?"

"Oh, I was invited." Using his left hand, he extracted a black, leather-covered flask from his inner pocket. He unscrewed the lid and pushed it my way. "A drink?"

"No, thank you."

"Irish whiskey." He put the flask to his lips and tipped back his head. "Ah. Just what the doctor ordered."

"I'd like the name of your doctor," I said with a laugh. "Mine tells me that drinking, smoking, eating too much sugar, pretty much having any fun at all is going to kill me."

"Don't listen to him then, Amy. Can I call you Amy?"

"Of course."

"You're young and healthy. You enjoy yourself. I may be stuck in this contraption, but I am not dead. I'm going to live forever. Just like my pappy."

He took another sip of whiskey as if to prove his point. He stuffed the flask back into his pocket. "I sit here and the world comes to me. I see things and I hear things."

Gar pointed to his eyes and ears. "Write it all down, I do. If it's important. Hand me that pole, would you?"

I picked up the slender fishing rod and handed it to him. "Would you like me to bait the hook for you?"

"Nah. That won't be necessary."

That was a relief. He rolled over to the bait bucket and placed a chunk of raw pink flesh on the end of a hook. With a smooth and efficient move of the arm, Gar flung the line out into the center of the pond. From the edge of the pond, Pep barked as if applauding the cast.

"You mentioned murder," I said.

"That I did," Gar said crisply. He folded his hands in his lap with the end of the fishing rod firmly between his legs. His eyes fixed on the point where the line had disappeared into the water.

"So you heard about the shooting?"

"Of course. Who hasn't? The police came by twice to question me and all the rest of us out here. For all I know, they've questioned everyone in the county."

"Chief Kennedy thinks an escaped convict named Alan Spenner is responsible."

"That could be so," Gar replied. "Someone has killed Yvonne. Someone should take the blame. That's the way it is supposed to work, isn't it?"

I agreed. How could I not? "Did you know Yvonne?"

"She came along to introduce herself. Invited me to her housewarming party about ten days or so later. I thanked her for the invitation."

"But you declined."

"That's right. Like I said, I don't socialize much."

"What about the others?"

"You mean my neighbors?"

I nodded.

"What about them?"

"Do you know them well? Even if you don't like to socialize much, as you say, you must be well acquainted with them."

"I've been neighbors with most of them for twenty years or more. Barnswallow over there," he pointed across the pond, "is the newest, and he's been here a decade or so himself. He's always on the warpath about one thing or another. Always banging on my door trying to get me to sign one of his petitions.

"The next cabin along after mine belongs to Kay Calhoun." He shifted his position. "That's Murray Arnold's place with the big yellow station wagon parked alongside it. And, of course, you visited with Madeline Bell already."

"She said some teenagers pillaged her garden."

Gar snorted and thumped his pipe against the tire of his wheelchair. "I suspect Madeline's grip on reality isn't quite holding."

"How do you mean?"

"Nothing. Forget I said anything." Gar sighed heavily. "I'm an old man. My grip on reality may be no more firm than anybody else's around here." He spat into the pond.

"I find that hard to believe." I wondered what had caused him to be in the wheelchair and how long he'd had to use it but did not dare ask.

"For instance, Kay," he turned his neck in the direction of Kay Calhoun's cabin, "she believes in fairies. Leaves them treats outside her front door at night."

"Sounds harmless."

"She is. But she says they eat them." Gar watched my face for a reaction.

"Raccoons?" I suggested.

"That's my guess. Then there's Barnswallow." He maneuvered the wheelchair toward the cabin across the pond. "There's something about him that concerns me."

"What's that?"

"Probably nothing. Some folks seem to have a cloud over them. He's one of those people."

"And Mr. Arnold?"

"Murray?" Gar wiped bits of tobacco from his lap to the dock. "He's the only one around here with any sense. Keeps himself to himself for the most part, although he is sort of the designated handyman around here. He's done a few jobs for me and done them well. Repaired the shingles on my roof after the tornado blew through here three years back. Fixed my kitchen sink when the pipe burst."

"He sounds like a good man to have around."

"I suppose he isn't completely useless. It is hard to get tradespeople to come out this far for small jobs."

That sounded like high praise coming from Gar Samuelson. "I don't suppose you've seen any strangers around?" I asked.

"Nope." There was a tug at the fishing line. Gar cursed and gripped the rod tighter. I watched as he reeled his catch up to the dock. Bending over and plucking the foot-long fish from the hook, he remarked, "Catfish. I don't care much for catfish, but Pep likes them." He deftly plucked the struggling fish from the hook and dropped it into the bait bucket.

I thanked Gar Samuelson for his time and gave Pep a friendly pat. "Who lives out there?" I pointed to the cabin at the far side of the pond. It stood relatively removed from the others and appeared neglected.

"The old Fritsch place? It's been empty for years."

"Did the police check it?"

He grinned. "You think Spenner might be hiding out there?"

"It has crossed my mind."

"Two police officers checked it out. It was empty. I told them it would be."

"You seem to know everything."

"About this place?" Gar tapped his pipe against the side of his chair. "I know most. Not all. This place holds its secrets close to its chest." He looked at me carefully. "We aren't all what we seem."

"Care to share?"

"No," he said flatly. "Wrote a story about it once, though. Sort of a diary."

"You are a writer?"

"Hardly." Gar brushed tobacco from his jacket. "You might say I wrote it for my own preservation."

"You mean satisfaction?"

"Yeah, that too." A smile appeared. "You might call it my *buried* treasure." His accompanying hearty laugh turned into a cough. Red-faced, he took another drink of his whiskey.

"I'd like to read it sometime."

"Who knows? Things are changing fast," he said, eying the sky cryptically. "You should go."

Dismissed, I thanked him once again for his time.

He nodded and rubbed his chin sagely. "You take care, Amy. Sometimes a body is dead," he intoned, his eyes falling on the fish flopping noisily, desperately—yet in the end, futilely—in the bait bucket, "and it doesn't even know it."

I promised I would and headed toward shore.

11

On those ever so slightly chilling words, I returned to my van.

Had Gar Samuelson's last words been a warning? A threat?

Murray Arnold was walking slowly behind a gas-driven lawn mower. Puffs of blue smoke came spitting from the engine's exhaust. Shredded green confetti shot out the side of the grass chute.

He waved to me as I passed.

I stopped at the edge of the road as he came toward me in long strides, having left his mower sitting in the middle of the lawn. "Good morning, Murray."

"Hello, Amy." He pulled off a red knit cap and ran his arm over his damp forehead. He smelled of fresh-mown grass. "Any news on Yvonne's murder?"

"Nothing that I've heard. I was just going to pay my condolences to her brother, Lani."

Murray wiped his neck with a red handkerchief. "Mind if I come along? I've been meaning to pay my respects as well."

I said, "Of course," and waited a minute while Murray hurried inside. He washed quickly and threw a brown flannel jacket over his green flannel shirt.

"What did you think of Gar?" Murray asked as we bounced along the narrow road leading to Yvonne's cabin.

"He's very...colorful."

Murray chuckled. "That he is. He's an old goat, but he's a friendly old goat."

"How did he end up in a wheelchair?"

"I believe it was a stroke. He lost the use of his legs."

"I'm sorry."

Murray shrugged. "He seems to have compensated well. What he lacks in leg power he makes up for with upper-body strength."

"Really?" Gar hadn't looked all that strong.

"Yes. You ought to see him when he's out here shooting his bow. He bends it like it's made of butter."

"He enjoys archery?"

"He enjoys hunting."

I was having a hard time picturing Gar Samuelson trudging through the woods during hunting season with a wheelchair attached to his butt.

Murray must have read my thoughts because he said, "He doesn't go much farther than the edge of the woods. He sits there, silently, patiently, with Pep at his side. Waiting, just watching and waiting. Then, when a deer comes—" Murray pretended to pull back a bow, banging his elbow against the passenger side window. "Ouch."

He rubbed his elbow, then pulled back his imaginary bow once more, angling side to side, then shouted, "Twang!"

I pictured Gar sitting in his wheelchair, puffing on his pipe, chugging Irish whiskey, with herds of deer skittering past and mocking him. "Is he any good? I mean, has he ever hit anything?"

"He's a crack shot. I've seen Gar drop more than one buck. From a hundred yards or more. He's asked me and Barnswallow to help drag them back to his cabin for him. You have no idea how heavy a full-grown deer can be."

Murray stuck his hand between himself and the seat. "My back hurts just thinking about it."

Half-watching the road and half-watching Murray's antics, I almost missed Yvonne's cabin and was forced to slam on the brakes.

"Sorry," I said as Murray threw his hands against the dashboard.

"No problem. Who are they?" He squinted out the window. "Wish I'd worn my glasses."

I followed his gaze to where several young men in jeans and leather jackets sat on the bench and front steps. Two had acoustic guitars in their hands. The third fellow, seated on the top step, had a pair of fancy bongo drums stuck between his knees.

"Aloha!" The musician banged out a rhythm on his drums with the sides of his hands. The drums had been fashioned from highly prized koa wood and finished with steel hardware polished to a mirror-like finish. He set the bongos on the middle step, then stood.

"Hello," I answered.

Murray and I stepped from the van, giving each other puzzled looks.

"You must be Lani, Yvonne's brother." I extended my hand in greeting. He had to be the brother. He was only an inch or two taller than me and had black hair, near-black eyes, and a beautiful Polynesian skin tone. I caught a glimpse of a shell necklace around his neck, a brown leather loop with small cream- and rose-colored shells. The other two young men were too tan and too blond. They looked nothing like Yvonne. They looked like every California poster boy.

I could see Yvonne in this man's features. And it made me sad all over.

"Lani Rice." He squeezed my hand firmly, then turned and did the same for Murray. "Hi-ya."

"Murray Arnold." Murray winced and waved to the others watching from the porch.

"And I'm Amy Simms."

"Hello, Amy. Wait." Lani stepped back, eyes narrowing. "You're the reason my sister is dead."

"Don't be ridiculous," Murray snapped, his face a picture of anger. "Amy never harmed Yvonne. She's never harmed anyone."

I was liking Murray more by the minute.

"Ms. Simms and I have come to pay our respects."

"That's right, Lani. Yvonne was a wonderful young woman. While she was new to the community, we all are very sorry for her loss."

The two men on the patio had set down their guitars and stood on either side of Lani. Murray and I were outnumbered.

"If it wasn't for you, lady," crowed the man to Lani's right, "Yvonne would still be alive."

The second belligerent fellow on his left added, "That's right. We heard all about you. You are bad luck."

"This is ridiculous," Murray grumbled. "Let's go, Amy. If these, these louts," he pointed his finger at the young men, "can't accept our condolences, we might as well leave them." He turned around and started for the van.

"Just a minute," I said. "Lani, I had nothing to do with Yvonne's murder. Did you talk to the police?" He remained mum but allowed me to continue. "The police believe that an escaped convict, a violent criminal named Alan Spenner murdered your sister."

"How do I know you didn't lead him here?" Lani's face was dark and his voice low. It held an undercurrent of threat.

"Me? Why would I do that? I would never—"

He held up a hand to stop me. "Not physically. Spiritually. Your spirit draws murder to you." His friends nodded their agreement.

Was the whole world going crazy?

"My spirit?"

Lani ran his hands along the curves of my body, never actually physically touching me, yet I felt ice with every move. "Your spirit attracts mayhem, sin, and murder." He looked toward the sky. Silvery gray clouds hung over us. "You bring evil."

"You are cursed, lady," snapped the young man on the left with a none-too-flattering goatee.

Fury and indignation filled me head to toe, but Lani had just lost his sister—and violently. I drew in a deep breath and let it out. I owed him my sympathy and compassion. "Please," I began, "accept my condolences for your loss. If there is anything I can do to help you, give me a call." I pulled a Birds & Bees business card from my wallet and handed it to him.

Surprisingly, he slipped it into the pocket of his jeans. I had been expecting him to rip it to shreds. I got the impression that that was what he wanted to do to me.

Murray and I jumped in the van and burned rubber. Okay, no rubber was burned. Still, I was mad. Mad enough to burn rubber.

You try burning rubber in a decade-old Kia minivan. On a dirt road, no less.

"You okay, Amy?" Murray inquired.

"I'm still shaking," I said, pulling my right arm from the steering wheel for him to see. Sure enough, it shook like a willow branch in the wind.

Murray invited me in for coffee. I gladly accepted.

We took our coffee on the back porch seated in a pair of faded Adirondack chairs. We had an idyllic view of Webber's Pond and the cabins surrounding it.

Murray Arnold lived alone. "I had a dog once, but he died." Murray rested his cup and saucer on his right knee. "Then I got another dog, and she died too."

"Did you ever think about getting another dog? It must get lonely out here."

"I thought about it, but I don't want to put myself through the pain of loss anymore." His gaze shifted across the pond.

"I can understand that." I helped myself to a flaky buttered biscuit on the table between us. Murray said he had baked them that morning. "If you don't mind my asking, do you have any family?"

Murray shook his head. "No."

"No wife? No children?"

"I am afraid not. I seem to be one of those persons destined to remain alone."

"You never know," I said, reminded of Esther and Floyd's sudden late-blooming relationship. "What about the others?"

"You mean my neighbors?" I nodded, and he continued. "Barnswallow has a girlfriend. She spends the night occasionally. I don't know much of anything about her. The rest of us live alone." The beginnings of a smile formed on his face. "It must be a disease."

He stood, and I listened to his knees crack. "Maybe it is something in the water."

I looked at my nearly empty cup of coffee. "I hope not."

"Your Derek strikes me as being a good man."

"He is."

Murray folded his hands behind his back, his eyes on the horizon. "Maybe the spirit board was his way of letting you know that he was contemplating marriage." He shot a glance at me.

I blushed and choked on my biscuit. "Sorry," I said, wiping crumbs from my lap.

Murray laughed, then turned somber. "Yvonne told me she had come here to escape her past, you know."

Alarms went off in my head. "She did?"

Murray returned to his Adirondack chair. "I believe there was a young man who was pursuing her rather aggressively and who wouldn't take no for an answer."

"Where was this?"

"In Hawaii, I imagine. She did not specifically say."

"Ruby Lake is a long way from Hawaii." I thought a moment. "That could explain her being here, though."

"Did she say who this man was? Did she give a name?"

Murray frowned. "She did." He tapped the side of his head. "I'm sorry," he said with a shake, "but the memory isn't what it used to be. If I think of it, I'll tell you. Do you think it's important?"

"I don't know," I admitted. "I just don't know."

"It's the oddest thing," Murray said. I waited as he bit into a biscuit and chewed with his mouth open. After swallowing and washing it down with coffee, he continued. "That whole *I am murdered* thing. I don't believe in ghosts or spirits or voodoo magic, Amy. Somebody had to have written that. Why? Was it a warning? A threat?"

"That's what I would like to know."

"Then again, the episode could have been nothing more than a silly party game. Mere coincidence. Alan Spenner might have broken into her home and shot her." He squeezed his fingers over his knees. "That's what the police think."

Murray took it upon himself to refill my cup from the insulated pot he had carried outside. I sipped slowly. Murray's coffee was thousands of times better than mine. "This is good. Usually I don't care for decaf." In fact, I'd never tasted decaf that was better.

"I grind the beans fresh every day. Just enough to make a cup or two."

"Shade grown?" I couldn't help asking.

"Shade grown? What's that?"

I set my saucer carefully on the wide arm of my chair. I gave Murray a brief overview of the benefits to people and birds and the world in general to shade-grown coffee. He promised to pick some up the next time he was in town.

There was something I wanted to ask but hesitated to for fear of offending him. Finally, I couldn't help myself. "I hope you won't take this wrong…"

"What?"

"Do you suppose that one of the dinner guests could have shot Yvonne?"

Murray smiled. "I don't see how, Amy. We were all together."

"No. I mean after we all left. Maybe somebody went back to her cabin."

Murray leaned into his chair and gave it some thought. "I don't believe that is possible."

"How can you be sure?"

"We all drove together. In my car. I have the only vehicle big enough. It's that station wagon out front. You must have seen it. I drove us all back here. Barnswallow walked straight to his place, while Kay and Madeline stayed for a nightcap. We were all here when Officer Reynolds came and broke the news of the murder."

I couldn't hide my disappointment. "Ross Barnswallow could have driven to Yvonne's afterward."

"Why?" asked Murray. "What reason would Barnswallow have for wanting her dead? No motive, no murder? Isn't that what they say?

"Besides," Murray insisted, "I and the others would have heard his truck if he had left to go murder Yvonne. He'd have to pass right by my cabin. And that little truck of his makes quite the racket, I don't mind telling you. When he drives his girlfriend back to town late some nights, it wakes me, and I have a devil of a time getting back to sleep.

"No, if you ask me," Murray said, "it was Spenner. It's the only thing that makes sense. Several witnesses have reported seeing Spenner in Charlotte."

"I hadn't heard that."

"The woman on the radio reported it this morning."

I thanked him for his time and told him to let me know if he heard anything about a funeral or memorial service for Yvonne.

"And please, do the same for me, if you should hear something first."

I promised I would as I climbed wearily into my van. "Tell me, Murray, if Alan Spenner did not shoot Yvonne, who might have? Can you think of anyone?"

"No, I—"

"What? Who?"

Murray looked over his shoulder and across the pond toward Gar Samuelson's place.

"Gar? You think he might have shot her?"

"No, of course not. It's just that—" Murray hung his arms over the edge of the open driver's-side window.

"It's just that what?"

"Gar does not like what he calls in-comers."

"No?"

"No. Why do you think the Fritsch place is still empty after all these years?"

"Because of Gar?"

"Anytime someone comes sniffing around looking to buy the place, he causes a fuss. Acts all crazy like, sics his dog on them, accidentally sends arrows flying into the side of the cabin. Once, he nearly hit some poor soul who was only out there to appraise the property. Not that it is worth anything. Not now."

"Does he bother the rest of you?"

"No. We've been here long enough. He tolerates us."

"But Yvonne didn't live here. Her cabin must be nearly a mile away."

"Not quite that far, I believe." Murray shrugged. "Gar has been getting odder and odder as the years go by. Did you know the man rides around naked every full moon?"

I shook my head. A naked man in a wheelchair chasing the full moon? That was an image I could have lived without. "He seemed so...normal when I talked to him."

"Come back on the next full moon. See what you think then." Murray tapped the side of the door with his knuckles. "I guess I had better finish the lawn."

I made a U-turn and headed back the way I had come.

The whole paying my condolences and setting Yvonne's brother straight thing had backfired big-time.

"You just keep driving nice and calm, and nobody is going to get hurt," came a chilling voice from the back of the van.

12

My foot hit the brake.

Hard.

"Hey!"

"Sorry!" I shrieked, spinning to see my assailant, who looked vaguely familiar—in an I'm scared to death and about to die so I don't really have time to process who you are now, thank you very much kind of way—then spinning back around again to see where I was going. I had lifted my right foot from the brake pedal. That foot seemed to have a mind of its own, and it insisted on pressing the gas pedal to the floor.

We were accelerating quickly. Fifty miles per hour...sixty!

"Slow down! You're going to get us killed!"

"I know!" I jerked the wheel hard to the right to keep from going off the side of the road and down the embankment to the left. It was a lot closer than it had looked on the way out to Yvonne's house. The van's tires spun in the loose dirt. The Kia wobbled. I turned the wheel hard to the left and then the right again.

"Slow down!" the man behind me hollered once again. "Stop already!"

"I-I can't!" I shouted back. And I couldn't. I wasn't saying that because I was trying to scare him. I was probably more frightened than he was. "My foot is stuck. I can't seem to lift it!"

The more I tried, the more my foot seemed glued to the gas pedal and the gas pedal seemed glued to the floorboard.

The man scrambled forward on his hands and knees. "Just lift your foot!"

We both looked in horror at a four-way interchange ahead. Cars were coming from every direction. Unfortunately, the nearest vehicle was a truck the size of Mount Rushmore. And probably just as solid.

For a quiet country lane, the world had become quite crowded. What were the odds?

What were the odds we weren't going to be at the epicenter of a major collision?

I didn't have time to calculate either of them. The next thing I knew, my attacker had squeezed his way up between the front seats. He gripped my right thigh and yanked.

"Ouch!" I cried as his fingers dug into my flesh. I closed my eyes because Mount Rushmore was getting closer by the second. I had always wanted to see Mount Rushmore, but not like this.

A car with a driver who had more guts than brains dove quickly through the intersection, moving at high speed from left to right.

"Hit the brakes!" the man commanded.

"What?"

"Never mind," he growled, and the next thing I knew he was jamming his left foot down on the brake pedal, slamming his leg between my two legs in the process and callously mashing my foot.

"Yeow!"

The trucker at the wheel of Mount Rushmore leaned on his air horn and didn't stop until he was a hundred yards down the road.

We skidded. The back of the van wiggled like a worm on a hot sidewalk, then came to a grinding halt at the side of the road. One driver slowed to ask if we were all right. Another stopped to ask us if we were crazy.

I smiled lamely at both. What was I going to answer? I wasn't all right, and well, I wasn't about to answer that question about crazy. There are laws in the United States about self-incrimination.

Besides, I had a vicious killer slash hijacker in the van with me. He probably preferred me to keep mum.

"Are you crazy?" That was my hijacker, not the anonymous driver of the car we'd come within kissing distance of sideswiping.

I spun. "You!"

The man in the van wasn't a complete stranger. He was one of Lani's musician friends. The one without the scraggly goatee.

"What are you doing in my van?"

"I wanted to talk to you. Now I'm beginning to wish I had never bothered." He shoved a lock of blond hair from his eye. "You really are crazy, lady. Lani just might be right about you."

"What? That I'm bad luck? Hounded by a cloud of evil spirits?" I jammed the van into park but left it idling. I was practically frothing at the mouth.

He nodded, which only infuriated me. "Something like that."

"And what was the big idea of hiding in my van and threatening me?"

"Threatening you? What are you talking about?" The guy really did appear oblivious.

I scowled. "You told me to keep driving, and nobody would get hurt."

He rolled his eyes. "Yeah, and look where that almost got me. It was a joke. You know, like in the movies."

He had one hand on the dashboard and the other on the steering wheel. "I didn't want anybody to see me talking to you. I don't want word to get back to Lani. So when I saw your van parked at the side of the road, I popped inside and waited for you to come out. It took you long enough."

"Sorry I kept you waiting. Next time there's a hijacker waiting for me in my van, I'll try to be more prompt."

"Couldn't hurt," he replied oh too glibly.

I lasered my eyes at his left leg, which was still nestled between my right and left legs. "Do you mind?"

"Not at all," he replied with a very annoying smirk. "But you're gonna have to let go first."

I blushed bright red. In my fear, I had locked my legs around his. I quickly pulled them apart. "There." I gestured to the passenger-side door. "You can leave now."

A bead of sweat ran along his hairline. He swiped it with a finger, then wiped the finger on his jeans. "We need to talk first."

His hair was sun-bleached and his skin suntanned. His eyes were as blue as a woodland kingfisher's plumage. It made me uncomfortable when he looked at me because his leg had been way too close to my crotch.

"Can we go somewhere?"

"Sure," I said, feeling my courage return. Slowly, but surely. "How about the police station, where we can talk about how you broke into my van and hijacked me?"

This caused him to chuckle. A not unpleasant sound. "And how you tried to kill us both? Besides, the van wasn't locked, so technically that's only entering." He wagged his finger at me. "No breaking."

I fumed.

He glanced out the rear window. "You know, it wouldn't surprise me if somebody hasn't already called the police about that little stunt of yours."

I felt a prickle at the back of my neck. I did not need Jerry Kennedy giving me grief over my driving skills.

"Look," he said softly, no doubt feeling he'd won, "how about if we go somewhere and have a beer?"

When I failed to reply, he added, "My treat."

"I'm not sure we have anything to talk about, Mister—?"

"Phillip Sloan." He extended his hand. "Call me Phil."

I had picked out a lot of names for him since discovering him hiding in my van, and Phil wasn't even close to being one of them.

"And you're Amy. Simms, wasn't it?"

Phillip Sloan settled back into the passenger seat and buckled up. Whether that was his usual practice or a reflection on my driving, I couldn't know. "So, know someplace we can get a beer? How about that truck stop out by the highway? I noticed it when me and the guys drove into town."

"Truckee's," I said, reluctantly shifting into drive. "Fine. But I still don't see what we can conceivably talk about. Your buddy, Lani, has made it clear that he doesn't like me. What can we possibly have to discuss? Did Lani put you up to this? What's his game?"

"Lani doesn't know I'm here." Phil wound his window down an inch or two to let some cool air in as we moved. "I told him I was hitching into town to scope things out."

"In the back of my van," I said.

"It worked out great seeing your van parked outside that old guy's cabin."

"Mr. Arnold wouldn't appreciate being called old."

Phil merely shrugged. "How old is the guy? Sixty? Seventy?"

Phil was probably correct in his guess. He looked all of twenty-five, so Murray was probably ancient in his eyes.

"If Lani didn't put you up to this, what is it you want to speak to me about?"

"Isn't it obvious?"

"No, it is not."

"Yvonne, of course."

"I barely knew her." I glanced at him quickly, then took the on-ramp. Truckee's was only an exit away. "I am sorry she's dead."

"Me, too," Phil said. He looked straight ahead toward the mountains.

I cast nervous looks in my rearview mirror. Phil's words had gotten to me. Chief Kennedy or one of his minions could show up any minute, lights flashing.

"I think Lani killed her."

My foot slammed down on the brake pedal. We both flew forward.

Phil cursed me.

The car riding my butt honked furiously. I lifted my foot and accelerated. "Sorry! Sorry!"

The exit ramp was coming up quickly. I put on my blinker and slid over as the car behind me raced past.

"What did you say?" My heart was thumping so strongly, my tongue vibrated with each beat.

"I said I think Lani killed his sister."

Strange words coming from Lani's friend.

Truckee's Road Stop sprawled over several acres of pitted blacktop and several more acres of gravel and dirt. It was owned by Greg and Martha Tuffnall. Greg's granddad had built the place by hand, and a Tuffnall had been running it ever since.

Greg was an old schoolmate of mine. The two had been married only seven years but already had three kids.

Some people's lives moved faster than others. I was single with zero kids.

I pulled up to a spot in front and climbed out. Though there was a separate bar, I led Phil to the diner, and we grabbed a table.

"Are you always so skittish?" Phil asked once the waitress had delivered two cold beers.

"What do you mean?"

Martha, a stout woman in her forties, waved from the serving window. I waved back.

"The way you reacted to finding me in your van."

"You were *hiding* in the back of my van. How else would you expect a person to act?"

"Well, not so crazy, I guess."

"I thought you were Spenner."

"The convict?" Phil looked both amused and confused. "What would he be doing in the back of your van?"

"Oh, I don't know. Trying to escape? Trying to murder me? Maybe take me hostage?"

"Wow." Phil's head bobbed up and down. "You've got a vivid imagination. Not to mention an overinflated opinion of yourself."

"Me?" I said indignantly. "Look who's talking! You're the one who thinks Yvonne's brother murdered her."

"How about keeping your voice down?" Phil looked anxiously around the simple, no-frills, no-nonsense dining room, filled mostly with truckers intent on their food and the TV monitors playing every sport imaginable.

"How about telling me what's going on?" I noticed I was drinking faster than Phil. I slowed down and munched on some salty bar mix that the waitress had supplied in a paper-lined basket.

"What makes you think Lani killed his sister? In the first place, he is, was, her brother. In the second place, and it's a big one, he was in L.A., from what I hear. You *all* were, right? Don't tell me he did it telepathically." Maybe this guy in front of me was the killer and was merely trying to confuse me.

If so, mission accomplished.

Phil ignored the taunt. "Sure, we're from L.A. But that's not where we *were*."

I felt a tingle. "Oh?"

"We had a gig in Charlotte."

That got my attention. "Charlotte, North Carolina?" That was less than a two-hour drive from Ruby Lake.

"You know another one?"

"Not offhand."

He nodded and fisted his glass. "After the gig, Lani left with some chick he met."

"When was this?"

Phil eyed me steadily. "The night Yvonne was murdered."

"And you think Lani, *your friend*, pulled the trigger?" I leaned back. "Why?"

"Lani's got a temper. Don't get me wrong. He's one of my best friends, but Yvonne...well, she was special."

"You cared for her?"

"You could say that."

I didn't bother saying that I just had. "You're the one she was trying to escape from."

Phil banged his fist on the table. "That's a lie!" He leaned close. "Who told you that?"

"Yvonne told somebody. That somebody told me." I wasn't about to give this unpredictable hothead Murray's name.

"She wasn't escaping me," Phil insisted. "We were simply taking a little time off from each other."

"I see."

"No, you don't, but it's the truth. You see, Yvonne and me, we sort of grew up together." He drew a Y on the table with his finger. "We were meant to be together."

This guy was spooky.

Was that a tinge of something deeper than sadness I noticed in his eyes? "What time was this gig of yours?"

"About five o'clock. We played the happy hour at a local brewery. We finished at seven."

While happy hour was technically illegal in North Carolina, it only meant that establishments could not offer free or reduced-price drinks. They could, however, offer food specials.

He rattled off the name of the place. I'd never been inside but remembered seeing it downtown near the Charlotte Hornets' basketball arena.

Phil's face suddenly lit up. "Hey, you should come check us out sometime. We play traditional Hawaiian music with a modern flair. Sort of like Don Ho meets the Beach Boys meets Prince."

"Thanks." I couldn't begin to imagine what Phil had just described. Two guitarists and a bongo player performing a mashup of those three disparate acts? I wasn't going to commit myself to anything.

"We're playing a spot in downtown Wilmington next Saturday."

Wilmington was along the North Carolina coast. "You guys are a long way from L.A."

"Lani lined us up a whole string of gigs out this way."

"How convenient."

Phil merely shrugged. "We try to get around."

Still, Yvonne moves to town, and Lani and his band show up soon after. Shortly after that, his sister is dead. Phil might have been onto something. "So you believe Lani had plenty of time to drive to Yvonne's cabin?"

"I wasn't sure until we drove out here."

"When was that?"

"The morning after the murder. Lani got a call from your police."

"Do you remember? Did he seem upset?"

"Well, yeah, I guess he sort of did."

"That doesn't sound very convincing."

"Lani doesn't show his emotions."

"He sure showed them to me."

Phil chuckled. "Maybe it was all an act."

I was wondering if I had been witnessing an act myself the last twenty minutes. "Meaning?"

"Meaning he wanted to stir things up. Create some confusion. You were convenient. Plus—" He swallowed a handful of pretzel-and-nut mix and chewed while I hung there waiting. His Adam's apple bobbed up and down; then he said, "Plus, he said he'd heard things about you."

"What sort of things?" I could only imagine. "Not good, I'll bet. From whom?" I demanded.

"I have no idea. Ask Lani."

"I just might." My fingers drummed the table. The waitress had taken Phil's side and brought two beers. I ignored mine. "Do you remember what this woman Lani left with looked like? Did you get her name?"

"A hot blonde. I didn't get her name."

"Did they leave together? Did you get a look at her car?"

"Never saw it. Lani had our van. Maybe they went together. Maybe they drove separately," he said unhelpfully.

"He abandoned the two of you?"

"It was no big deal. It's part of the code. If one of us meets someone special, the others fend for themselves. We hitched back to our motel and crashed."

Phil leaned his elbows on the table and beckoned me closer. "Lani didn't get back until after midnight. He sounded strange."

"Strange how?"

Phil gave my question some thought before answering. "Upset somehow. Me and Teddy—"

"Teddy is the one with the goatee?"

Phil nodded. "We asked him how things went. He told us to shut up and go to sleep."

I nibbled a pretzel stick. "Did you know that Yvonne was here in Ruby Lake?"

"Of course. Lani knew too."

"Had he seen her?"

"No. He said he called her. Who knows? He might have been lying. They were going to hook up."

"Why would Lani lie?"

"Because he can."

That was an interesting answer. "Did they get along well?"

Phil shook his head. "When they were kids. Not so much now. Yvonne didn't like Lani's habits much."

"Such as?"

"Running around playing his music, chasing women. Spending money he didn't have."

Phil grinned.

"What?" I demanded.

"Well, he's got money now, doesn't he? Now that Yvonne's dead."

"You're saying Lani inherits Yvonne's estate?"

"He must. They were all the family each other had."

The waitress sidled up to the table and asked if we wanted another round. Phil said yes. I said no. The waitress left to go figure things out for herself.

"Does Lani own a handgun?"

"Does a revolver count?"

13

It was date night at Derek's apartment above his downtown law office. That meant dinner and a Broadway musical on the TV across from the sofa. It also meant refilling the bird feeder I had installed outside his window. I had given him the feeder as a gift. According to Derek's twisted thinking, that meant it was my job to refill it on a regular basis.

Derek's job was to watch me do it.

He was good at his job.

To his credit, Derek had provided dinner. He was a whiz in the kitchen when he wanted to be.

"He called me that murder lady." Sitting cross-legged on the sofa, I watched my foot bounce there at the end of my leg, and I couldn't stop it. I was mad.

Derek smiled. "It's a step up from *that bird lady*, isn't it?"

I pinched my brow. "Is that what people call me?" My foot stilled.

"Sometimes," Derek said with a wicked grin. "The nice ones."

"Very funny." I tossed my dinner roll at him. He dodged. I'd just buttered it too. I picked it up off the rug and tossed it in the trash can. What a waste. "Can I get you anything while I'm up?"

"Another beer will do." Derek held up his empty. "Why does this guy Phil think Lani killed his sister?"

"Money." I settled back on the sofa and snuggled up against Derek's shoulder.

"Money is always a motive. Was Yvonne that well off? I didn't get that impression."

"I have no idea. She had the cabin and property. I don't know if she had any other assets."

"Doesn't sound like much, but sometimes a little money is all it takes when you have none yourself. I'll see if I can find anything out."

"Would you?"

Derek shrugged. "I figure I might as well volunteer because you were going to ask me to anyway."

I slugged him in the upper arm. He pretended not to notice.

"Dad told me that the official consensus is that Spenner is heading south."

"Far south, I hope. Like South America."

"Two people claimed to have seen him in Charlotte. There was another purported sighting in Atlanta the next day. Dad says the police think he's heading to Florida."

"Maybe he's thinking of retiring." I glanced out the window. It was cold and dark out there. "Florida sounds good."

"Spenner has a stepsister near Orlando. That may be where he's destined."

"That would be stupid."

"Beating people up with a baseball bat isn't exactly Einsteinian." Derek kissed me suddenly, and I felt my toes—and several other unmentionable places—tingle. "I'm just glad that he's far away. Otherwise, you might just be tempted to play bounty hunter."

"Oh, no. Not me," I insisted. Dinner finished, I rose and moved our bamboo trays to the kitchen peninsula counter. "My days of getting involved in murder are over." I rinsed the plates and placed them in the dishwasher. "It all started by accident anyway. I never meant to get involved in anything other than running Birds and Bees."

Derek headed toward me. "What's up? You sound defensive."

"Nothing." I tipped the dirty napkins into the trash.

"Really?" Derek pointed out the discarded napkins. "Those are cloth."

"Oh." I fished the napkins out of the trash can and gave them a shake to get the coffee grounds off them. "Sorry."

"You don't have to apologize." Derek arms went over my shoulders, and his fingers massaged the sore spots I didn't know that I had until then.

"What's going on? Is Yvonne's murder worrying you, or is it Spenner?" He planted a delicate kiss on my neck, just under the ear. "Or are you missing your mom?"

"Do you think I'm a bad influence on Maeve?" I blurted out, surprising even myself. I cringed, instantly wishing I could vacuum the question back up and bury it somewhere deep, deep inside me.

Derek drew back, bumping into a bar stool. He caught it in his hands as it wobbled precariously. I was wobbling pretty precariously myself.

Fortunately, Derek noticed this too and took my hands in his. "What are you talking about, Amy? A bad influence how?"

I pulled free and grabbed my unfinished beer from the coffee table. "Nothing." I took a big swig and gulped it down quickly. "Can't we just forget that I said anything?"

"A bombshell like that?" Derek crossed the room in two strides and motioned for me to sit.

He turned off the TV.

We'd both been ignoring the movie anyway. What a shame. Bernadette Peters's portrayal of Lily St. Regis in *Annie* was a favorite performance of mine, with Kristin Chenowith's depiction of Rooster's airhead girlfriend a very close second.

"What's this all about, Amy?" Derek gave my hand a squeeze. "How could you possibly be a bad influence on my daughter?"

When I didn't answer, he continued. "I've seen how much ice cream she scarfs down when we go to the ice cream parlor together. You always try to match her scoop for scoop." He grinned. "If anything, she's a bad influence on you."

I sniffled and wiped my nose. I didn't even realize I had been crying. "Sorry," I mumbled.

"You've got nothing to be sorry about." He took my chin in his fingers. "Except that you still have not explained what you are talking about."

"I wouldn't want you to think that I would do anything that would harm her."

"Of course not," Derek blurted. "That's not even worth discussing."

"I mean, I think the world of her and only want the very best for her."

"That's good," Derek said, eyes twinkling. "So do I."

I pouted. "You're not taking this seriously."

"No, sorry. I guess I'm not. But you have to admit, this whole conversation is ridiculous."

"Ridiculous?" I pulled free of his hug. "Now you are calling me ridiculous? Just because I'm worried about Maeve?" My lips were moving quickly—my brain maybe not so much. "Just because I don't want Maeve to grow up like me?"

"What would be wrong with that? I sort of like you." His hand brushed softly against my cheek.

"A-a murder magnet?"

Derek's mouth fell open. His hand dropped to the sofa cushion. "Is that what this is all about?" Fingers, his, pushed away the tears that fell from my eyes.

I could only nod. "People think I'm the murder lady." I looked away. I couldn't bear to look at Derek.

He snuggled up beside me. "That's ridiculous. What people?"

"Just people," I said at a whisper. I knew I couldn't dare tell him it was his ex.

"Well," Derek said after a moment, "those people are wrong. Dead wrong."

I shot him a look.

"Sorry," he said. "No pun intended. Look, you're smart, you're beautiful. You are a successful businesswoman—"

I cringed a little at that. Derek was not as intimately familiar with my checkbook as I was.

"Funny. Did I mention beautiful?"

"Yes," I sniffed. "But you can mention it again."

He did.

"So you don't think I'm the murder lady?"

After a kiss that lasted a lifetime, his lips melting into mine, he said breathily, "You know, Amy..."

"Yes, Derek?" I whispered. Was I about to hear the L word? Was I about to say the L word myself?

"You'll always be the bird lady to me."

I couldn't help smiling—just a little—despite the unexpected twist. Part of me was disappointed. Part of me wondered if it would have been too soon to mention love.

"Besides, as far as murder goes, you've probably solved more crimes in this town than the police. Don't tell Dan I said that," he added quickly. He and Dan had become good friends.

I laced my fingers with his and squeezed. "Thanks. I needed that."

"Don't mention it. Speaking of Dan, he stopped by the office today."

"What's up? Something to do with a case?"

"No, nothing like that. He said Kim went nuts on him."

I puzzled over his words. "Define *nuts*."

Derek shrugged and reached for a now-cold dinner roll. "Apparently she went to his house and created quite the scene in front of his houseguest. Some old classmate of his. What's with you two? You coordinate these things?"

"Are you talking about Paula?"

"Yes, that sounds right. Dan said she was staying with him for the week."

"Did he tell you she was gorgeous?"

Derek hesitated before answering. A sure tell. "He mentioned she wasn't unattractive."

"Going the evasive lawyer route, I see."

"I don't know what you are talking about." Derek reached for the remote. "Shouldn't we be getting back to our movie?"

I let him have his way. I threw my legs across his lap and my arms over his neck.

I wasn't about to give him a hard time.

He'd been too sweet.

14

The next morning, AM Ruby was reporting that Alan Spenner had been seen in central Florida. I breathed a sigh of relief.

"Maybe the bum wants to visit Disney World," Esther said as she busily swept the area around the entrance of the store. "If that bum shows his face around here, I'll show *him* how to use a baseball bat."

The broom moved faster than a hummingbird's wings. This meant more dirt and dander was heading up to the ceiling than toward her dustpan, but I was not going to say anything.

A busy Esther was a pester-free Esther.

"Maybe." I turned off the radio. "Nearly noon and not a single customer."

"Some days are like that," Esther said, sounding none too concerned. I didn't know why. She now had nearly as much money tied up in the store as I had.

Esther looked up and toward the street. "Don't look now, but here comes a customer."

"Really?" I perked up and practiced my best smile.

The door jingled brightly as it was opened.

"Oh, it's only you," I said.

Dan Sutton smiled. "I can't say that's the warmest welcome I've ever received, but I'll take it."

"Sorry, Dan." I moved from around the counter to give him a hug.

"What is it? The uniform?" He tugged at the brown material of his police uniform.

"No, sorry. I didn't mean anything. Esther and I were just talking about our lack of customers this morning." I looked at Dan with renewed interest. "I don't suppose you'd be interested in a bag of birdseed?"

Dan grinned and threw out his arms. "Sorry. No bird feeder, remember?"

"I remember." I turned to my not-so-secret weapon. "Esther."

Esther cackled and suddenly appeared at Dan's side with a slick, antibacterial, eight-rung feeder with a clear plexi tube and dark green trim. "On sale. Today only," she said. "Forty-nine ninety-nine."

When Dan hesitated, she thrust it at him, and he was forced to take it.

"Police officer's discount," Esther said. "How's about I ring you up?" She gripped him by the upper arm and pulled. With both hands clutching the bird feeder, Dan was helpless to fight back—despite his police training.

Face it, even if he'd had both hands free, he'd have found it futile to fend off Esther when she was in attack mode. "Amy, he's going to need birdseed. Twenty pounds ought to do." Esther had reappeared behind the sales counter and slapped the cash register to life.

"Twenty pounds—" Dan spun around.

"You're right," Esther said. "Amy, make that the forty-pounder!" Esther was determined to get a return on her investment.

"Forty pounds, right!" I found myself reacting like a soldier in battle. I gripped a forty-pound bag of sunflower seeds and dragged it to Dan's feet as he stood by the counter.

"Trust me," she told Dan. "It's cheaper when you buy more."

Dan's thick leather wallet was on the counter. I wasn't sure if he had pulled it out himself or if Esther had slipped it out of his pocket when he wasn't looking. As confused as Dan appeared, I didn't think he knew either.

Dan cast a dubious look at the feeder in his hands. "Where am I going to hang this thing?"

Esther moved with the alacrity of a nimble crab skirting the shoreline as she swept along the length of the counter. A moment later, she was yelling from aisle four. "We sell three kinds of mounting hooks. One looks like an actual tree once you get all these thingamabobs together."

I heard the sounds of clashing metal.

"This one here," she continued, all voice and no physical presence, "you assemble all the pieces and—" More crashing metal.

Esther emerged at the end of the aisle, hair disheveled, a mishmash of black rods extending from under her arms and one long, skinny piece oddly protruding out of the neck hole of her sweater.

I pictured fresh dents in the hardwood floors.

"Well, I, uh…" Dan pressed his back against the counter.

I decided it was time I came to Dan's rescue. "You could just screw or nail it into a tree or hang it from a tree branch, Dan. If you aren't worried about squirrels getting into it."

"Thanks, Amy." Dan gulped. "I've got nails. And I like squirrels."

Esther gave me a dirty look that I'd be seeing the rest of the day.

Rather than listen to her rant, I walked Dan out to his squad car. "Derek tells me you and Kim are having a little trouble?"

Gripping the feeder in one hand, I held the passenger-side door open.

"Not that one. Better put this in the back."

I shut one door and opened the other. Dan dropped the bag of seed onto the rear floor.

"Yeah. Funny thing is, I don't know why." Despite the coolness of the air, a line of sweat had formed on Dan's brow. "She came over to meet Paula, and before either of us knew what was happening, she stormed right out. Weird, huh?"

"Yeah," I sort of agreed. "Weird." Kim definitely had a weird piece to her puzzle. "Didn't she bring you cupcakes?"

"Yeah, she brought them." He folded his arms across his chest. "She came to the house the next morning unexpectedly. Not that I wasn't happy to see her."

Dan repositioned the bag on the floor and nestled the feeder against it.

"And?" There was definitely an *and*.

"And then she proceeded to throw them at both me and Paula."

I winced, picturing the scene. It wasn't pretty. Colorful, yes. Pretty, no. "I am *so* sorry."

He shrugged. "It's not your fault."

"Actually," I hated to admit but did, "it was. I was the one who suggested cupcakes. I thought they might help clear the air."

"Well," chuckled Dan—really, he was simply too sweet—"I don't know about clearing the air, but they sure went flying through it."

I groaned. "Did any hit their targets?"

"Oh, yeah. Paula and me. I guess we should all be grateful you did not suggest something harder, like cantaloupe."

"Sorry, Dan. Kim's just going through some stuff," I said in my best friend's defense.

"Oh? What sort of stuff?"

"Huh?" I hadn't been expecting the question. I'd made the comment only as a vague social cover-up. I should have kept my big mouth shut.

I thought a moment, letting my gaze drift up and down the street. A beautiful young woman came strolling out of Ruby's Diner with a to-go bag in her arms. Long dark hair danced on the breeze. She wore skintight denim jeans, a matching denim jacket rolled up to the elbows, and thigh-high black leather boots that lifted her derriere.

"I think Kim just wants to know where things stand with you two."

"How do you mean?" Dan waved to somebody across the street. "I'm crazy about her."

"Does she know that?"

"I thought she did." Dan frowned. "You think she doesn't?"

I could only shrug. "Kim is my best friend. Even when I know what she's thinking, I don't know what she's thinking." I slammed the door shut. "You know what I mean?"

"Not a clue."

The beautiful brunette stepped up to us. Her eyes were the delicate golden brown of a kestrel's wing feathers. "You're just in time, Dan. I've got lunch." She held up the bag.

"Toss it inside." Dan looked at the sky. There was nary a cloud in sight. Those that were tarrying above were puffy white and cute as marshmallows.

It was a near-perfect Carolina blue day. Weather-wise, at least. On a personal level, I'd see how things went before calling it one way or the other.

"Sure thing."

"Amy, this is Paula. Paula, Amy."

"It's a pleasure to meet you finally," I said. "I've heard so much about you." Seeing Paula up close it was no wonder Kim was homicidal *and* suicidal.

"Amy is a friend of Kim's."

"Oh, I—Oh! *That* Kim," Paula exclaimed.

I squirmed. "I'm afraid so. She's harmless, really."

"Nobody's ever been killed by a flying cupcake," Paula said equably.

"Not that I've heard," Dan added.

Paula peered around me toward Birds & Bees. "Is she working now? Maybe we can stop in, Dan."

"Kim won't be in for another hour," I explained. "Why don't the two of you go enjoy your lunch and stop back at the store afterward?" I took Dan's hand. "I think it will do you all good to clear the air."

"Clear the air of flying cupcakes at the very least," Paula said, but she was laughing as she pulled open the passenger-side door. "Hey, what's all that in the back seat?"

"Dan has decided to take up backyard bird-watching," I answered.

"I have?" asked Dan, working his way around the front of the car to his side. "Or did Esther decide to take it up for me?" He slid behind the wheel. "And with my credit card."

Dan wasn't wrong, so I didn't correct him.

"Who's Esther?" Paula asked.

"She works with me," I explained.

"Yeah." Dan started his engine. "I'll introduce you to her later. But you might want to prepare yourself first."

Paula looked puzzled. "Prepare? Prepare how?"

"Carry a loaded weapon." Dan threw the car into gear and waved goodbye. "And leave your wallet at home."

As they drove toward the lake, I spotted another familiar figure. A not-so-friendly one.

Lani Rice.

He was covering the distance between Yvonne's matte black pickup truck and the diner's entrance.

I waited for a gap in traffic, then hurried over.

By the time I got inside, Lani was seated at a stool and hunched over the green counter.

"I saw that cop talking to you." Lani stuffed a huge onion ring, hot oil dripping, into his mouth and chewed. "Good. Questioning you about my sister's murder, I hope."

My taste buds went into attack mode. It was all I could do not to help myself to the jumbo basket of fried heaven beside him. Onion rings are my Achilles' heel. Okay, one of my Achilles' heels.

I cupped my hand and pulled the smell up to my nostrils. I sniffed. Fried heaven, for sure. I ignored Lani's insults and plopped myself down on the stool beside him.

I waved to Tiffany, then pointed to the basket of onion rings.

She smiled and nodded.

To make sure I had something healthy to go with them, I ordered up a strawberry milkshake, too. What? The milkshakes at Ruby's Diner are made with good, old-fashioned whole milk, not powder, plenty of protein and vitamins there, and fresh strawberries—none of that frozen stuff.

"What are you doing?" Lani eyed me curiously.

Fortunately, I was saved from having to reply by the appearance of Tiffany. She slid a fresh-from-the-fryer basket of rings under my nose.

"Your shake will be up in a minute," Tiffany said, sashaying toward the milkshake machine.

Lani's eyes followed her backside. Tiff gets a lot of that. Me, not so much.

I grabbed a boiling-hot onion ring and gave it a whiff before biting into it. "Speaking of Yvonne's murder, have you heard anything new?"

"Nothing much." Lani took a gulp from his cup, then dumped so much milk in the coffee that it turned ecru. "They questioned all the people who were at her house that night. Plus, everybody in the surrounding area.

Nobody saw anything, and nobody heard anything." He gnawed another ring in half. "That's what happens when you choose to live alone in the middle of Nowheresville."

"I take it you didn't approve?"

Lani shrugged. "Like it mattered to her one way or the other." He pushed his hand across the side of his head. "She was only three years older than me but acted like she thought she was my mother."

"If you don't mind my asking, what will you do with the house?" I thanked Tiffany for the milkshake and planted my lips over the fat, striped straw.

Lani stared at me.

"You will inherit it, won't you?" The milkshake was icy cold, sweet, and fruity. His hard, glassy eyes were making me uncomfortable. I took another sip and felt a brain freeze coming on.

I clenched my fist and rubbed the tip of my tongue furiously across the roof of my mouth. I'd read somewhere that this was supposed to help. I couldn't remember why. The article had presented a rigorous rationale.

It didn't work. Now I had tongue freeze. Sometimes science sucks.

Tears welled up in my eyes. My brain slowly melted back to normal. Such as it is. "I heard you were her only living relative."

"In the first place, I do mind you asking. In the second place, it's none of your business whether I'm her only living relative or one of hundreds."

Lani whipped out his wallet and threw down a couple of bills on the counter. "Nor is it any business of yours what I do or don't do with the cabin. That contractor guy is supposed to stop by so we can get started tearing things down and ripping things up tomorrow. The cabin and those smelly stables."

Lani slid off his stool. His feet slapped the tile. "Maybe I'll turn the place into a recording studio. Maybe I'll rent it out to a family of circus clowns." A flash of malice sprang up in his eyes. "Maybe I'll turn it into a bird shop."

Lani grinned evilly. "How would you feel about a little competition for that joint of yours?" He stabbed a finger in the direction of Birds & Bees, then fumbled with the zipper of his black leather jacket.

"Your sister and I discussed transforming the property into a suitable gold-throated warbler habitat. The birds are threatened, you know." There was an edge to my voice.

Lani spat. "Better still. Maybe I'll turn the place into a cat sanctuary. For feral cats. The world's full of them."

"Cats and birds don't get along," I snapped. "Cats eat birds."

"Cats gotta eat, don't they?"

"You are impossible!"

"Impossible?" Lani said. "I don't think so. "In fact, the more I think, the more possibilities I come up with."

I was beginning to wish that if a Rice had been shot it would have been this one. It was an evil thing to think, but I couldn't help myself.

"I don't understand why you are getting so upset." With a tip of my head, I indicated to him that his raised voice was raising concerned eyebrows.

"Everything okay out there?" Len, the lead cook, stuck his head out the serving window.

"Fine, Len," I replied. Len had been a longtime employee of the diner but had left inexplicably for a time. I was happy to see him back. Moire Leora never said so, but I believed it had something to do with her one-time lover, a man who had insinuated himself into her life and business. Fortunately, he was now out of the picture.

Lani grimaced and leaned into me. "Look," he began, suddenly appealing to me, "I've just lost my sister. My only living relative. It's not easy."

"I know." I fingered a couple of onion rings. They were getting cold. I nibbled the crusty breading off one. "Do you have any idea who might have wanted to kill your sister?"

"Not a clue." Lani fell back onto his stool. His elbow bumped his cup. "Rats." He dabbed at the counter with a couple of napkins.

Tiffany came to his rescue, cleaning up and taking everything away when he said he was finished. She didn't ask me if I was finished, as I had plenty of onion rings left in my basket. She knew better.

"I mean, she was new to town. She wasn't here long enough for anybody to hate her." A chuckle escaped his lips.

I wondered what that was all about.

"Did she have any enemies from her past?"

"Not really. No."

I wasn't sure how to phrase this next question, especially without getting shot, but I had to know. "You carry a gun," I began softly. "Why?"

Lani bit down on the corner of his lip. "It's a big scary world, isn't it?" There was a harshness to his response. "My sister's death ought to prove that. You live in this cutesy little town, dreaming about birds and strawberry milkshakes. Let me tell you, the real world isn't so pretty."

Lani pressed his hands into the counter. "Oh." Comprehension filled his eyes. "That's it, isn't it? You think *I* shot my sister."

"Did you?" I whispered. Out of the corner of my eye, I saw Tiffany watching us as she ran a cloth over a coffeepot, pretending to dry it.

"No. I did not."

"I suppose the police checked your weapon." I helped myself to a room-temperature onion ring and chewed slowly. I didn't want to miss a word.

"Listen, lady, if you want to help and insist on poking your nose around where it doesn't belong, why don't you ask that Barnswallow character?"

"Ross Barnswallow? Why?"

"I saw him skulking around a couple of times on my property."

"You mean Yvonne's property."

Lani merely shrugged. "It will be mine soon enough. I saw him lurking about."

"When was this?"

"Once in the morning. Once in the afternoon. I thought I saw him out by the shed one evening, too, but I can't be certain.

"And it isn't just him," groused Lani, on a tear. "There's some goofy invalid scooting around the property on a doped-out golf cart like he owns the place. I'd put a ten-foot fence around the perimeter if it wasn't so expensive. Maybe I'll get a guard dog. A nice Rottweiler. The bigger the teeth, the better," he added, opening wide to show his own teeth.

"You think Ross Barnswallow might have killed her? Why?"

"Why not? Somebody did. If it wasn't Spenner, then he's as good as anybody."

"But not you?"

"Not me."

I wrapped my fingers around my ice-cold glass and sipped. "A certain someone told me that you and your sister didn't get along."

Lani cursed. "Phil. It was Phil, right? It couldn't have been Ted. Teddy only talks to himself. And there's nobody else around this burg who could know a damn thing about me." He nodded. "That leaves Phil."

"I really don't remember," I lied. It was not a very smooth lie, and both of us knew it.

Lani plucked a laminated menu from the napkin holder and flipped to the drinks page. "Why don't they sell beer in this dump?"

"I really wouldn't know."

Lani cursed some more. "Phil's got a lot of nerve pointing fingers at me. He's the one Yvonne was running away from."

"He was?"

"That's right." Lani's hand dove into my basket. He extracted the biggest onion ring in the batch, balled it up, and tossed it in his mouth.

I gasped. I couldn't help it—I'd been saving that monster ring for last. After recovering my senses, I said, "Yvonne had mentioned something about wanting to get away from someone."

"That someone was Phil." Lani folded his arms over his chest. "I'll bet he didn't tell you that, did he?"

"No," I admitted. "As a matter of fact, he said she wasn't running away from him. Merely that they were taking a break from each other."

"Give *me* a break," replied Lani. "I mean, the dude's my friend, but he couldn't understand that when my sister said she'd had enough, she'd had enough. And she had definitely had enough of Phil. Enough to have called the police on him one time." He wiped his face with his sleeve. "I'm beginning to feel that way myself."

"There's no one else from her past that she could have been trying to get away from?"

"What? You back to accusing me again? Give it up. I did not kill my sister."

This certainly changed things.

Had Phil been harassing and stalking Yvonne? Had she rebuffed him? Had that led to rage and then murder?

Maybe with Lani's gun?

He had the opportunity, or so it seemed. Did he have motive, too?

There was more going on beneath the surface here. I could picture Lani pulling the trigger as well, judging by his words and actions. I wasn't impressed with either man and wouldn't rule out either of them as suspects.

The only thing I could be sure about with those two was that they were willing to throw each other under the bus. Even when that bus was the murder bus.

For being pals, Lani and Phil sure seemed to treat each other as enemies. Did that same principal apply to brother-sister relations?

"About your gun…"

"As a matter of fact, I lost it."

"Where?"

Lani made a sour face. It seemed to be his specialty. "The police asked me the same thing. I'll tell you the same thing I told them: 'If I knew where it was, it wouldn't be lost, now would it?'"

He didn't wait for my answer and stalked out the door.

Someone tapped me on the shoulder, and I swiveled on my stool.

"Hello, Murray. I suppose you heard all that?"

Murray nodded. "The whole diner heard Lani, I'm afraid." He buttoned up his burgundy pea coat. He had his bill in his hand. "I guess he intends to stay in Ruby Lake."

"Apparently. Lani has an appointment with Cash Calderon. They are going to start on the stables tomorrow."

"You mean they are going to tear them down, after all?" Murray said. "Why?"

"It seems Lani and his buddies have big plans. They intend to build a recording studio." I assumed that Lani's other options involving circus clowns and bird shops were mere venting. "Maybe they figure they can record their own tunes plus rent it out to others to cover their expenses," I suggested. "You knew they were musicians, right?"

"We saw them playing on the porch, yes." Murray scratched his head. "So they want to build a recording studio? Are they even allowed to run a commercial enterprise on the property?"

"I guess so. If Cash is involved, it must have been approved. Cash is a licensed contractor. He wouldn't do anything that was illegal or even questionable."

"I suppose so." Murray crossed to the cash register and handed Moire his bill and a credit card.

When I finished my shake and licked my basket of onion rings clean and went to pay my own bill, I learned that Murray Arnold had paid for my meal as well.

It was nice to see that there were still some good people in the world. I left a fat tip for Tiffany under my milkshake glass. Before returning to Birds & Bees, I was determined to hit the lakeside trail to work off at least some of the calories I'd consumed.

Lani was sitting in the diner's parking lot, watching me in the rearview mirror of his vehicle as I headed toward the lakeside marina and park.

I didn't think I had anything to worry about, but just in case, I stuck close to a mother walking with a toddler and their pooch.

15

Esther, Kim, and I were gathered around my kitchen table. Brochures, maps, and Carolina birding books lay around us. The scent of lavender and rose petals hung in the air—the commingled scents of Esther's bath salts and Kim's latest French perfume.

My conversation with Yvonne's brother had left me feeling frustrated and glum. To rid myself of negative thoughts, I had spent the past few days focusing on business: bird business, not murder business.

I had posted the pictures of the yellow cardinal on the Birds & Bees bulletin board and web page as a tribute to Yvonne, without mentioning that the photographs had been taken on her property.

Solving Yvonne Rice's murder was a problem best left to the police—even when the man in charge of those police was Jerry Kennedy.

We had a new business venture starting: Birds & Bees Adventures. Esther had come up with the name. I had suggested Birds & Bees Expeditions. Esther's reply had been, "Expedition? You might as well say Death March."

"Yes, Esther," I'd replied, biting my tongue.

But Esther wasn't done yet. "You aren't going to get many senior citizens—and that seems to be the lifeblood of these trips, from what I've seen and heard—who want to go with you on some *expedition*."

She said the word like it was some sort of exotic poison. "*Expedition*. It makes it sound like they'll be forced to wear clunky, ten-pound hiking boots with forty-pound packs on their backs." Tsk-tsking noises followed. "In the pouring rain."

Esther could paint a vivid picture with words when she had a mind to. She often had a mind to.

It hadn't taken me long to realize that Esther was right, unfortunately, so Birds & Bees Adventures it became. And Esther was right again, *adventures* did sound way more fun and far more poetic than *expeditions.*

With luck, the new line of business would improve our bottom line, which at the moment was hovering somewhere near the bottom of the Mariana Trench.

I'd gotten the idea for the tours after attending a recent birding expo. Birding and other nature and wildlife tours seemed to be all the rage, as evidenced by the number of vendors at the expo and the numbers of people visiting their booths.

Truth be told, it was one of my fellow exhibitors who had suggested I consider branching out into the tour biz myself. I'd hesitated, but with her encouragement and the further encouragement of others at the store, including Derek, I'd finally not only gotten on board with the idea, I'd become excited.

Our inaugural tour, Birding the Carolina Coast with Birds & Bees, was only six weeks away.

"We've got a full house." Esther flipped through the registration forms one last time.

"I thought we had one spot left?" I raised the bottle of Riesling and refilled our glasses.

"Gertie took it." Esther didn't sound happy about it. Gertie Hammer was Esther's sister. The fact that they were sisters had remained hidden from me for quite some time. I still found it difficult to believe.

As for their relationship, Esther said it was complicated. Then again, practically everything that had anything at all to do with Esther was complicated.

And that was putting it mildly.

"Does she understand that she's going to have to ride in the van with the rest of us?" Kim giggled. "And spend nearly every waking hour for four days with us?"

Kim had a point. Birds & Bees was renting a fifteen-seat passenger van. Kim was going to drive it. I'd follow in the Kia, which would also hold the bulk of our luggage and birding gear.

We'd be eating meals together, staying in the same small beachside inn, going on birding walks—all as a group. Gertie wasn't much for socializing, and she wasn't a fan of mine. I had bought this big, old house from her and paid way too much money for it. Of course, I had only myself to blame for that.

Myself and my eagerness to return to Ruby Lake and open a business near my family and friends, and far from the man who had broken my heart.

Later, Gertie Hammer had tried to buy the place back for her own greedy purposes. Failing that, she'd tried to have me evicted via a push to have my property taken through a public-domain action instigated by her, the mayor, and several sleazy businessmen.

Fortunately, she had failed in the attempt.

Still later, Gertie had quietly been responsible for saving one of Ruby Lake's oldest and best-loved attractions, Christmas House Village.

Go figure.

Sometimes I got the feeling she was just messing with me.

Throughout all this, Esther had lived on my second floor, and I'd had no idea the two crazy ladies were sisters.

In retrospect, why hadn't I known?

"Gertie wants to go on a birding tour?" I fingered one of the full-color brochures we'd had printed as I mulled over the news.

"Maybe she thinks we're going bird *hunting* and wants some feathers for a hat." Kim giggled again. In her defense, she was on her third glass of Riesling. Or was it her fourth?

"The point is," Esther said, "I've got her bank check right here." She waved a green check in front of my nose. "The full amount, too, not just a deposit. And," she added, tucking the check into her purse so she could deposit it at the bank the next day, "I told her *no refunds*."

"Smart." As much as I had reservations about the prospect of spending four days with Gertie *and* Esther, I knew that Gertie's check was good. The woman was so closefisted, she made Scrooge McDuck look like a spendthrift. Plus, she'd paid in full.

The Disney-anthropomorphized Pekin duck had been a personal favorite growing up. A presage of the bird lady I'd become?

Watching McDuck cartoons as a girl, I had dreamed of having a rich uncle like Scrooge to shower me with love and presents. What I'd gotten was Esther the Pester, a deep-pocketed woman of intrigue, mystery, and the uncanny ability to push every one of my buttons at once.

They do say to be careful what you wish for...

"I like the sound of that." Kim raised her glass, and she and Esther shared a toast.

I was beginning to think I'd better make some whole wheat toast and get it down Kim's throat. She was going to need something to soak up all that alcohol. "Are you sure you wouldn't like something to eat?" I asked her.

"No, thanks." Kim hiccoughed. "Dan's picking me up here for dinner in a little while. I don't want to spoil my appetite."

There was a knock on the apartment door.

Kim jumped up. "That must be him now."

She pulled open the door. Dan stood sheepishly on the doormat. Close beside him, stood Paula d'Abbo.

"Uh-oh," I whispered for Esther's ears only. I grabbed the wine bottle. It was empty, but I stuck it in the refrigerator before Kim came for it with the intent to cause bodily harm.

Remarkably, she did neither. "Hi, Dan. Hello, Paula." She daintily kissed Paula on the cheek and Dan on the lips.

Esther and I shared a look that said we'd talk later.

Dan was wearing his best suit, dark blue, with a pale gray and pink striped tie. Paula might have been wearing her worst navy dress, but she still looked stunning.

Speaking of stunning, Kim's laissez-faire attitude was the most stunning thing going at the moment.

"Come on in. I'll grab my coat." Kim waved for Paula to go first.

I held my breath. Would she clobber the poor woman from behind?

Would Dan dare arrest her for the crime?

"Can I get either of you a drink?" I offered when I realized nothing bad was going to happen.

Was Kim waiting to ambush her enemy? Take her by surprise?

Esther was the first to reply. "I'll take one." She moved to the kitchen cabinet that held the wine bottles and deftly opened a fresh liter. She refilled her glass.

"Nothing for us. We have a reservation at Lake House," Dan answered.

Lake House was a romantic, upscale restaurant in the Ruby Lake Marina. Probably the most romantic spot in town for dining.

"What's all this?" asked Paula. She picked up a brochure outlining our upcoming Carolina coast birding trip.

I explained how we'd soon be offering birding trips. "That's the plan, anyway. We'll see how the first one goes and if we turn a profit."

"We'd better." Esther sat at the table and scowled.

"We will. According to the spirits," Kim began, "new ventures will be successful, remember?"

"Spirits?" Paula asked.

"Don't ask," I replied.

Kim ignored me. "The Ouija."

She pointed to the sofa where a Ouija board and planchette rested on the sagging cushion. The open box it had come in was on the floor, out of sight. Kim had dug the game up from her guest-bedroom closet. I couldn't believe the thing hadn't been donated or trashed by now.

Dan paled. "That's not Yvonne Rice's spirit board, is it?"

"No. Kim brought it. It's our old board from when we were kids." I wagged my head at her. "I still can't believe you kept the silly thing all these years."

Kim shrugged into her coat. "You never know when talking to the spirits is going to come in handy."

"I just hope they're right this time." As for spirits, Kim had been drinking most of hers. I hoped she wasn't bottling things up emotionally and saving them for a veritable volcano that would erupt at Lake House.

Kim moved to the door. I locked my fingers over her shoulder. "A word before you go, please."

"Um, I guess so."

I pulled Kim into my bedroom and eased the door shut.

"What's with you?" I demanded.

"What's with me?" Kim threw back. "What's with you? You said you wanted a word with me."

"Why are you being so nice to Paula?"

Kim planted her hands on her hips. "Let me get this straight, you want me to apologize for being nice?"

"Don't give me that. The last I heard, and that was yesterday, you hated the evil trollop, wanted her dead and then expelled to the gulags until, as you so colorfully put it, she turned into a hellish hag with wrinkled flesh and sagging boobs."

Kim flecked an imaginary speck from her black and white houndstooth coat. "That was yesterday. I'm over it."

I narrowed my eyes suspiciously. "Over it? That is so, so un-Kim-like."

"I'm sure I don't know what you mean. Dan and Paula are friends. Nothing more."

"Sure," I replied, "*I* know that. But you?"

Kim sniffed. "If you must know, the spirits told me not to worry. We do have a reservation to keep." She made a show of looking at her watch.

"The spirits?"

"That's right," Kim said rather haughtily.

"Might those spirits be speaking to you via the Ouija board?" If so, the only fingers moving that board had been her own. Didn't she realize that?

She didn't deign to reply to the question. "According to the spirits, Paula and Dan are nothing more than good friends. More like brother and sister, really. And—"

Kim turned to see that the door was closed. "And the spirits tell me that Dan is going to ask me to marry him."

On that jaw-dropping remark, my best friend yanked open the bedroom door and rejoined the others, who had all gathered around Esther at the kitchen table.

My head was pounding. I helped myself to the wine.

"Ready?" Dan asked Kim.

She said she was.

"Great. It's been a long day," Dan said wearily. "I requested a table near the fireplace. There's nothing I'd like better than to unwind with a cold drink, a fine meal, and some fine company." He placed his arm around Kim's waist.

Kim turned and stuck her tongue out at me.

I wished them a pleasant evening and prayed there would be no burning logs being flung across the restaurant.

"Poor Dan," Paula rubbed the back of Dan's neck.

I saw Kim flinch, but a smile soon masked any other emotion she was feeling.

"Why do you say that?" I asked.

"Didn't you hear?" Paula replied. "There was an accidental death out in the country, and Dan and Larry spent hours at the scene. Then Chief Kennedy had them filling out endless piles of paperwork at HQ for hours."

"I'm sorry to hear that," I said.

"Me, too." Kim's hand went to the nape of Dan's neck and remained there possessively.

"Who was it? Anybody we know?"

"What did you say his name was, Dan? Gar something?"

Dan nodded. "Gar Samuelson."

I sucked in a breath. "Gar Samuelson? From Webber's Pond?"

"That's right."

I leaned against the counter. "What-what happened?"

"He drowned. Apparently, his wheelchair malfunctioned or something, and he fell in. A neighbor found him this morning." Dan looked at the clock on the wall. "Hey, we're going to be late."

I locked the door behind them and leaned against it for support.

"What's wrong with you?" Esther brought her glass to her lips. "You look like you've seen a ghost."

I hadn't seen a ghost, but I had definitely felt one. He had run his ghostly fingers over my bones and whispered in my ear.

I am murdered, he said.

16

I do not like coincidences. Gar's drowning at Webber's Pond seemed too suspicious to have been a fluke. Especially when a woman had been shot dead in the vicinity a short while ago.

I tossed and turned all night. In the morning, it was no use. My curiosity had gotten the best of me.

I had to learn what was going on.

And who was behind it.

I drove to Webber's Pond. There was no sign of Murray, but smoke drifted lazily from his chimney toward the lowering sky. In her side yard, Madeline Bell leaned against the handle of a rake. I waved and continued to Ross Barnswallow's cabin.

His home was the same basic shape as the others, built for function more than style. Unlike the others, however, with their lacquered wood doors, his front door was painted bright red, though the paint was chipped and smudged with dirt and grease.

A small green rowboat was covered by a tin awning at the edge of the pond.

I knocked. Somewhere a dog barked.

Finally, a face, moving too quickly for me to see more than a glimpse, peered out from between the white curtains, then was gone. I heard a few muffled words inside.

A moment later, there came the sound of a lock turning, and Ross Barnswallow opened his door. Out came Ross, followed by an Irish setter. One of them smelled of tobacco and beer.

I was guessing it was Ross. His eyes were bloodshot, and his hair needed combing. He looked like he needed a bath. A red-and-black-checked lumberjack shirt hung over a pair of baggy jeans with scuffed knees. His feet were housed in thick wool stockings. "What do you want?"

"Is this Pep?" The Irish setter wagged its tail and nuzzled its nose against my leg. I scratched him behind the ears.

"That's right. I'm keeping an eye on him." Ross chuckled, a guttural sound like gas escaping from a crack in granite.

"That's nice."

"You could say we're keeping an eye on each other. Isn't that right, boy?" Ross slapped his thigh, and Pep retreated to his side.

"I heard about Mr. Samuelson." I shifted my gaze out across the pond to Gar Samuelson's cabin. Ragged gray clouds crowded around as if drawn to the scene. Was it my imagination, or did Gar's cabin appear lonely and abandoned?

Ross joined me on the porch, moving silently in his stocking feet. "I was the one who found him, you know."

I returned my attention to Ross. I could smell beer on his breath. It was barely noon, but who was I to judge? "No, I didn't know that."

I'd been meaning to ambush Kim and see if she'd gotten any further details of the accident—if it was an accident. I had my doubts and wasn't going to accept that verdict until it had come down officially. Preferably from someone higher up the food chain than Jerry Kennedy.

I had called Lance at the *Weekender* before departing Birds & Bees. He told me that the police were treating the incident as an accidental death. "I heard his wheelchair malfunctioned."

"Mmm." Ross rubbed his whiskers. He grabbed a maroon cap from a hook just inside the door. A pair of dirty boots rested at the side of the door. He picked them up, banged the heels together to shake the mud loose, and then hastily laced them.

I followed him. We were heading toward the still waters of the pond. "What happened exactly?"

"I found him out there." Ross pointed in the general vicinity of Gar Samuelson's cabin and dock. "Gar was floating out in the pond."

He coughed. "The police found his wheelchair at the bottom at the end of his dock. In the muck."

"So he really did drown then." I watched a lone mallard scoot along the weedy shoreline.

"That's what the police say."

"Do they say when exactly?"

"Not that they told me. They spent hours out here, too. Tromping all around the place. Chief Kennedy drove all over in his car. Look at those tire tracks," Ross complained, pointing to rows of deep tracks like wounds in the grass. "It's gonna take years for the traces of his disrespect for the land to disappear. Longer if I don't get some soil to fill them in."

He cursed. "And that's going to take money I don't have and labor hours I don't feel like spending."

"Maybe you could ask the town to take care of it?"

Ross laughed.

I thought the idea was pretty funny, too, now that I'd said it out loud. The Parks and Recreation Department had limited funding and limited personnel. They focused most of their energies on the places most visited by tourists.

No surprise there.

"Had you talked to Gar recently?"

Ross dug his toe into the moist red earth before answering. "Not so much. Just to say hello. Nothing special. We weren't close."

"Did he seem okay to you?"

Deep lines formed in Ross's forehead. "Okay, how?"

"I don't know, worried? Upset?" Like guilty over having killed Yvonne?

"You think he killed himself?" Ross shook his head. "That doesn't sound like Gar. You never know, though." He threw a stick, and Pep bolted after it. A moment later, Pep and stick were back. Barnswallow pried the crooked stick from the dog's mouth and threw it again, farther this time.

"If he had shot Yvonne, he might have had a guilty conscience."

"Why would old Gar shoot her?"

"I heard he wasn't exactly the neighborly sort."

That made Ross laugh. "None of us here are. I guess that's why we live out here. Not in town."

"Is that why you moved to Webber's Pond?"

Ross shambled over the uneven ground and adjusted the canvas covering his rowboat. "It works for me."

"When did you discover Gar?"

"Why do you want to know? The man's dead. End of story."

I stared him down.

"Fine. I heard a dog barking in the night." This time he took the stick from the dog's mouth and tossed it to the center of the pond. Pep bounced along the shore as if unsure what to do next.

"Pep does that sometimes, so I didn't pay much attention. Then when I heard the dog still barking yesterday morning, I got curious. I went to look, and there he was. Floating like that."

Ross's words struck me as false or maybe only well-rehearsed. Was that because he had rehearsed his words, or was it merely because he'd thought it over in his mind and had to tell the same tale to the police?

"I hope Gar's place doesn't sit empty too long. That's all we need around here."

"What happened to the wheelchair?"

"The police took it."

"Oh." I'd been hoping for a look at it. Not that I had any idea what I'd be looking for. If somebody had sabotaged Gar's wheelchair or even simply shoved him off the end of the dock and into the pond, there wasn't likely to be any evidence of that.

I thanked Ross for his time and drove off. Walking the length of Gar Samuelson's dock, I saw nothing that seemed amiss. Then again, the police had been up and down the dock, the grounds, and probably inside the cabin, too.

I stooped and studied some scuff marks, but they did not appear to be fresh. Standing at the end of the dock, I studied the water. Near the edge, it was reasonably clear. Small, dark gray shapes swam lazily, disappearing under the dock. I noticed two deep gouges on the bottom of the lake several feet from shore.

Something about those marks nagged at me. I squeezed my eyes shut, trying to get the hidden thoughts to push out, like toothpaste from a tube, but it was no use.

According to Lance, Gar had probably been in the water six to eight hours, give or take. Ross Barnswallow had discovered the body, according to him, a little after eight that morning.

I wondered what Gar Samuelson had been doing outside on the dock so late at night. Chasing the moon?

"Miss Simms!" Kay Calhoun was surprised to see me on her doorstep. She recovered quickly.

"Hi, Kay. I hope you don't mind me stopping by unannounced."

Kay Calhoun smiled. Wrinkles formed around the edges of her lips. She wore a thick navy-blue rope sweater with a high collar and beige slacks. "Come in, Ms. Simms. I was just about to have tea."

To prove her statement, she held up a delicate porcelain teapot whose slender handle was curled in the fingers of her left hand. A tendril of steam rose from the spout. I found myself watching, mesmerized, holding my breath and waiting a moment to see if the smoky wisps might turn into a genie.

When they didn't, I followed her inside. "Wow, this is nice." I ran my fingers over a polished live-edge wood table near the door. "I like the way you've decorated. Very cozy." The décor wasn't what I had been expecting at all. There was an elegance to the furnishings that the other cabins had lacked.

"Thank you." She motioned for me to sit. "I think so. Excuse me. I'll fetch a second cup."

I settled in a comfortable leather seat close to the fireplace. A stack of wood sat on the hearth, ready to go. A tangle of kindling rested in a basket to the left.

Kay returned with two cups of tea and a sugar bowl that matched the teapot and cups.

"This is lovely china," I said. The delicate white china was gold-trimmed and featured small butterflies, ladybugs, and various flowers in shades of pink, blue, and yellow.

"Thank you." Kay brought her cup to her lips. "It's hand-painted. Imported from England." She sipped. "The tea is English breakfast tea. It's said to have been the Queen's favorite."

"Are you English yourself?"

"No, not at all. My family is from Oklahoma."

"Have you lived here long?"

"Yes."

Kay offered nothing further, so I didn't press her. Some people don't like to talk about their pasts. There are certainly parts of mine that I wish I could forget and didn't like to share with anyone.

She held forth a tray matching the rest of the tea set. It held a half-dozen flat, yellow cookies covered with black speckles.

I looked at it closely before trying a bite. Was that pepper? "Delicious."

"These are my English breakfast cookies. The specks are bits of tea, you see."

"These are very good." I finished the cookie and didn't hesitate when she encouraged me to have a second. "I never thought about putting tea leaves in cookies."

Kay topped off my cup then her own. "I'll give you the recipe before you leave."

"Thanks." I didn't have the heart to tell her the odds of me doing any baking were slim. My mom had a knack for cooking. That knack seemed to have skipped a generation. "Do you live here alone, Kay?"

Kay settled her cup and saucer on her lap. She had taken a seat at the small dark sofa to my left. "I have my Tabitha."

"Tabitha? Is that your daughter?"

"Oh, dear. No." Kay carefully set her cup and saucer on the side table and pushed herself to her feet. "I'll fetch her. You wait here."

Puzzled, I sipped my tea. It was quite good. I helped myself to a third tea cookie, too.

After a minute, Kay returned from her bedroom with a large orange... something. Poofy throw pillow? Furry hand muff?

"This is Tabitha."

I leaned closer. She'd named her hand muff?

"Say hello to Amy, Tabitha."

The thing in her hands squirmed. Whatever it was, it was alive.

Kay turned her orange something around, and I saw a pair of suspicious eyes the color of pumpkin pie glaring at me.

"Yikes!" I caught myself. "I mean, what a lovely cat."

Kay dropped the beast in my lap.

"Isn't she, though?"

My eyes teared up as the creature sank its dragon-like claws into my thighs. The giant cat was all puffy red-orange fur yet still felt like it weighed as much as a goat. How was that possible?

"What-what breed is she?" I had been about to ask her what planet the creature had come from but caught myself in the nick of time.

"Tabitha is a tabby Persian. She's special."

She was *special*, all right.

Tabitha leapt from my lap. She hit the floor, setting off a 2.5 on the Richter scale earthquake. With a kick of its paws, the beast retreated once again to the bedroom. I looked at the claw-sized tears in my slacks. I'd just bought them a month ago, too, *and* paid full price.

I'd never in my life seen a cat so big, so hairy—so much like I pictured Sasquatch if Sasquatch were to walk around on his hands and knees.

I grabbed another cookie to steady my nerves. I felt like I had just witnessed a miniature orange star exploding.

"Don't mind Tabitha. She is not much for company. Plus, she likes to look at the lake from her perch on the bedroom window ledge."

I minded the beast very much but kept quiet. "Speaking of the lake," I said as I dabbed at the blood leaking through my pants with my thumb, "isn't it sad about Gar?"

The blood was spreading, and my actions were only making things worse. But I didn't dare soak my blood up with one of Kay Calhoun's embroidered linen napkins for fear of offending her.

"Yes, quite. He was a neighbor, you know."

That was stating the obvious. I let her statement hang there, a piece of fruit not worth picking.

"To think," Kay said, picking up a square of yellow yarn and resuming her knitting, "we had dinner just that night."

"You and Gar?" This could be interesting.

"No, Yvonne." Kay seemed surprised by my question. "You were there, Miss Simms. You should recall that Gar had not come although he had been invited, I hear."

"Oh, right." Kay seemed to exist in a world all her own. "Yes. Have you met Yvonne's brother, Lani?"

"Ugly fellow."

"I'll take that for a yes."

Kay stabbed a knitting needle into the arm of the sofa. Judging by the pockmarks, it wasn't the first time she had done so. "He and his friends will cause nothing but trouble."

"I'm not real fond of them myself."

Kay nodded abruptly. She extracted her knitting needle and resumed her task.

I listened to the snick-snick of the needles. In the other room, I heard a dragon hiss.

"Tabitha must see a bird near the window," Kay remarked, glancing casually toward her bedroom.

I had just opened my mouth to make my escape when Kay said, "I woke up groggy."

"Sorry?"

"Ross was knocking on my side door," Kay sort of explained. "He told me the news."

"Right, about Gar? I heard he was the person who had discovered him floating in the pond."

"No, Miss Simms." Her fingers paused. Whatever she was knitting looked cat-sized. Well, freak-of-nature cat-sized. Maybe a dressing gown for Tabitha. "Miss Rice. Yvonne."

"I see." I sank bank into my chair. Was I losing my mind? Were those cookies laced with LSD?

"I thought you were with Madeline and Murray that night and that it was Officer Reynolds who told you about Yvonne?"

"Did he?" She blinked as if to clear the reception in her head. "Yes, I suppose he did."

Though what Kay had said was interesting. Ross had been the one to find Gar, too.

Interesting and convenient.

"What about Gar?"

"Gar is dead, Miss Simms. Hadn't you heard?"

One of us seemed to have one foot outside the real world, and I was beginning to wonder whether it was her or me. "Were the two of you close?"

"Marian and I? Oh, yes. Quite close."

"Excuse me? Who is Marian?" I dug my fingernails into the arms of my chair.

Kay's eyes seemed to glaze over. "Marian? I don't know." She blinked rapidly. "Why?"

I tried again. "Were you close to Gar Samuelson?"

She thought my question over before replying. "Not so much. He wasn't a cat person. He preferred that dog of his."

"Did you hear anything odd that night?"

"Which night?"

I sucked in a breath and counted to three. "The night Gar drowned."

"Not a peep. I am a very sound sleeper."

"Can you think of any reason why Gar might have been out on his dock in the middle of the night?"

Kay blinked. "Why shouldn't he be? It was his dock. If he'd been standing on my dock in the middle of the night, I'd have given him what for."

"'What for'?"

Kay pointed a knitting needle in the general direction of the door. A shotgun leaned against the wall next to an umbrella. "It's filled with rat-shot."

Note to self, do not step out on Kay Calhoun's dock without express permission from the owner.

"Do you have any idea who might have wanted to see Gar dead?"

Her answer surprised me. "Why, everybody wanted to see him dead, Miss Simms. Leastwise, they didn't care if he lived."

"Anybody in particular?"

"More tea, dear?" She waved the teapot in my direction.

"No, thank you. I really should be going."

"Don't you want to hear my answer?" she asked as I hurried toward the front door and some sliver of reality that I hoped and prayed dwelt there on the other side.

"Yes, of course." I rested my hand on the doorknob.

"You see, I know exactly who killed Gar."

"You do?" I felt my pulse rev. "You said you hadn't heard anything."

"I hadn't. That doesn't mean I didn't *see* anything, does it?"

No, it did not.

"You saw something?"

I could almost see the memories replaying on the screen of her face. "I saw something," Kay whispered. "Shadows. Dark shadows at first. Then I saw the murderer. And I wondered, is it a banshee? Is it the Devil himself?"

I was on the edge of my metaphorical seat now. "Did you tell the police this?"

"Oh, yes. They didn't believe me."

Based on the last fifteen minutes of my life, that didn't surprise me.

"Who did you see? Who was it, Kay?"

"The same person who shot Yvonne, wasn't it?"

"Was it?" Was any good going to come from this conversation?

"Of course. You know him yourself."

"I do?" Was she going to accuse one of my friends? A member of my family? Was it too late to go back in time and choose *not* to knock on Kay Calhoun's door?

"It was the baron, Miss Simms."

I pinched my brows together. Twin headaches exploded in my temples. "The baron?"

"That Baron Samedi fellow, you know."

"The Lord of Death?"

"That's the one."

"How can you be sure?"

"I saw him myself. He drove Gar straight into Webber's Pond."

17

Back at Birds & Bees, I shared my intel with Kim.

"That's what Kay Calhoun said?" Kim asked in disbelief. "She said she saw Baron Samedi push Gar Samuelson into Webber's Pond?"

"That's exactly what she said."

"Wow." Kim sank back in her chair and crossed her legs.

"Yeah, wow." I turned at the jangling sound of the front door opening. "Didn't you lock up?"

It was after hours, and the store should have been empty and locked up tight as a drum.

Kim frowned. "I thought I did."

I went to see who it was and ran into Dan Sutton coming in. "Oh, it's you. Kim's in the kitchenette. She must have left the door unlocked."

"No, she didn't." Dan shook a set of keys in front of my eyes. "These are her keys. She left them at my place."

"Thanks." I thumbed the lock and invited Dan to join us in the rear of the store.

Was there anybody who didn't have free access to my store?

Dan helped himself to hot cocoa after helping himself to Kim's puckering lips.

"What are you girls up to?" Dan leaned back on his heels.

"Since you asked," I replied, "we were talking murder."

Dan groaned. "Sorry I asked." Balancing his mug, Dan took a seat on the rope rug at Kim's feet. She plopped her legs over his shoulders. "Careful," he said, gripping the mug tightly.

"Sorry." Kim ruffled his hair. Dan was still in uniform but was off duty. "Amy was telling me that Kay Calhoun saw who it was that pushed Gar Samuelson off his dock."

"Did she recognize them?" Dan asked.

"Sort of. She told me it was Baron Samedi, the Lord of Death. She also said that she told the police."

"Right." Dan chuckled, then sipped. "I remember now. Truth is, we didn't take her seriously. You should have seen the look on the chief's face when she told him that. He thinks she's batty."

"I hate to say this and will deny it in a court of law, but this might be the first time that Jerry and I agree on anything."

I offered Dan a vanilla cupcake with cherry frosting, and he flinched as if I might launch it at him.

"Very funny." Kim pinched his neck then took the cupcake from my hand. She held it in front of Dan, and he took a bite. She took the next one.

It was nice to see the two lovebirds getting along so well. I had refrained from bringing up the subject of Paula d'Abbo with Kim. I figured if she wanted to talk, she'd talk, and if she wanted to throw cupcakes, well, she'd throw cupcakes.

Sometimes you've just got to let a friend do what a friend's got to do and pick up the pieces, whether psychological or cupcake, afterward.

"Dan, I thought you said Gar's drowning was an accident?"

Dan extended his legs and pushed off his shoes. "I did. But..."

"But what?"

"But it is possible that his wheelchair was tampered with. At least, that's what we've heard from the lab. The technicians are taking a closer look at it."

"Meaning that it is possible that Gar's death was not an accident or even a suicide." I tapped the counter.

Kim clutched her head and groaned. "I could be responsible."

"What do you mean?" Dan asked.

"I'm the one who gave Yvonne the Lord of Death. First, she's dead, and now..." Her voice trailed off as she shook her head.

Dan looked to me for the rest.

"Like I said, Kay Calhoun told me that she saw Baron Samedi push Gar Samuelson into the pond."

It was Dan's turn to groan. "Oh, brother. I do not want to have to go back to the chief and tell him that Kay Calhoun may have actually seen something. I mean, not the Lord of Death." He scratched the top of his head. "But maybe she really saw somebody after all. The chief won't like it. He said he had half a mind to have her committed to a psychiatric hospital for observation."

I grinned. "Has he met Tabitha?"

"Who is Tabitha?" Kim and Dan asked as one.

"Ms. Calhoun's tabby Persian. Although, you'll never convince me it's not the disturbing love child of Sasquatch and Chewbacca."

We decided to continue our conversation over dinner. Hot cocoa and cupcakes, as good as they are, can only take a person so far.

The night called for pizza and beer. We pulled ourselves together and walked next door to Brewer's Biergarten.

Kim hesitated at the entrance.

"What's wrong?" I asked.

"On second thought, I'm not sure I want to go inside."

"Huh?" Dan stood holding the door open. "Why not?"

"Kim sang karaoke here the other night, and she's a little embarrassed at her performance," I replied.

I shoved Kim through the door, despite her protests.

"I didn't know Brewer's had a karaoke night." Dan waved to the hostess and asked for a table indoors.

"They don't," I replied as we were quickly taken to a table near the dart action and sat. Kim kicked me under the table.

Okay, I guess I sort of had that coming.

While wolfing down our pizza, Kim reached for her mug, and it went crashing to the floor. "OMG! I am so sorry!" Kim blushed and fell to her knees to help the waiter soak up her suds.

Paul ambled over. "Everything okay?"

"I broke a glass," confessed Kim.

Paul leaned back on his heels. "What? Don't tell me you were singing again?" His eyes sparkled mischievously.

"Oh, you are so funny I forgot to laugh." Kim smoldered and chomped down on a slice of pizza. She turned to Dan. "You're a police officer. Can't you do something about him?"

Dan grinned. "How about another pitcher, Paul?"

"You've got it. This one is on the house." He flashed his eyes at Kim before departing. "And this time, let's try to keep it on the house and not on the floor."

"Ouch!" Dan's hand disappeared under the table.

I had a feeling he had borne the brunt of Kim's latest foot attack.

"Sorry, Dan," Kim said oh-too-innocently. "I had a twinge."

"Kim gets a lot of those," Dan said for my benefit.

"Tell me about it," I replied, giving Kim the evil eye. "Maybe you should see a doctor. Get that checked out. My mom gets those. She says it is part of getting older."

Realizing what I'd said, I quickly scooted out of range. Kim lashed out but hit only air.

Staring at the damp beer smudge on the floor as I returned my chair tableside brought to mind something that had been niggling at me. "There's something that's been bothering me about Gar's accident, Dan."

"What's that, Amy?" Dan asked, as eager to change the subject as I was. My shins couldn't take any more abuse.

Our server brought a cold pitcher of beer and topped off our glasses.

"I was out at Webber's Pond and—"

Dan groaned. "I don't think I want to hear this." He grabbed his mug and drained half of it in a single gulp.

"I was out at Webber's Pond to pay my respects and—"

Dan's elbows hit the table. "To pay your respects? To who? Gar Samuelson didn't have any kin, leastwise not at the pond."

I glared at him. "Are you going to let me tell this?"

He waved for me to continue.

"I was out at—"

"We know, Webber's Pond." This time it was Kim who had interrupted. "Get to the point, Amy."

I fumed at the two of them until they got the message, then continued. "I happened to be out at the end of Gar's dock, and I noticed what looked like the marks of the wheelchair where it landed in the muck."

"So?" Still Kim.

Dan was showing restraint.

"So, I'm not sure, but I got the feeling that if Gar had simply fallen in accidentally, the marks would have been directly at the edge of the dock. Like your beer." I pointed to the damp spot on the floor.

"I don't know, Amy." This time Dan dared speak. "I mean, you could be right, now that I think on it." He rubbed his chin. "It does sort of make sense."

"You mean you agree with Amy?"

Dan shrugged. "She can't always be wrong, despite what you and the chief are always saying."

"Jerry is a complete—" I came to a grinding halt and threw my half-eaten slice down on my tray. "Wait, are *you* saying I'm always wrong?" My question, like my attention, was all on Kim.

Kim burbled something unintelligible, so I turned to Dan. "Is that what Kim says?"

Dan had turned the color of a boiled beet. "Anybody for a game of darts?" He pushed back his chair and stood.

At that moment, Violet Wilcox came teetering out of the ladies' room and crashed into him. "Sorry!"

She tumbled into the seat between me and Kim and helped herself to a slice of our pizza.

Dan swiveled his chair around and sat on it backward, draping his arms over the back. He eyed her professionally. "You look like you've been celebrating, Ms. Wilcox."

"I am." She smiled broadly. "Didn't you hear the news?"

"What news is that?" I asked. Being Ruby Lake and not New York City, it probably involved a scandal at the annual pie-baking contest or the fact that the town had ordered a new streetlight.

"Alan Spenner has been caught." Her impossibly big smile got impossibly bigger. "And I was the first one to get the scoop in all the Carolinas, the entire country maybe."

"Are you sure?" Dan asked.

"Sure, I'm sure. I've got this friend—" She stopped and turned to Kim. "Do you mind?"

"Do I mind what?"

Without explaining, Violet grabbed Kim's glass and washed down her pizza. "Thanks." She licked her lips. "I've got this friend down in Nassau—"

"In the Bahamas?" I interrupted.

"That's right. She works for a news bureau there. She told me that Alan Spenner was shot dead in a police raid not two hours ago."

"Wow." Dan followed his word with a low whistle.

"I reported it on the air several times. I'm trying to set up an interview with the head of the police there for tomorrow. It will be another exclusive."

Violet raised her glass—well, Kim's glass—with Violet's plum lipstick smeared on it. "In your face, Lance Jennings!"

"I hadn't heard. Congratulations," I said.

Violet frowned. "Don't you people listen to the radio?"

None of us dared answer. We'd all heard her *Town Gossip* show at one time or the other, and everybody in town lived in fear of being spotlighted on it.

"I can't say I'm sorry he's dead," Kim said. She helped herself to a clean mug up at the bar and returned to her seat.

"The chief will sure be glad to hear this," Dan said, filling Kim's fresh mug.

Kim was looking at me. "What's wrong, Amy?"

"If Alan Spenner is dead, we may never learn who murdered Yvonne."

Kim sighed. "You're right."

"Say, Dan," Violet leaned across the table, flashing blood-red nail polish, "my spies at the crime lab tell me Gar Samuelson's death is being treated as a possible homicide. What do you think?" pressed Violet.

"I think," said Dan, "that you've had enough to drink and are going to need a ride home."

Violet smiled seductively. "With you?" She winked at me. "I thought you'd never ask."

Violet rose suddenly and wobbled like a ship on a stormy sea. She planted her hands on the back of her chair to steady herself. "I'll get my coat."

Dan looked like he'd been trapped between a rock and a hard place. That hard place being Kim.

Violet wasn't just sexy, she was persistent.

But Kim was having none of it. "No problem, Violet. We will be happy to give you a lift. Won't we, Dan?"

Dan was quick to agree. Despite my protests, he paid our bill.

I insisted on leaving the tip.

"Aren't you coming, Amy?" Kim asked, as she buttoned up her jacket.

"No, thanks. It's only a short walk for me. Plus, I've got some thinking to do."

And I did.

18

That thinking led me to the Kia, which led me to Webber's Pond at twelve-thirty in the morning.

I never said it was *smart* thinking, merely thinking. Okay, dubious thinking.

And if necessary, I could always blame the pizza overdose (didn't artichoke hearts possess certain psychotropic properties, or was I imagining things?), the excess of beer, and the lateness of the hour.

Already, with the cold seeping through the steel and glass of my van and worming its way into my bones, and the clouds scudding across the low, dark sky like hungry ghosts seeking doomed human vessels to occupy, I was beginning to regret where it was that my thinking had led me.

Here.

Nowheresville, as Lani Rice had so poetically put it.

I shut off the engine and listened to the tick-tick-tick of the radiator cooling down. I had turned off the headlights as soon as I was close enough to make out the shape of the cabin and stopped a good fifty yards away from my target.

There were three vehicles in front of Yvonne's cabin, her truck and a white van that I knew belonged to Lani and company. The third, a creamy metallic Lexus sedan, looked vaguely familiar.

There were lights on inside the cabin and smoke coming from the chimney.

"This is crazy," I muttered. My van remained mum on the subject. Probably for fear I'd send her to the junk heap if she dared agree with me.

I knew that the Lord of Death could not have possibly been responsible for Gar Samuelson's death. And I knew that Kay Calhoun could very well have been dreaming or hallucinating when she had recounted seeing the spirit push him into the pond. Probably OD'd on English breakfast tea and cookies.

I also knew for sure that Baron Samedi, if Lani hadn't tossed him on the scrap heap, would be sitting right where Yvonne had placed him—on the mantel.

I just wanted to see for myself.

I opened my van door as silently as possible and only half-closed the latch for fear of calling attention to myself.

As I bathed myself in darkness, a woman screamed bloody murder. But that was okay, I knew it was only a coyote doing his or her coyote thing somewhere out there in the mountains.

At least, I hoped so.

I tiptoed up to the window. There was a several-inch gap in the front curtains. All I needed was one look. One look, and I could go home satisfied. Get some sleep. Wake up in the morning refreshed and with a clearer head and smarter ideas.

Because as ideas went, they didn't get much dumber than this.

It wasn't just Kim who had gotten under my skin. There was also Kay Calhoun.

Worse yet, it was Baron Samedi who had worked his insidious soul-sucking self into my life.

But that was okay. I was just going to take one quick look, then skedaddle.

The first porch step creaked maddeningly as I put my foot down on the sagging board. Rusty nails on the ends of the step fought their way upward, screaming to be set free.

I held my breath and counted to ten. No one came to the window, and the front door remained closed. I skipped the second step and put my weight gingerly on the porch.

So far, so good. I moved stealthily to the window to my left. From there, I should have a decent view of the table and fireplace. I inched my way closer, trembling for fear that Lani and his friends might see me.

What would they think?

How could I explain myself?

Sleepwalking? Not even Kay Calhoun would believe an explanation like that. No, for her I could always say I'd been under the spell of the Lord of Death. My gut told me that Lani might not prove as gullible.

I held my breath and hoped for the best. I leaned closer, my nose almost touching the glass.

I could see shapes inside, people. The back of a woman's head.

Bony fingers clamped around my wrist. "Don't make a sound," a voice whispered in my ear.

I gasped and cursed myself for taunting the gods by daring to hope for the best.

"Lani," I started to turn, "I can explain—" But it wasn't Lani.

"Phil," I whispered harshly. "Let go of me!"

He did. With a smile. He motioned for me to follow him.

We slid off the side of the porch.

"I never took you for a peeper." Phil leaned against a pine tree and smirked.

"It isn't what you think." A sweet odor hung around him. He'd been smoking, and if memory of my college days served me right, it hadn't been a cigarette.

"I think you were spying on us. Or at least trying to."

"Kay Calhoun said some things and..." How was I going to explain myself? "I just wanted to see if the Lord of Death was still there."

"Who?" Phil angled his eyes toward the cabin. "Are you talking about Lani?"

"No." I explained about Baron Samedi and how Kim had given him to Yvonne as a housewarming present.

"Wow," Phil said softly, "some welcome to the neighborhood present. Why not just give her a box of matches and tell her to use them to burn down her house?"

I was glad it was pitch-black because my cheeks were burning red. "It wasn't my idea."

"No," Phil said. "Your idea was to come sneak around on private property in the middle of the night and peek in the windows."

Having no real defense, I opted for going on the offensive. "What are you doing out here?"

"Come on, I'll show you."

I hesitated.

"Come on. I'm not going to hurt you. I haven't yet, have I?"

On that rather dubious assurance, I reluctantly followed Phil as he moved in a wide circle away from the cabin. We ended up at their van. He rapped on the rear door, then opened it without waiting for a reply from within.

The smell of marijuana filled the air.

"I brought company," Phil said. "Move over."

I peered inside. A candle burned on the bare metal floor in the center of the van's cargo hold. Several rumpled sleeping bags and a couple of pillows that I recognized as belonging on Yvonne's sofa filled the edges.

Ted lay sprawled against the back of the passenger seat, the nub of a joint in his left hand. He sucked noisily. "Hey. What's up?"

Phil had scrambled inside. He held out his hand to me.

"No, thanks. I really should be going."

"Come on," Phil coaxed. "We should talk."

I studied the Lexus beside us. "Whose car is that?"

Phil grinned. "Have a seat and I'll tell you."

"Fine." I pushed aside several crushed beer cans and climbed aboard. The van was cramped, it stank, and the bare metal hurt my knees.

Other than that, it was paradise.

Ted extended the joint toward me once again. I declined with a shake of the head.

The candle flickered wildly as Phil tossed about the sleeping bags and blankets. "Aha!" His hand came up with an unopened can of beer. "Here you go."

"No, thanks."

"Are you sure? It looks like the last one."

"I'm sure. So who does the car belong to?"

Phil took an annoyingly long time in answering. He popped open the beer, which proceeded to explode in his face. This caused both him and Ted to laugh hysterically.

Personally, I was ready to run for the hills.

After they had settled down, Phil took a swig and answered. "It belongs to you."

"Me?"

The index finger of his left hand wavered in my direction.

Now I was mad. I'd waited around in this smelly van just to hear a drunk and high-out-of-his-mind druggie tell me that the car sitting next to us belonged to me?

Just in case I was wrong about him, I tried again. "I am talking about the Lexus, *not* my Kia."

"I know."

Ted giggled.

"I'm out of here!" I groped for the rear latch.

"Wait, wait!" Phil grabbed me by the jacket and urged me to stay.

I twisted, bumped my skull against the roof of the van, and faced him down. "I really need to be going now. Do I have to scream?"

"Boy, you are a handful. I'm only trying to have some fun."

"Your idea of fun and mine seem to be miles apart."

"Tell me about it." Phil snapped his fingers, and Ted handed him the roach. He sucked it, then spat. "The car belongs to Amy."

"Amy?"

Phil was smiling, not a bad sight by daylight but somewhat gruesome in the confines of the van and by flickering candlelight. "That's her name."

Then reality hit me. And it was about time. "You don't mean..." Could it be? "Amy Harlan?"

"Could be," Phil replied.

"You know her last name, Teddy?" Phil inquired.

"Not a clue." Ted curled up into himself. "All I know is that Lani said he had a date and for us to stay out here till he was through. I'm tired." He tucked a pillow between himself and the back of the front seat. "I'm going to sleep."

He put his hands under his head and shut his eyes.

"Do you know her?" Phil asked me.

"If it's who I think it is, yes, I do." The woman I had seen through the slit in the curtains had blond hair. It could very well have been Amy Harlan. "Can you describe her?"

"Sure." And he did. "She's the chick that Lani met in Charlotte. Sure was funny him running into her again."

"Yeah, funny."

19

I drove home in a daze and maybe just a bit of a haze.

I changed out of my day clothes and into a pair of thick purple plaid pajamas. My toes were toasty in a pair of gray felted slippers with hand-painted holly branches laden with bright red berries and cardinals for decoration. They had been a holiday gift from one of my suppliers.

They weren't subtle, but they were cute.

I filled a coffee mug to the halfway mark and sat down on the sofa. I switched on the TV and settled in to watch the oldies movie channel. They were running *Seven Brides for Seven Brothers*, the fifties classic. Our own little theater group had put on a production several years ago at the Theater On The Square. My cousins Riley and Rhonda had played supporting roles. Although since neither of them had ever been married, they knew about as much about the wedded state as I did—zilch.

I took a generous drink from my cup.

Did I mention my cup was filled with sangria?

I mean, coffee after midnight? That would practically be suicidal.

I dragged my feet up on the sofa and tossed the comforter over my lower half. Kim's spirit board and planchette taunted me from the coffee table.

I was half-tempted to give the whole shebang a good swift kick and get it all out of my sight. Lately, the spirits had been nothing but trouble.

I yawned, the sweet strong wine was already having its effect on me.

Unfortunately, I was also half-tempted to ask the spirit board for advice. I think that half-tempted part of me was controlled by the half-drunk portion of my brain.

Double unfortunately, the soused side won out.

I finished my sangria and stretched my arm back to place the coffee mug on the end table. I then leaned over the coffee table, one eye on the spirit board, one eye on the antics on the screen—Milly was teaching her six brothers-in-law how to dance—and one eye on my sanity.

Yes, I know how to count. Math just seems less precise and more fluid after midnight and alcoholic beverages.

I placed the planchette near the center of the board. "Oh, Ouija," I began. I couldn't resist rolling my eyes even though there was no one present to appreciate the gesture. Well, except the spirits.

Potential spirits.

"Oh, Ouija," I started again. "Share your wisdom with me." I thought a moment. "Who killed Yvonne Rice?"

T-H-E-M-U-R-D-E-R-E-R.

"Well, sure." I hiccuped. "That was an easy one."

I tilted my head ceilingward—number one, to think about my next question, and number two, to check for any kindly or malevolent spirits hovering silently overhead.

The coast was clear.

"Oh, Ouija." Thank goodness, Kim couldn't see me now. She'd razz me all the way to my grave!

I cleared my throat. "Will I ever get married?"

Trust me, it was the booze talking. Not me.

I waited. My fingers were sweating all over the plastic planchette.

U-R-M-A-R-R-I-E-D.

I gulped. The planchette jumped to GOODBYE.

My cell phone began singing, and I dug it out from between the cushions, where it had fallen. Sometimes the space between those cushions was like quicksand.

I read the screen: UNKNOWN CALLER.

Before I could answer, the call dropped.

Who had it been? A crank caller? A wrong number? The spirits playing tricks on me?

Or had it been my future husband?

I'd never know…I tossed the phone gently to the end of the table and went to bed.

I crawled under the covers and shut my eyes. I'd had enough fun for one night and made a big enough fool of myself for one night, too.

* * * *

I slept well but had strange dreams. Was it the secondhand smoke or all the odd and sinister goings-on?

I grabbed my binoculars from the bedside table and watched the titmice and cardinals as they attacked the feeders down in the yard. I'd have to refill them soon. This time of year, the birds seemed to double up on their feeder time.

I started the coffee and threw a slice of white bread in the toaster. Lamentably, the birds ate more nutritiously than I did.

I wished my mother would get home. There was something comforting about her presence.

I got downstairs late. Esther had already opened up the store. I had to listen to my employee berate me for my lack of commitment and poor work habits.

I sighed and shuffled off to the kitchenette, our little oasis of caffeine and sugar. There would be sustenance there. Sadly, it was bagel day, and I had to settle for half a toasted blueberry bagel rather than something more exciting, like a blueberry-filled jelly donut.

I carried my food and drink to the counter and watched as Esther popped a DVD into the machine. This one featured a series of lectures on bird-watching. We liked to keep something playing on the TV monitor for the customers to watch while they shopped. Hopefully, they found the videos educational, and just maybe, it led to impulse buying.

I wiped the sleep from my eyes for the umpteenth time. Where did all that crud come from? My only impulse was to crawl back into bed. Instead, I planted my elbows on the sales counter and dipped a chunk of bagel in my sugary coffee.

The phone rang like a bedside alarm, prodding me awake. "Hello, Birds and Bees."

"Good morning, beautiful."

I smiled. "Now, that is the way I like to start my day." It was Derek. His smooth voice washed over me like a warm, sensual wave. "Couldn't you call me like this first thing every morning?"

After the briefest of pauses, the reply was, "Better yet, I could whisper it in your ear."

My toes curled. Other parts made moves I didn't know they could.

"What's wrong with you?" barked Esther. She nudged me aside so she could ring up a sale for a customer who had come in for her monthly supply of seed.

I cleared my throat and moved to the storeroom. "What's up?"

"Can you come by the office? I have something to discuss with you."

I pinched my brows. "Can we talk over lunch? My treat."

"This is business. It would be better in the office. We can hit Jessamine's afterward," Derek replied. "*My* treat."

We agreed to meet at his office at one o'clock and rang off. Kim came in the back door, unwound her scarf from her neck, and threw it atop a stack of boxes. "Sorry I'm late."

"No problem."

And no surprise. So there was no point in making a big deal out of it.

Kim hastily tied on her store apron. "Anything special going on today?"

"No. It's delivery day. The truck should be arriving sometime after three. Other than that, all's quiet on the Ruby Lake front. And I, for one, am glad of it."

I followed Kim to the front of the store. Esther was stalking another customer in aisle two.

"Did you get Violet home okay?"

"Yeah." Kim idly checked the seed bins. "Did you know she lives at the radio station?"

"I had no idea. Makes sense, though. The woman lives for that station."

"I suppose." Kim moved from one bin to the next.

"And men," I couldn't resist adding.

"Amen to that," Kim was quick to agree.

"What are the others up to today?" The *others* being Dan and Paula. I wasn't sure if it was safe to say the P word.

"Paula and Dan are spending the day in Asheville."

Apparently, the P word wasn't verboten.

"Paula's never been, so Dan offered to show her around the city. She's only in town for a couple more days." That last sentence had a certain happy bounce to it.

The artsy city of Asheville was a close neighbor, a mere day trip away. "And you didn't go with them?"

"No. Dan asked me, but I decided to stay in town."

"Why?" That didn't sound like Kim at all.

"I figured they could spend the day together. They're friends. It will do them good." Kim rearranged suet cakes on the shelf in front of her.

All wrong.

She was sticking the cakes with the later dates in front of the ones that should be sold first. I'd fix it later.

"Besides, I want Dan to see how mature I am."

"Are you planning on driving up later and spying on them?" I teased.

"So I am going to need the afternoon off." Kim planted a kiss on my forehead.

"I was only joking."

"I knew you would understand."

But Kim wasn't listening. She untied her store apron and threw it in my face. "Thanks, Amy!"

By the time I had untangled myself and could breathe again, my best friend was out the door and hurrying to her car. Watching her alacrity, I wouldn't have been surprised if she had left the motor running the entire time.

I looked at my watch and sighed. It was only ten a.m.

I parked in the public lot near the town square and made a beeline for the offices of Harlan and Harlan. Ben Harlan was at his desk in front, speaking on the telephone. He smiled as he looked out the big window and waved to me.

I purposefully avoided looking at Dream Gowns, Amy-the-ex's boutique next door. It would only annoy me. I pulled open the door to Harlan and Harlan, expecting to find Derek and Ben's latest receptionist, a stiff-haired woman who was about as friendly as a kiss from a blooming cactus.

But no, my luck was worse than that.

Derek's ex-wife sat behind the heavy mahogany desk. She wore a tight white sweater designed to show off her significant assets, made all the more so by the sheerest of bras. Her platinum hair glistened in the light spilling in the windows. She smiled broadly as I entered and hung up my coat on the tree to the left of the door.

That smile did not reach to her eyes.

"Can I help you, Ms. Simms?" Amy-the-ex asked in a voice that held more frost than my freezer.

I looked around wildly. Had I gone in the wrong door? Had I somehow ended up in Dream Gowns? No. That shop held fancy wedding and ball gowns. This place held simple yet elegant furnishings and a reception desk behind which sat a...well, you get the picture.

Was I dreaming? Was I still asleep, deep in an alcohol and secondhand-weed stupor?

"I'm here to see Derek."

Amy-the-ex set down her nail polish brush, blew frost across her fingernails, shook her hands in the air like a pair of pinwheels. "I'll see if he is available."

She daintily picked up the phone at the desk and punched a button. "There is a Ms. Simms here to see you, dear."

Dear?

I fought to maintain my composure. So much blood was rushing to my head and filling my ears that I barely heard Amy-the-ex tell me to go on back to Derek's office. It was only when she waved persistently at me that I understood.

I stumbled down the narrow hall and through the open door into Derek's office.

"Hi, Amy." He smiled and greeted me with a kiss.

The merry-go-round that had replaced my brain went on relentlessly, moving in circle after circle after endless circle.

"Have a seat." Derek motioned for me to take one of the two comfy seats provided for clients. "I've missed you. I tried calling last night. I couldn't get hold of you. I couldn't get hold of my ex, for that matter."

"How is everything with the two of you?"

"Okay. Fine, I guess. Same old, same old. Why?"

"Just curious." I fingered the fancy silver pen and pencil set at the edge of Derek's desk—a gift from his father when he joined the office.

"Are you all right?" Derek peered at me with interest.

"Huh?"

"I asked if everything was okay." He swiveled as he talked and extracted a folder from the file cabinet behind the desk.

"Yes, fine." In a not-so-fine-at-all sort of way. I felt a bead of sweat forming on my brow and wiped it with a finger. "You wanted to see me about something?"

Derek nodded and opened the manila folder. "It's about this."

I crossed and uncrossed my legs, wishing I had changed out of my Birds & Bees clothes and into something sexier. "What is it?"

Derek leaned back in his plush chair and tugged at his red tie. "Gar Samuelson came to see me recently."

"Oh?"

"Yes. He wanted us to prepare his will. It didn't take long. It was quite simple, and he didn't have much." He tapped a finger on the typed sheets in the open folder. "This is it."

"You mean he came to town, had a will written up, and then—"

"And then he died," Derek finished my sentence. "Under somewhat murky circumstances."

"This is so odd. Did you tell Jerry?"

"Oh, yeah. Like you, he thinks it's suspicious. But," Derek folded his hands, "that is not why I asked you here."

"Why did you ask me here?" It couldn't be to rub my nose in the fact that his ex-wife was now working in the outer office. Derek was no cad.

"Mr. Samuelson mentioned you in his will."

"Me?" My hand flew to my heart.

"Yes, you. And Chief Kennedy finds that a bit suspicious, too."

"He would," I muttered. "Why on earth would Gar Samuelson mention me in his will? I barely knew the man."

"Apparently you knew him well enough that he named you his sole beneficiary."

"Me?" I said again.

"Well, his only human beneficiary."

"Excuse me?"

"Pep has been provided for too."

I smiled fondly. "His Irish setter."

"So he said. He really loved that dog." Derek picked up the sheets of paper and tapped them against his desk. "I'll skip the legal mumbo jumbo and tell you that, after funeral expenses, you've inherited a small sum of money in the local bank, enough to cover the current taxes and expenses, dog care, plus the cabin at Webber's Pond."

"I don't know what to say." And I didn't. "When is the funeral?"

"You'll have to ask Chief Kennedy that question. I believe it is still on hold, pending further investigation. At least, that's what Dan told me."

"I see."

"Speaking of funerals, I did hear there is going to be a ceremony for Yvonne Rice tomorrow at the lake. Her body is being returned to Hawaii."

"I hadn't heard." Why hadn't anybody told me?

"Amy told me."

I ground my teeth. "Speaking of Amy," I turned my head toward reception, "I didn't know she worked here now."

"Heaven forbid." He grabbed his suit jacket from the hook on the wall. "She's filling in while Mrs. Edmunds is out sick."

He slipped his arms into his coat and motioned for me to go first. "Nice of her to help out on such short notice."

"Yes," I managed to say, despite my sudden-onset lockjaw. "Nice."

There was a good crowd at Jessamine's Kitchen, a Southern-style eatery near Derek's office. We squeezed into a table for two in the back. Derek ordered the fried shrimp po'boy. I ordered a peanut butter and banana sandwich with cole slaw and a glass of Cheerwine, North Carolina's legendary cherry soda.

Forget comfort food. I needed a comfort feast.

"A cabin," I said, sucking at my soda. "What am I going to do with a cabin?"

"Move in?"

"It's more convenient living above the store."

"I know what you mean." Like me, Derek lived in an apartment above the law offices. "You could always sell it," he suggested.

"Is there a mortgage on it?"

"A small one."

"That is an idea. Still, I feel bad coming into it this way." I used my bread knife to carve off a chunk of Derek's po'boy. I popped it into my mouth and chewed. "Poor Gar Samuelson. Poor Pep. What's going to happen to him?"

"Ross is taking care of the dog for the time being."

"Yes, I know. I saw them together."

"Maybe he'd like to keep Pep."

"Maybe. That would be nice. Pep would get to stay at Webber's Pond. That is, it would be nice if Ross isn't the person responsible for Gar's death."

"What makes you say that?"

"I don't know. I guess I have a suspicious nature."

"That you do. Tell me," Derek took my hand, "were you suspicious when you saw my ex sitting at the reception desk?"

"Not at all," I replied. "Shall we order dessert?"

Derek laughed. "Pecan pie?"

"Sounds perfect."

Pie was served and mostly eaten by me.

"Are you sure you don't want more?" The tines of my fork hovered over the last bite on the plate between us.

"No, thanks. I enjoy watching you eat."

Judging by the grin on his face, that was no lie.

"Maybe you should consider keeping Pep," Derek said as I wiped the remains of crust from my lips.

I was stuffed. "I love dogs, but with my life, the way things are, I couldn't give him the attention he needs."

"Too busy running your business?"

"Something like that. And I don't have a yard."

Derek picked up his glass and began making damp circles on his place mat. "Have you ever thought about, you know, maybe having something more?"

My heart fluttered like the heroine's in a romance novel. "Do you mean—"

"Did you hear?" blurted our young waitress, Lulu. She planted two fresh glasses of soda on our table.

"Hear what?" Derek asked.

I was unable to speak because my heart had lodged somewhere up near where my tonsils sat.

"It was on the news. That dead guy they thought was that convict wasn't that convict at all." Lulu brushed a dark brown lock of hair from her right eye. "He was just some other dead guy."

I blinked in confusion.

"I think what Lulu is trying to say," said Derek, "is that Alan Spenner is still very much alive."

"Yeah, that's it." Lulu grinned. "Will there be anything else?"

20

As we exited Jessamine's, Derek's cell phone chirped. He extracted it from his inside coat pocket. "Yes?"

It was his ex. I shuffled my feet while he hemmed and hawed and finally agreed to meet with a client in the neighboring town of Swan Ridge.

"I forgot that I had a meeting with a client and his attorney this afternoon." We cut through the farmers market holding hands. "What are your plans?"

"Would it be possible for me to take a look at Gar's cabin?"

"I don't see why not. It will soon be yours. You can't remove anything from the premises yet, however."

"I only want a look around. Maybe it will give me some ideas."

"Why do I get the idea that you are planning to do some snooping?" Derek asked.

"Maybe because it is you who has the suspicious nature?" I countered.

He held the door, and we reentered Harlan and Harlan. Derek's ex-wife was daintily plucking at a green salad with avocado slices. The look Amy-the-ex was shooting me felt very much like I imagined it felt to hit a brick wall at high speed.

Nose first.

Derek rummaged in his desk and pulled out a key ring that held several keys of varying sizes and shapes.

I reached for the keys. Derek wrapped his hands around them. "Oh, no, you don't."

"What do you mean? You just said—"

"I just said I guess it would be okay for you to have a look around. I didn't say alone." He rose and grabbed his jacket. "I'm going with you."

"What about your appointment?"

Derek twisted his watch around. "I've got time. Besides, Webber's Pond is practically on the way to Swan Ridge."

Derek was driving to his appointment afterward, so we agreed to take separate cars. I led the way since I had been there several times now.

* * * *

We pulled up outside Gar's cabin.

"That's Pep." I pointed across the pond to where an Irish setter was dancing on the grass. The dog stopped and looked our way. "He's probably hoping to see Gar," I reflected.

"Come on," Derek said. "Let's go inside."

Gar Samuelson's cabin was no different from the rest, except a shed leaned against the western side. Next to the shed, there rested a dirty golf cart with underinflated tires and a tattered roof. Thick, untamed shrubs surrounding the cabin hid most of the windows.

"It doesn't look like Mr. Samuelson put a lot of care into managing the property," Derek noted. He thrust a key in the lock and turned it. "You might be disappointed."

I hovered behind Derek and peeked over his shoulder, trying to see inside, but it was too dark to make out anything much. "I wasn't expecting anything, so I won't be disappointed. Besides, he was wheelchair-bound. He could not have done much of the work himself."

"True." Derek's hand moved up and down the wall inside the door. An overhead light, nothing more than a shop lamp really, flicked on. The low-watt bulb cast a yellow glow on the room and its furnishings.

"That's good," Derek said, stepping inside. "Because this place is a mess." His whistle was absorbed by the thick walls. He fought his way through a jumble of upturned furniture and old newspapers. A lamp lay on the ground near the hearth. He picked it up from the floor, straightened its cracked green shade, and switched it on.

Derek held the lamp out, pulling its cord as far from the wall as he dared. "Either Gar Samuelson was the world's worst housekeeper, or I'd say somebody has trashed this place."

Derek was looking to me for the answer. "Was the cabin like this when you were here?"

"I never was here. I mean, not inside. I only spoke to Gar outside." I pointed. "On the dock. That's where I met him."

I moved gingerly through the debris-laden floor. "Who would do this? Why?"

I lifted a faded brown sofa cushion and set it back on the sofa. The sofa itself sat at a funny angle. Judging by the marks in the rug, it had recently been moved. "I can't believe Gar Samuelson lived like this."

"I take it he wasn't a slob?"

"I have no idea."

"He certainly wasn't the day he came to my office. In fact, he wore a suit and smelled like lime aftershave. That and tobacco."

"He smoked a pipe."

Derek picked something dark off the floor near the refrigerator. "Like this?"

It was Gar's pipe. "Yes." Pep's dog bowls, one for water and one for food, stood empty beside the stove. Ants crawled fruitlessly around them, their soldierly flank disappearing underneath the cabinet.

"I guess I'd better tell Chief Kennedy about this." Derek moved to Gar's bedroom. "Hey, it's just as bad in here."

And it was.

"Shouldn't you be going?"

Derek appeared confused.

"Your appointment?"

"I almost forgot." Derek checked the time. "I'm going to be late."

"You go ahead," I said. "I'll call Jerry and wait for him here."

"Are you sure?"

"Of course. I'll be fine."

I pushed Derek out the door.

"If you're sure?" He dropped the keys to the cabin in my hand.

"Go get 'em, tiger."

Derek backed his car up and started slowly down the dirt road. As he passed out of sight, I turned and studied the front-door lock. The door had been locked when we arrived, and there had been no sign of forced entry.

There was a second door at the back of the kitchen. It too looked perfectly normal, and I saw no signs of tampering there either.

Whoever had tossed Gar's home had either had a key or was a very clever locksmith. I made a mental note to mention the issue of the lock to Jerry. The police might be able to tell if the lock had been picked, whereas I could not.

I set my purse on the kitchen counter and pulled out my cell phone so I could take a few pictures of the interior. I knew I should be calling the police. I'd told Derek I would, but I wanted a look around for myself a bit before Chief Kennedy arrived and kicked me out.

I took a few photos and set my phone down beside my purse. I moved to the bedroom. The nightstand drawer stood open. Inside the drawer, I discovered a heavy black flashlight and a red leather Bible. Atop the nightstand was a leather pouch filled with tobacco and a small plastic butane lighter.

The bedsheets had been ripped off the bed, and the mattress lay askew atop the box spring. I lifted the side of the mattress and peered underneath. Nothing.

I returned to the main living area. There were a number of books scattered on the floor beneath the built-in shelves located on either side of the fireplace.

I riffled through the titles: some out-of-date history books, several classic American novels, including Robert Louis Stevenson, and a handful of old Reader's Digest Condensed Books, a series of anthologies that contained abbreviated versions of more contemporary novels.

Curious, I flipped through the table of contents of several of them. After reading a bit, I set the book on the lowest shelf. I picked up another. This volume appeared much older.

I sat in an old yellow chair with velvet upholstery that was covered with dog hair. I smiled. This must have been Pep's spot.

I curled my legs underneath me and flipped open the book. The volume had been printed in 1950. The first story was written by a man named Elmer Rice. His novel was called *The Show Must Go On*. It told the tale of a new playwright, his first play, and the accompanying and probably unavoidable trials and tribulations that went along with it.

I must have read a hundred pages before realizing I had lost track of the time. My throat was dry and scratchy. I carefully set down the book, making note of the page I had stopped on. I planned to continue it later, after everything was settled.

I moved to the kitchen. The refrigerator was filled with spoiling milk, fruit, and vegetables. I grabbed a tall, not-so-clean glass from the edge of the sink and filled it from the tap.

Drinking slowly, I glanced out the kitchen window. Obstructed by the wild shrubs that were in desperate need of pruning, a glint of light caught my eye. I paused and squinted out the smudged glass, focusing my eyes on a gap between the tightly packed leaves.

There was nothing out there in the distance but the unoccupied cabin and the woods beyond. A veil of darkness was now settling over Webber's Pond. The sun does not stick around long this time of the year in North Carolina.

Only one or two stars dared show their faces.

There it was again. The briefest of silver flashes. Then nothing.

Whatever it was, it had come from the abandoned cabin at the farthest edge of the pond. The one that no one had lived in for years and that Gar Samuelson was purported to have scared prospective buyers away from.

As I watched, the dark shape of a dog ran along the edge of the lake, coming from my left. The animal was jogging in the direction of the cabin. It then disappeared from my sight.

Was that Pep?

Did Ross know the dog was loose? Was Pep chasing Gar's ghost?

I decided to investigate. If it was Pep running around loose after sunset, Ross might not be aware of it. Although I had no doubt that Pep knew Webber's Pond and the surrounding woods far better than I did or ever could.

This would also give me a reason to visit the empty cabin. I didn't know why, but I was attracted to the cabin at the edge of the woods like a prothonotary warbler was attracted to a vacant nesting box.

Besides, Gar was gone now. There was no one to deter me from taking a closer look. There would be no more frightening prospective buyers away.

I stepped outside and pulled the front door closed behind me. I didn't bother to lock up. I stuffed the key ring in the pocket of my coat jacket.

Under the lowering sky, I walked to the last cabin. I looked all around and listened. Only the sounds of the woods and its creatures were audible.

"Pep?" I cupped my hands and called again. "Pep? Come here, boy!" I slapped my hands against my thighs.

A bird fluttered in the branches of a nearby oak, then flew off.

With no sign of the dog, I turned my attention to the cabin. The derelict structure appeared long neglected, with a sagging porch, cracked windows, and several loose shingles.

Glancing back, I saw lights on in each of the other cabins but no one out of doors.

The front door itself was warped and showed signs of age, with gray, almost silvery planks and pitted, rusty hardware. There was a gap at the bottom large enough for a fat rat to squeeze through.

Great.

Now that I'd thought it, I had probably created a whole family of the critters, and they would be waiting for me just inside the door, mouths wide open, sharp little teeth glistening with saliva, tongues hanging out, waiting for a tasty toe or two.

I wiggled my toes nervously and tried the doorknob. Surprisingly, it turned. Even more surprisingly, the door opened easily, without complaint.

Foul air swept over me like an ethereal plague. I pinched my nose and grunted. "Gross."

It smelled like Death itself was napping inside.

"Coming here was a bad idea," I whispered.

"Yes," a man's voice whispered back in my ear. "It was."

"Phil?" The jerk was trying to scare me again. "Is that you?"

"Inside!"

21

Rough hands shoved me forward through the open door. I tumbled inside. The room was as black as it was foul-smelling. I banged against a hard, cast-iron woodstove and spun around. "Who-who are you?"

A match flickered to life. The face of a man danced before me. He was unshaven and unbathed. He wore a dark ski mask over his face. A baggy shirt hung loose over a pair of muddy blue jeans.

The match burned down to his fingertips. He cursed, tossed it over his shoulder, and lit another. From that, he lit the stub of a candle that he pulled from the front pocket of his pants.

"Who are you?" His voice was breathy and menacing. Hard black eyes studied me from behind the mask.

"Amy Simms," I said. "Who are you? What are you doing here? This cabin is supposed to be empty." As my eyes adjusted to the little light that was available, I inspected my surroundings.

The floor was filthy, covered in dirt, caked mud, dried leaves, and every manner of debris. The dusty old woodstove sat on a raised hearth in the center of the room. Beside it, there was a small, portable camp stove, the kind that uses canned gel for fuel. I noticed other signs of camping: a slender LED flashlight, a tattered blanket, food wrappers, and empty plastic water bottles, one of which was filled with cigarette butts.

"You live here?" I asked.

The stranger rubbed his face. His lips looked like two purplish scars. "You live in one of these cabins?"

"No. You didn't answer my question."

I probably should have kept my mouth shut or at the very least been more polite, but something about this man was getting under my skin. "You shouldn't be here. Aren't you cold?" I wrapped my arms around myself. "If you need a home, I'm sure social services could help."

"Shut up, lady. Just shut up."

He rubbed his face some more, and I wondered if it was the itchy nature of the ski mask or a nervous condition.

"Fine." I stepped toward him. "If that's the way you're going to behave, I'm leaving."

I reached for the door.

He threw himself against it and grabbed my arm. "Sit over there!"

I winced as he twisted my right arm and threw me toward an upholstered chair that definitely looked like it was home to an entire colony of toe-biting rats.

Hey, I gave it a shot.

"I don't know who you are or what you want, but everybody knows I'm here." I struggled to keep the fear I was feeling from revealing itself in my voice.

I clamped my hands over my knees to cover my trembling and looked madly about the room for a means of escape.

Barring that, a good weapon.

But neither a plausible escape route nor a possible weapon leapt to sight or mind.

"Don't even think about it," he snarled, as if reading my mind.

The room smelled of smoke and stale sweat. "The only thing I'm thinking is that you really could use a housekeeping service."

"You volunteering to be the maid?"

"You can't afford me."

"You got that right."

The way he said that was chilling.

He tugged at the end of his dark blue ski mask. "Don't move."

He stabbed a finger at me. It may as well have been a knife or a gun. I wasn't going anywhere.

He moved to the window and peeked out. "You got a car?"

I debated lying but couldn't see what my advantage might be. "Yes."

I debated lying again, but I was also afraid he might not like it if he discovered I had misled him. "It's a van. It's parked outside Gar's cabin." Unfortunately, I couldn't help myself from adding, "You know, the invalid you drowned?"

My captor didn't confirm my statement, but neither did he bother to deny it. Was that a sign of guilt?

He breathed heavily through his open mouth and blinked at me. "Is the key in it?"

"Yes. It is." I realized leaving the key in my vehicle was getting to be a very bad habit. The last time I'd done so, some kids had taken it for a joyride. That was probably the fastest and hardest the van had been driven in its lifetime. While the Kia may have enjoyed itself, I hadn't been a happy camper.

"You can have it if you want. There's plenty of gas."

"Good to know." He grabbed the poker from the fireplace and slapped it forcefully against his meaty palm. "Let's you and me go for a ride."

"And if I say no?"

My captor loomed over me, both hands clasped tightly around the poker. "I don't think you are that stupid."

I stared him down for all of three seconds, but he was right. I wasn't that stupid. If he attacked me now, who would hear my screams? The nearest occupied cabins were hundreds of yards distant.

Pep to the rescue? I'd seen no further sign of the dog, if it was a dog and if it was the Irish setter.

Maybe, if I went with him, one of the residents would notice and notify the police. I groaned. I should have telephoned the police hours ago—as I had promised Derek I would.

If I got out of this alive, I promised myself that I would be wiser in the future. Face it, I couldn't get much dumber.

"Open it," he said, indicating the door.

I did and stepped out onto the porch.

"Oh!" My heart jumped.

Derek stood with his back pressed to the wall outside the open door. He held a finger of caution to his lips. His left hand gripped a broken shovel handle.

I forced myself to look away for fear of giving Derek away.

"Quiet and get moving." Rough hands gave me a push.

I stumbled down the steps.

I heard a muffled shout and turned around. Derek and the man in the mask struggled on the porch. The broken shovel handle lay between their feet.

Derek was taller than his assailant by approximately a head. I ran toward the porch. Derek saw me out of the corner of his eyes and yelled. "Stay back, Amy!"

Derek was distracted. His attacker cursed and pummeled him in the face and chest. Derek fell backward, hitting the porch hard. He scrambled and grabbed the handle of the shovel. He took aim at the other man's shins.

The man jumped but not high enough. There was a sickening yet satisfying—for me anyway—crack as wood met bone. The masked man howled in pain, kicked savagely at Derek, then spun away.

Derek staggered to his feet and threw himself on the man's retreating legs. The masked man fell half in, half out of the front door and struggled on his elbows to detach himself.

Derek slowly climbed over the man's back. The man kicked and bucked like a wild animal fearing capture.

Derek struggled to hold on. Finally, he sat on him. The man threw a couple of awkward backward punches. Derek pressed the masked man's face into the floor.

"You got him!" I threw myself on Derek.

"Careful!" he shouted, tumbling sideways and throwing out his right arm for support.

"Oops!" I climbed off and ran around to the front. I had picked up the busted shovel on my way in the door, and I waved it threateningly at the man on the floor.

"Sorry! Sorry!" I hollered breathlessly, my eyes on Derek.

"Let's see who we've got here."

Ignoring the man's snarls, Derek yanked the ski mask off his face.

Holding the broken shovel out like a lance, I studied the red, unshaved face by candlelight.

"Recognize him?" Derek asked.

When the man tried to heave himself up, Derek raised himself up momentarily, then dropped his weight mercilessly on him. He then pushed the man's face even harder against the wood floor.

"It's the guy." My mouth hung open.

"The guy?"

"Lulu's guy. That dead guy that they thought was that convict that wasn't that convict at all." I gulped. "It's that convict."

Only he wasn't dead. Although I almost was. And if it hadn't been for Derek, I probably would have been.

"You mean it's—" Derek leaned over, trying to catch a glimpse of the man's face.

"Alan Spenner," I answered.

22

"Well, well," said Derek. "A lot of people are going to sleep better tonight knowing where you are."

Spenner snapped at Derek. Derek pressed his forearm against the back of the escaped convict's neck.

"What do we do now? Can you hold him?"

"I think so. But look around and see if you can find something to tie him up."

"Right." I looked around for some rope or, better yet, some heavy chain.

"The police should be here any minute," Derek said.

I rummaged through the debris for something, anything. My shoulders sagged. "Actually, I forgot to phone them," I confessed.

"I called them," Derek said. "Rather, I called Anita at dispatch. She said she'd send a car."

"How did you know to do that?"

"When you weren't at the cabin but your van was, I knew you had to be up to something. And with you, that something usually spells trouble."

"I'd resent that remark if it wasn't patently true."

"I got worried that something might have happened to you. Even that you might have gone off into the woods for some reason and gotten lost," Derek explained. "Anita told me to sit tight and wait for Chief Kennedy. But then Chief Kennedy himself called while I was waiting. I explained what was going on. He said you had never called the station like we had agreed."

"I sort of lost track of time." It was a lame excuse but the only one I could come up with at the moment.

"Chief Kennedy sounded angry when I told him about us visiting Gar Samuelson's cabin and the mess we discovered inside."

"I'll bet."

Derek grunted and reapplied pressure to Spenner's neck as the convict tried to buck him off. "I saw a couple of footprints outside Mr. Samuelson's place and figured you had come this way."

I rummaged through the kitchen cabinets.

"Then I heard your voice and this guy's when I got close to the cabin. I was trying to figure out what to do when the door opened," Derek explained.

"I'm not finding anything to tie him up with," I complained.

"Maybe in your van?"

"Sorry, I'm a bird-watcher, not a mountain climber."

"Okay. Don't worry. I've got him."

"You'll pay for this!" warned Alan Spenner. "When I get out of here—"

I cut him off. "I can't believe this killer has been hiding out here all this time." I felt much safer insulting my masked attacker now that Derek had subdued him.

"Not so tough now, are you?" I lowered my face to look him in the eye. "Murderer!"

"You're crazy!" snapped the escaped convict. "I didn't kill anybody!"

"No? Tell it to the police, buster!" I shook my finger at him. "And what about all those other innocent people you beat up? Huh? What about them?'

Alan Spenner's dark blue eyes burned with hatred. "You talking about that kid I roughed up with a baseball bat?" He struggled to move his arms, but Derek had them tight. "He was trying to run off with my daughter. I had to stop her. I was a father protecting his daughter. For that I went to prison." He spat on the floor. "Would you have done any different?"

A strong voice broke through the chaos that was my mind.

"The police are here." Ross held Pep by the dog's leather collar.

Startled by the voice from behind, Derek lost his concentration. As Derek released his grip, Alan Spenner took advantage of the moment. The escaped con pushed off from the floor, shoved me aside, and ran toward the bedroom.

"He's getting away!" I cried for absolutely no good reason. I mean, we could all see that.

Pep barked and lunged, but Ross was holding him tight. Derek leapt up and surged past me. I shouted incoherently as Derek leapt in the air and tackled Spenner halfway out the bedroom window.

"Get him!"

I spun around to see who had hollered.

It was Chief Kennedy. Extracting his weapon with one hand, he waved to Dan and Larry with the other. The boys took hold of a writhing and fuming Alan Spenner by the arms. Those arms were quickly pulled behind him and cuffs applied.

"Nice tackle," I said, taking a seat on the floor next to Derek, where he sat nursing his right shoulder in the bedroom. "Did you ever play football in high school or college?"

"No." He massaged the shoulder. His voice sounded pained. "And I don't intend to start."

I kissed him on the cheek. "Thanks." I stood and extended my hand. "Come on. We'd better get you to a doctor. That shoulder is going to need looking at. Plus, there could be bad cuts, scrapes, bruising. You'll need to bathe those wounds and probably could use some disinfectant."

Derek winced as I pulled him to his feet. "I don't need a hospital," he said mulishly.

I grinned. "Who said anything about a hospital?"

"Huh?"

I arched my brow in the seductive manner that I had been practicing in the mirror since I was sixteen years old, just waiting for the right time, place, and person to practice it on.

It took him a moment, but Derek got the message.

"Oh!"

Derek leaned against me. We walked to the front threshold. Officer Larry Reynolds stood on the porch. He had hold of the prisoner. Officer Dan Sutton was frisking him.

Alan Spenner watched, sullen and fuming. He looked like a man far from having given up.

I was going to give him a wide berth.

"Hold up there, you two," Chief Kennedy waved us back. He had holstered his gun, probably disappointed that he hadn't had a chance to shoot at something or someone. "We've got our killer," Jerry said. "In some small way, thanks to you two," he added grudgingly.

"But what if Spenner didn't kill Yvonne?" I asked.

"He did."

"He told us that he only beat that boy with a baseball bat because the boy had forced his daughter to go with him."

"That daughter," Jerry replied, "was nineteen years old and had a mind of her own. From what the state police tell me, she not only went willingly with the young man in question, she prodded him into committing several burglaries. Seems she liked pretty things." Jerry's frown said he didn't think much more of the daughter than he did her father. "Alan Spenner probably took a baseball bat to the kid because he didn't like his daughter doing side work with some other crook besides himself."

"That puts a different spin on things," Derek said.

That it did.

"As for the second time," Jerry continued, moving inside the cabin, "Spenner didn't like what some unfortunate journalist wrote about him concerning the first incident."

"I didn't know that," I admitted, suddenly deflated.

"No, you didn't." Jerry ran a big flashlight around the cabin. "It looks like Spenner's been hiding out here for some time." He turned to Ross. "I'm surprised none of you people noticed."

He said "you people" like the residents of Webber's Pond were some sort of strange subspecies.

Surprisingly, Ross Barnswallow, usually so quick to flare, merely stroked Pep and nodded.

"How's the shoulder, Mr. Harlan?" Chief Kennedy asked.

"It's been better," Derek said through gritted teeth. "But I'll be fine."

I kissed him on the cheek. His left eye was swelling up, and there was a cut on his chin.

"Glad to hear it," Chief Kennedy barked. "The EMTs will be here any second. I think I hear them now."

A siren played its one-note score in the background and crescendoed a moment later as the van skidded to a stop outside the cabin.

While the driver remained seated behind the wheel, two EMTs rushed up to us.

"Give me a minute, folks," the chief said to the man and woman who began checking over Derek's wounds.

The two EMTs took a step back, their eyes falling with curiosity on the prisoner.

"As much as I appreciate you two nabbing a killer and escaped convict, how about you telling me what you're doing here in the first place?" Chief Kennedy stuck the flashlight back on his belt and folded his arms under his armpits.

I debated how to answer the question before opening my mouth. No matter what I said, Jerry wasn't going to like it. "I heard that Gar had willed me his cabin, and I—"

Jerry interrupted. "Yeah." He spat. "What was he? Some sort of lunatic?"

"Gar Samuelson was a very nice man, Jerry."

"I thought you barely knew him?"

"That's true but—"

"And didn't I hear that you thought he might have murdered Ms. Rice?"

"Who told you that?" It was true, but I didn't remember telling him that.

"Doesn't matter." He turned to Derek. "Maybe I can get a straight answer out of you."

"I've got a straight answer for you!" I shoved my hands in my pockets before my fists did something stupid that I couldn't control and would regret later.

Derek rested his fingers on my elbow. "Don't mind Amy, Chief. She's been through a lot."

Jerry was smirking, which was only making me madder.

"We all have."

"Yeah, yeah," conceded Jerry. "I suppose."

"And like you said yourself, it is because of Amy that you've caught Mr. Spenner."

Jerry took pause.

"Yes, this is quite a coup," Derek said. "This will be quite a feather in your cap."

I rolled my eyes.

"Wait until the news reporters get hold of the story," Derek added.

Jerry's brows twitched.

"Front-page news. Right, Amy?"

"I think I'm going to be sick," I muttered.

Derek raised his voice over mine. "It wouldn't surprise me if you and the entire Ruby Lake PD didn't get some kind of commendation. Maybe from Mayor MacDonald himself."

"Maybe even the governor." Jerry rubbed his chin.

"Maybe Mickey Mouse," I mumbled.

Derek prodded me with his elbow. "How about if Amy and I go home, get some rest, and meet you down at the station tomorrow? We'll give you our statements then. Right, Amy?"

"Right," I said grudgingly. I had several statements I wanted to give Jerry right then and there, but I supposed they could wait.

"Nine a.m.?"

"Nine a.m." Derek laid his hand on his chest.

"Fine. Get out of here. I've got a department to run and a murder investigation to wrap up. I'm sure you have little birdies to feed."

He hustled me to the door. "But you, Mr. Harlan, are not going home."

"I'm not?"

"Nope. You are going to the ER."

"What for?" Derek halted on the porch's bottom step. "I'm fine. Really, Chief."

"That's the rules, counselor. There's liability issues. We can't go having the Town of Ruby Lake being sued if it turns out later you have serious injuries that we neglected to treat you for."

Derek reluctantly agreed.

"I'll meet you there."

Sigh. So much for playing the role of Nurse Simms. We kissed, and Derek climbed into the EMS vehicle.

"Wait. What about my car?" called Derek as one of the medics applied some cream to the cuts on his chin and hands.

Dan stuck his head in the back of the vehicle. "Don't worry, Derek. I drove up with the chief. I'll drive the Civic to town and park it outside your office."

Reassured, Derek nodded and allowed the medic to strap him in.

"Thanks, Dan," I said as Derek and company headed down the road. "I'll catch up with you later."

I waved to Ross Barnswallow, who stood on the lawn outside the cabin, still holding Pep, still saying little.

I imagined the shock he must be feeling. I was feeling it too. Alan Spenner was now locked in the back of Officer Larry Reynolds's squad car. Larry started his engine and drove off, following the EMTs to the medical center so Spenner could get checked out by a physician, too.

Derek had hit him pretty good.

Dan pulled me aside. "Before you go, I'd like a word."

"Sure, Dan. What is it?"

Dan glanced toward the cabin. Jerry was interviewing Ross Barnswallow now. That is, Jerry was talking, and Ross was mostly nodding. Ross had on a baggy brown coat that hung practically to his knees, brown corduroy pants, and a red hat.

"It's about Kim."

"What about her?" In the midst of capturing an escaped convict and the man responsible for murdering one and possibly two innocent people, he wanted to talk about Kim?

Dan shifted his hands on his duty belt. "Did you know she was seeing somebody?"

"What do you mean?"

Dan's lower lip sagged.

"Oh, Dan. You don't think she's cheating on you?" I was shocked. Kim was a lot of things, but she was no cheat. "Kim would never—"

"No!" He threw up his hands. "Please, Amy." He admonished me as he glanced nervously over his shoulder at his boss. "Keep your voice down. Okay?"

I nodded and he continued.

"I didn't mean 'seeing somebody' like that. I meant seeing somebody like a shrink."

"Huh?"

"A shrink. You know, a psychiatrist."

"Are you crazy? Oops." My hand flew to my mouth. I giggled. "Sorry. That just slipped out." I grabbed his wrist. "But are you crazy?"

"Sutton!" Chief Kennedy boomed.

Dan colored and turned. "Yes, Chief?"

"Get over here! Anita says the county and state boys are on their way. I don't want them thinking we don't know how to do our jobs!"

"Yes, Chief." Dan mouthed "We'll talk later" to me, then lumbered off.

"I want this cabin and these grounds searched top to bottom," Jerry instructed. "If there is anything here to find, I want us to find it before they do. That means I want the neighbors interviewed. Again. And I want—"

Jerry froze midsentence.

It was me he was looking at.

"I want you out of here."

"Yes, Jerry." Why fight it? Besides, I was anxious to check on Derek. Despite his assurances, he could have sustained some serious injuries—all on account of me.

"And I don't want to see you again until nine o'clock tomorrow!"

I frowned. "What's at nine o'clock tomorrow? I've got a business to run, in case you've forgotten."

Jerry looked like a kettle about to blow its top.

Dan came to my rescue. "You and Derek need to give your statements. Remember?"

"Don't worry, we'll be there." I smiled at Ross and Pep. "Good night, neighbor. Hang in there."

Pep eyed me like a potential playmate. Unfortunately, now was not the time.

Ross looked at me like I was nuts. I didn't let it bother me. I get a lot of that.

23

In the morning, after a fortifying breakfast of pecan pancakes smothered in real maple syrup and butter at Ruby's Diner—I always consider it best to face Jerry on a full, well-sated stomach—Derek and I drove together to the police station.

Derek was behind the wheel.

I was wishing I'd worn a looser pair of slacks.

"Uh-oh. What's this all about?" Derek said as we drove slowly along Barwick Street looking for a spot to park.

The AM Ruby van was parked at the curb. Lance's car, a metallic green Beetle with *Ruby Lake Weekender* signage, was squeezed in beside it. A much larger white truck, with enough electronics on its roof to host a small convention, loomed over them both. That truck belonged to a Charlotte television station.

Violet Wilcox was banging her fist on the police-station door. Lance was peeping through the window.

Good luck with that.

According to Anita, those windows hadn't been washed a single time during Jerry's tenure as chief of police. Not to mention the odd assortment of half-dead greenery and faded file folders on the inside that blocked the view from the outside.

"Let's park in back," I suggested.

"That parking lot is for official use only." Derek motioned for the car behind us to pass us.

"This is official business," I countered. "Jerry told us to be here."

"I suppose." Derek didn't sound convinced, but since he saw no other option, he lifted his foot off the brake and cruised around to the rear of the police station. He pulled in between a pair of freshly washed squad cars.

A white bandage ran along Derek's jawline, and another was plastered to his forehead. I felt sorry for him, but I also thought he looked sort of adorable. He groaned as he slid from behind the wheel and his feet hit the pavement.

Maybe I'd get to play Nurse Simms yet.

I rang the bell at the back entrance. Officer Pratt peered through the tall, skinny bulletproof glass in the door.

He led us down the narrow corridor that held a couple of small holding cells. I'd personally experienced one of those cells not long after moving back to town. Long story.

The insides of those cells were invisible to us, but I pictured a sullen and cowering Alan Spenner sitting on the hard bench inside one of them.

Chief Kennedy's desk sits at the back of the room. He likes to keep an eye on his officers. I waved to Larry, who sat at his desk doing something on his computer. For his sake, I hoped he wasn't playing solitaire.

Dan was nowhere in sight.

"The chief is in a mood," Officer Pratt said quietly. "I'll leave you two to it." He abandoned us, retreating to his desk, where he picked up a set of keys. He jangled the keys and grabbed his hat.

"Tell the chief I'm going on patrol," Pratt said to Larry.

Jerry Kennedy was yelling into the phone on his desk. "I don't care! Next time, somebody needs to talk to me first!" He slammed down the receiver. "What do you two want?"

I opened my mouth. Derek placed a calming hand on my upper arm and stepped in front of me. "We're here to make our statements, Chief."

Jerry appeared pacified. He glanced around his squad room. "Reynolds!"

"Yes, Chief?"

"You busy?"

"I'm writing up my report for the—"

Jerry did not care what it was for. "It can wait. Take Mr. Harlan's and Ms. Simms's statements. I suggest you start with the counselor first. Maybe then you'll be able to make sense of anything Simms says afterward."

Derek pulled me away before I could do or say anything stupid. That was probably for the best, no matter how satisfying it might have felt in the heat of the moment.

"Have some coffee and a piece of coffee cake," Derek suggested, leading me to the refreshment setup on the other side of the room.

"I don't want any pastry," I sulked.

"They've got bananas and green apples."

Yuck. "I'll have coffee cake. Just a small piece." I pulled loose a corner slab the size of a playing card and nibbled.

Derek took a seat at Larry's desk after first removing his coat and draping it across his lap.

Mollified by the sugar rush, I plopped two big pieces of coffee cake on a paper plate, filled a sort of clean Ruby Lake PD mug with hot coffee, and placed it on Jerry's desk.

He looked like he could use a little mollifying, too.

Jerry looked up at me, suspicion in his eyes. "What's this?"

"You looked like you could use it."

Jerry frowned but pulled the plate closer.

"Rough night?" I sipped my coffee. It wasn't bad. That meant Anita or Larry had probably brewed it. Those two knew how to make a decent cup of coffee.

Dan barely knew one end of the coffee maker from the other. As for Jerry, the only coffee he ever considered decent had been that brewed by Cozzens Coffee, a shop at the edge of town—and they had shut down years ago due to a lack of customers.

Jerry was on a coffee wavelength all his own.

Usually, I like my coffee sweetened, but since I was probably far over the Surgeon General's recommended daily allowance of sugar for the day due to the pastry and pancakes—and it was only nine-fifteen in the morning—I skipped it.

I watched with sugar envy as Jerry ripped open the two packets that I had placed on his plate for him. He poured them into his mug without a care in the world as to what that sugar might be doing to his heart or his teeth.

His eyes locked onto mine. "I like milk."

"Right. I'll get that." I set my coffee on the corner of his desk and hurried to the micro fridge under the refreshment counter.

"None of that soy stuff Anita keeps sneaking in here!" Jerry hollered. "Real milk."

I brought the pint-sized carton of full-fat milk and watched him pour. In the tiny time I'd been gone, one of his two pieces of coffee cake had disappeared but for a trace of white icing on his upper lip. As if reading my mind, his pink tongue lashed out like a striking viper and destroyed it.

"Have you gotten much out of the prisoner?" I asked, sliding my thigh over the edge of his desk.

166   *J.R. Ripley*

Jerry drank. His telephone rattled, but he ignored it. "Mr. Spenner is not the talkative sort."

"Has he admitted to murdering Yvonne Rice and Gar Samuelson?"

Jerry narrowed his eyes. "What makes you think Gar Samuelson was murdered?"

"Wasn't he?"

Jerry looked past me. "Where's Pratt?" he asked Larry.

"Gone on patrol, Chief."

"You didn't answer my question, Jerry."

"That's because I don't want to, Simms."

He pushed my leg off his desk.

I lost my balance. Coffee flew upward from my cup. Unfortunately, it did not come straight down. It went sort of sideways and down the front of Jerry's shirt.

Jerry cursed. I raced over to the refreshment counter and returned with a handful of paper napkins. Jerry continued cursing while swiping at his shirt.

"Look on the bright side," I said with a smile, "with that brown shirt, the coffee is going to blend right in."

Well, except for the bits of wet, white paper napkin that were now ground into the fabric.

Jerry cursed some more as he picked at the white spots.

"Don't worry," I said. "That's gonna wash right out."

Jerry squeezed his eyes shut.

I could imagine what he was thinking but refused to. What was the point?

Finally, he spoke, his voice controlled and strained. "Did Spenner say anything to you about the murders? You were alone with him for a bit in the cabin. Did he confess to either of the killings?" Jerry leaned closer, his hands gripping the edge of the desk.

"No," I had to admit. "In fact, he insisted he hadn't killed anyone."

Jerry chuckled. "Gee, what a surprise. A convict who says he's innocent."

"So you do think he's your man?"

"I've got a theory or three that I do not feel inclined to share with you," Jerry answered. "Or anybody," he added loudly.

Why was he looking at Larry when he said that last part?

"Whatever." I was used to Jerry holding out on me. Probably made him feel macho. And it probably had something to do with me holding out on him during our one disastrous date in high school.

I picked up the remaining piece of coffee cake from the plate on Jerry's desk and bit it in two.

"Hey!"

"Sorry." I extended the remaining bit, but he refused it.

"It's got your germs on it."

"Really, Jerry? Germs? That didn't stop you trying to make out with me on our date!"

I'd never seen Jerry's face turn redder. "Me? You tried to make out with me, Amy Simms!"

"Ha!" I threw back my head. "You were the one who—"

Derek cleared his throat loudly. "Everything okay over there, kids?"

I smiled weakly.

Jerry yanked open a desk drawer and then slammed it shut again, apparently just for the hell of it.

"Look, Jerry, I'll get you another piece." But when I turned around, I saw Anita popping the last slice in her mouth.

Jerry shot daggers at me but, hey, that was better than bullets.

It was time to move the subject beyond dates and coffee cake to something safer. Like murder.

"Did Alan Spenner say why he shot Yvonne?" I pressed.

"No, he did not."

"And who called 911 using Yvonne's cell phone? Was it him? Why would he do that? Did you ask him, Jerry?"

Jerry pressed his knuckles into his temples.

"I'm ready for Ms. Simms now," Larry called from his desk.

"Thank you, Lord," mumbled Jerry, eyes to the ceiling.

"Jerry," I said before leaving him, "do you think it would be all right for me to talk to Spenner?"

"Why would you want to do that?" Derek appeared at my side, his coat draped over his left arm.

"I want to hear what he has to say for himself."

"I'm not sure that's appropriate, Amy," Derek said. "I'm not defending the man, but he is entitled to legal counsel."

"I suppose…"

"Even if I wanted to say yes," snarled Jerry, throwing his feet on his desk, "which I don't, I wouldn't."

"Why not?" I huffed.

There were so many things wrong with that sentence, but I let it go. Pointing out Jerry's deficiencies, as much as I enjoyed the exercise, never helped when I wanted a favor from him.

And our morning, so far, wasn't off to a good start.

"Because the state police have hauled Alan Spenner's butt off. So if you would like to have a little chat with him, I suggest you first go have a nice chat with them."

Jerry pointed to the station door. "If you leave now, you just might make it before nightfall to Charlotte, which is where they took him."

Dan Sutton came through the back door with Ross Barnswallow limping along at his side.

I formed a question with my eyebrow. Dan gave an almost imperceptible shake of his head in reply.

"There you are, Sutton." Jerry's feet hit the ground. "Have any trouble?"

"No."

"Good." Jerry shooed me away. "Give your statement to Officer Reynolds, Ms. Simms. Then you are free to leave." Jerry was suddenly all business. "In fact, I insist that you do."

"Being here was not my idea, Jerry. I'll be happy to go." I turned to Ross Barnswallow. "Good morning, Ross. How are you? I see Jerry has dragged you downtown, too?"

"Hi, Amy. Derek." Ross thrust his hands in the deep pockets of his wool coat.

"Here to make your statement?" I asked. "That was crazy last night, wasn't it? Where's Pep?"

"Back at the cabin. Murray said he'd keep an eye on him."

Larry shouted my name.

"Be right there." I dropped my hand onto Ross's shoulder. The poor fellow looked like he had barely slept. Unless I was mistaken, he was wearing the same clothing I had seen him in the night before.

"Hang in there," I said. "Jerry's bark is worse than his bite." I fetched him a cup of coffee and threw in some sugar.

"Thanks." Ross gulped gratefully. He didn't look like he had shaved in days.

"Is the media still out outside?" Chief Kennedy asked Dan.

"I'm afraid so."

Jerry drummed his hands on his desktop. "Tell them to leave."

Dan dared a smile. "I'm not sure they will listen. Especially Violet Wilcox. You know how she gets."

Jerry snorted. "Tell them they've got five minutes. If they aren't all gone, each and every one of them will be spending twenty-four hours in a cell with each other. And I'll impound all those expensive vehicles they've got illegally parked on my street."

"Yes, Chief." Dan saluted and left the way he had come.

As Larry led me to his desk, I heard Jerry say, "Have a seat, Mr. Barnswallow. Then explain to me why you failed to share with us your relationship to Alan Spenner."

My head spun around so fast I thought it might achieve liftoff. "You know Alan Spenner, Ross?"

Ross looked troubled.

"How?"

"I'll ask the questions, Simms," Chief Kennedy snapped.

Larry dragged me away. "Come on, Amy. Have a seat." He motioned to the chair across from his desk.

I tried to tune Larry out as he questioned me. I grunted a lot of *yeses*, *nos*, and *I don't knows*. I might have been confessing to murder myself.

I tilted my ear toward Jerry and Ross.

"If you lean over any farther, you'll hit the floor!" Jerry hollered. "Get her statement in the interview room, Reynolds."

With no choice but to follow Larry, I mouthed for Derek to pay attention to whatever was going on.

I'd grill him later.

I scooted into a hard chair across the table from Larry. He set his notebook on the table, along with a digital recorder. "Be right back, Amy," he said. He patted his pockets. "Forgot my pen."

"No problem." Once Larry left the room, I found my finger reaching for the button on the small, beige intercom on the table. Again, from experience, I knew that the intercom connected the room to a companion intercom on the corner of each officer's desk, including Jerry's.

If memory served, turning on one switched on the others.

I accidentally hit the ON switch. And not so accidentally leaned closer for a listen.

Chief Kennedy was talking. "Why did you hide your previous relationship with Alan Spenner, Mr. Barnswallow?"

"Yes, why?" I whispered. Oops. I clammed up. I strained my ears.

The intercom went dead.

A few seconds later, Larry's face loomed in front of me.

I smiled.

He didn't.

24

Deemed guilty by association by Jerry, Derek was ejected with me.

After being booted out of the Ruby Lake PD, I invited Derek for a bird walk around the lake and an early lunch, but he had work to do. Back to the office he went.

I had work to do, too, but I was more interested in what was going on with the Alan Spenner situation and the two murders. Because I was certain that Gar Samuelson had been murdered just as surely as Yvonne had.

The methods may not have been the same. But the results were.

I needed to think.

Why was Chief Kennedy so interested in Ross Barnswallow? Perhaps more importantly, what sort of previous relationship with Alan Spenner did Ross have?

Esther was alone in the store. By alone I mean the only employee and not a customer in sight.

Despite the blow to our bottom line, that suited me just fine. I climbed the stairs to my apartment and booted up the laptop at the kitchen table.

It was time for some serious digging.

I dug back through the years, scanning article after article on Alan Spenner and Ross Barnswallow. There were the usual stories about Mr. Spenner's exploits, and there was absolutely nothing on Ross.

It wasn't until I hit on the search engine's IMAGES option that I got lucky. It was a picture of Ross standing outside a government building of some sort.

Only the scanned newspaper article wasn't calling him Ross Barnswallow. No, they were calling him Ross Barnard.

I tilted the screen for a better look. Was I mistaken?

A little younger, a little thinner. Definitely better groomed.

Still, there was no doubt about it: Ross Barnswallow was Ross Barnard. And this Ross Barnard had been one of Alan Spenner's victims. The man on the screen, the same man who owned a cottage at Webber's Pond, which was where Alan Spenner was hiding out and subsequently captured, had been the person Spenner had taken a baseball bat to.

I about fell out of my chair.

What was going on?

And how on earth were Yvonne Rice and Gar Samuelson caught up in all this? Had they been innocent bystanders? Been in the wrong place at the wrong time?

What was Alan Spenner doing at Webber's Pond?

Then it struck me.

There could be only one answer.

I slammed the lid on the laptop and poured myself a drink.

Alan Spenner had very nearly beaten Ross Barnswallow aka Barnard to death once. He had escaped from prison only to come to Ruby Lake to finish the job he'd started.

Lucky for Ross, the man had been captured before he could follow through on that plan.

I needed somebody to talk to.

I drove to Kim's place. Her car was in the drive. I parked behind it and strolled around to the backyard. There was no point grabbing the key beneath the flowerpot because I could see my best friend milling about in the kitchen.

I climbed the rear stoop and peeked in the window. Kim's hair was done up loosely atop her head and held in place with a skinny red hair band. She was leaning over, peeking in the oven window, her backside to me.

I rapped on the door and let myself inside.

Kim spun around. She wore a rumpled purple sweat suit that I was pretty sure belonged to my old boyfriend's new girlfriend. A pair of heavy wool socks covered her feet.

"Hi, Amy. I'm making brownies."

"So I see." I sniffed. "And smell." I was hungry all over again, despite the big lunch I had indulged in. "Aren't those Cindy's clothes you're wearing?"

Kim plucked at the sweatshirt. "Yeah, how did you know?"

"I recognized the *Juicy* behind."

Kim colored. The kitchen timer went off. Kim slipped on an oven mitt and pulled out a tray of dark chocolate brownies. She transferred the tray to a wire rack. "Hungry?"

"You won't catch me saying no to a brownie."

"I thought not." Kim fanned the glove across the top of the tray. "I'm afraid these are going to need to cool a while. How about a glass of wine?"

"Thanks." I bent over the tray and took a whiff. "They look a little funny, but they do smell good." I turned to Kim. "I don't recall you ever baking brownies before. In fact, I don't recall you ever baking."

"I'm trying something new," Kim said somewhat defensively. She pushed the wire rack closer to the window and farther from me.

I grinned. "Trying to impress Dan with your homemaking skills?"

"Do you want a drink or not?" Kim snapped as she reached for the bottle and two glasses.

We took our drinks to the living room and sat side by side on the sofa.

I told her about my little adventure at Webber's Pond. Of course, she had already heard Dan's version of it. At least, as much as he felt he could, as an officer of the law, tell her without giving up any information that could jeopardize their investigation.

I also described to her what had occurred down at the police station earlier that day.

"Wow." Kim pulled her knees up to her chin. "I hadn't heard. Dan has been busy, and I haven't talked to him all day."

I was nodding. "Believe me, you could have knocked me over with a feather when I heard Jerry asking Ross Barnswallow about his connection to Alan Spenner."

"That is weird," Kim agreed. "And spooky."

"If it wasn't Spenner who murdered them, then it had to be Ross. I just can't figure out why."

"If you can't, don't expect me to." Kim took a thoughtful drink. "Did you ever stop to think that maybe they were in it together?"

I slapped my forehead. "Bird poop." I drained my glass and quickly refilled it. "Why didn't I think of that?"

"Because you are not as smart as me?"

We batted around a lot of theories, but none of them made sense. Murderers do not kill for nothing. There had to be a reason that our killer decided that Yvonne Rice had to die and then Gar Samuelson.

What was it?

"Let's say that Alan Spenner killed Yvonne because he was on the run. He barges into her cabin. There was no sign of a break-in, but she could have simply left her door unlocked." I played the scene in my mind. "He shoots her, steals her cell phone—"

"Why does he steal her phone?"

"Maybe he was thinking he could use it and then decided that he couldn't risk it because it could be traced."

"That makes sense," Kim agreed. But then she had to ask, "Where did he get the gun?"

"It could have been Lani Rice's weapon." I explained that he owned a handgun he claimed had gone missing.

"How would Alan Spenner get Lani Rice's gun?"

I had to think about that one for a bit. Finally, I came up with an answer. "Maybe," I speculated, "Yvonne borrowed the gun from her brother."

"Without telling him?"

"That's right."

"Why would she do that?"

"You said it yourself. Suppose you were right, Yvonne knew she was in some kind of danger. She borrowed her brother's gun to protect herself."

"And instead it was used on her."

"What do you think?"

"I think your theory has more holes in it than one of those purple martin houses we sell at Birds and Bees."

"Such as?"

"Maybe Yvonne had some connection to Alan Spenner and was worried for her safety."

Kim scrunched up her face. "Was the news even out at that point about his escape? Did she know?"

"Not helping," I snapped, feeling a drumming building in my skull. "Okay, how about this—"

Kim yawned. "How about if I go check on the brownies?"

I followed her, furiously constructing theory after theory in my brain as we entered the warm kitchen. Each carefully built theory fell apart as quickly as I formed it.

Kim pulled a long-bladed knife from the drawer and sliced into the tray of brownies.

I squinted, distracted from my thoughts. "They look sort of yellowish inside. Are you sure you cooked them long enough?"

"Forty-five minutes, like it said on the package."

The inside of the brownies looked more like some sort of yellow-white alien guts than a dessert food. "What recipe did you use? Not your mother's, I hope?" Kim's mom was a notoriously bad cook.

"No. I took it right off the box."

I picked up a fork and probed the side of a brownie. "It looks more like a chocolate omelet. How many eggs did you use?"

"Maybe it's just that one section that is funny." Kim took her knife and cut a wide slice at the opposite end of the tray. "The oven cooks uneven at times."

But the brownie guts here looked as bad as they did on the other side. "I don't understand it." Kim studied the ugly stain on the knife. "I only used the one dozen."

I dropped my fork. I was just about to slide a bite onto my tongue. "One dozen eggs? That doesn't sound right." I scooped up my scrambled egg brownie and plopped it down in the kitchen sink, where it settled in over the dirty dishes. "Let me see this box."

"Okay, okay." Kim pulled open the door under the sink and plucked a box from the trash. I noticed an empty carton of eggs in there too. "Here."

I read quickly. "One egg."

"Huh?" Kim was cutting the remaining brownies into somewhat equal squares.

"Read here." I pressed my fingernail to the side of the box. "That's one egg per batch."

Kim came closer, squinting. "One egg. Yep, you're right. You think it makes a difference?"

"Only if you intend to eat them."

"Very funny."

"Go ahead." I picked up a yellow-white-chocolate alien slime bar and lifted it to her mouth. "Try one."

Kim pushed my hand away. "No, thanks. I'm not hungry right now."

"Right." Kim's phone, sitting on the kitchen counter, rang. I looked at the screen. "It's Dan. Aren't you going to answer?"

"Maybe later," Kim said inexplicably. She retreated to the living room once again, and I followed her.

Plopping down on the sofa—a touch irritable since I'd been deprived of my promised brownie—I said, "This whole thing just has to be about Alan Spenner and Ross Barnswallow. Where's your laptop?"

Kim pointed, and I retrieved it from her small desk near the front door. I fired it up on my lap.

"Alan Spenner has been locked up for years," I said after sifting the internet. "And there is no record of any Yvonne, Rice or otherwise, as ever having been connected to him, victim or otherwise."

"Plus, Yvonne only moved to the mainland from Hawaii a short while ago. Face it, Amy." Kim picked up the TV remote and began flipping through the stations. "There is no reason on earth why Ross Barnswallow would want to help Alan Spenner kill anybody. Spenner almost beat him to death with a baseball bat."

Kim landed on a glitzy fashion show and turned her attention to the screen. "If somebody practically turned me into mush with a baseball bat, you wouldn't see me helping them take out the trash, let alone commit murder."

"If not them, don't you think that it must be one of the other guests at the housewarming party?" I insisted. "I mean, it has to be, hasn't it? Somebody at the Ouija board wrote *I am murdered*."

"Could be. Or it could be that Yvonne wrote that herself like we already talked about."

"That's the same thing that Murray Arnold said when I asked him about it. But why? What possible reason could she have to write such a thing? I don't know."

Kim shrugged. "We've eliminated any connection with Alan Spenner. Maybe it was just a random home invasion."

"I could accept that, maybe," I said, "if it had only been Yvonne. But Gar too?"

"Maybe you're making too much out of that whole *I am murdered* thing," suggested Kim. "Maybe Dan got it wrong."

"I suppose you could be right. Could it have been meant as a joke? A premonition?"

"If it was a joke, it was a sick one."

"I agree. But you have to agree that if it was a joke, Yvonne paid the ultimate price for it."

"Her life."

"Exactly."

"The more I think about it, the more I maintain that somebody at the housewarming party that night just has to be the murderer. And that somebody is Ross Barnswallow."

"So he killed Mr. Samuelson, too?"

"It stands to reason."

"Why? Why would he kill Yvonne and then, later, Mr. Samuelson? According to you, Alan Spenner is the person Ross Barnswallow would have wanted to dead. And," Kim just had to add as if adding salt to a wound, "Spenner is the one who had been hiding out in that empty cabin."

"I haven't quite figured all that out yet."

Kim's face suddenly fell. She switched off the television.

"What's wrong?"

"You don't think this is my fault, do you?" Kim wrung her hands. "I mean, you don't blame me, do you, Amy?"

"You? Why would I think you would want to shoot Yvonne? It's not like she was after your boyfriend."

"Thanks, I think." Kim frowned. "I'm not talking about jealousy, thank you very much. I'm talking about Baron Samedi."

"Ah. Your housewarming gift. Welcome to Ruby Lake." I thrust out my arms. "Here's the Lord of Death. I thought you might enjoy him."

Kim squirmed uncomfortably. "I didn't want—I didn't mean for anything bad to happen to Yvonne," she said softly.

"Of course not." I refilled our wine glasses. "Let's stop talking about it now. Maybe the answer will come to us."

"Better yet, let the police handle this one. Jerry might be a little challenged in the gray-cell department, but Dan is really smart."

"A little?" I chuckled. "Speaking of Dan, he said the oddest thing to me."

"When was this?"

"The night of Alan Spenner's capture."

"What did he say?"

"He asked me about you."

"How do you mean?"

I ran my finger around the rim of my glass. "He asked me if you were okay."

"Okay?" Kim scrunched up her nose. "That's funny."

"That's what I thought." I tipped back my head and drank. "He said something else funny."

"And that is?" Kim joined me gulp for gulp.

"He asked me if you were seeing somebody."

"What? That's preposterous. I would never do a thing like that!"

"That's what I said."

"Good." Kim slammed her glass down. "Seeing somebody," she muttered between curses. "The nerve. He's the one with that-that woman staying with him in his house."

"Turns out," I said, ignoring Kim's rant, "Dan didn't mean *seeing somebody* quite the way I thought."

"That's good," Kim huffed, still brimming with indignation over the remark.

"No. You made the same mistake I did. What Dan meant was seeing somebody as in a psychiatrist." I stared steadily at Kim waiting for a reaction. "Have you any idea where he would get such a—pardon the pun—crazy idea?"

Kim's breath caught in her throat. "Uh…"

I could see by the anguish and embarrassment written on her face that she had more than an idea. "Kim," I said, "what did you do?"

Kim stood and paced the floor.

"They caught me," Kim lamented.

"Caught you what?"

"Not what." Kim faced out the front window. "Where."

"Okay, where?"

"In Asheville. I rounded a corner downtown. You know, near the park where they have the drum circle on Saturday night?" Kim turned back to me.

I knew the place and said so. "Paula and Dan caught you spying on them?" I groaned. "What did you do? What did they say?"

"They were surprised to see me," Kim replied, pink-faced. "I said the first thing I could think of."

"What was that?" If I'd been in her shoes, I had no idea what I might have said in my defense. Nothing believable or even plausible sprang to mind.

"I told them I was in Asheville because I had an appointment."

"Okay, okay." I nodded. "That's not so bad." I took the idea and ran with it. "You told them you had an appointment that you had forgotten about earlier and only remembered at the mention of Asheville. Good." I rubbed my hands together. "Good. I like it."

Kim's face told a different tale. She looked miserable.

"Who did you say you had your appointment with? For what?"

"With Dr. DiNizio."

That was a new one on me. "Who is Dr. DiNizio? GP?"

Kim shook her head in the negative.

"OB/GYN?"

More negative head shaking.

"Dentist?" I ventured. "He's not a pediatrician, is he?" Kim could act rather childish.

Kim hung her head and mumbled, "A psychologist."

I cupped a hand over my ear. "A what?"

"A psychologist," Kim repeated through gritted teeth.

"What did you tell them that for? Why not just say that you were doing some shopping or seeing a dentist to get your teeth cleaned? A psychologist!"

"I panicked," Kim said. "It was the first thing I could think of."

"Psychologist was the first thing you could think of?" What would a psychologist make of that interesting tidbit?

Kim huffed. "There was a sign for a psychologist on the door of the building I was standing beside when they caught me."

"Dr. DiNizio, Psychologist?"

"Yes."

I pictured the scene and smiled. Did that make me a bad friend? "Then what happened? What did you do?"

Kim's head hung impossibly lower. "What could I do? I had no choice. I couldn't let them know I'd been spying on them. I went inside."

"You went into Dr. DiNizio's office?"

Kim nodded reluctantly.

I rubbed my jaw, a poor attempt to hide my grin. "So now Dan and Paula think you're not a spy, just some crazy psycho?"

Kim groaned.

"Cheer up," I said. "It's better Dan should know the truth about you now rather than finding out later."

For once, Kim didn't have a comeback. I almost felt sorry for her, then I remembered the time when she switched out my best moisturizing lotion with the cheapest, cheesiest orange self-tanner, and the feeling passed.

I draped an arm over her sagging shoulder. "Look, I'm sure it will be fine. Why not simply admit that you—"

"You want me to admit that I was spying on them?"

I gave her a reassuring squeeze. "Of course not. How about this? You tell them you had changed your mind about joining them. Yes!" I snapped my fingers. "So you got in your car and drove up to Asheville to surprise them."

Kim sniffed and swiped the bottom of her nose with a balled-up tissue. "That's not bad," she said. "But how do I explain what I said about visiting Dr. DiNizio?"

"Oh, that's easy," I replied. I slid back my chair. "You tell them you are crazy!" I jumped and ran for the kitchen door.

I was rounding the corner of the house when the wet brownie hit me in the back of the head.

Hey, it was better than a cupcake.

Or a rolling pin.

25

The next day was like an eternity. It was Esther's day off, and I'd had to work for a change. Of course, Esther the Pester's response when I'd asked her to postpone her free day so I could do some snooping had been to tell me that it was about time I worked for a change.

Knowing I was on shaky ground, I had not bothered to argue the point with her.

The highlight of the day was looking out the window and seeing Derek striding up the path to Birds & Bees in his dark blue wool suit. He had a takeout food bag in his hand.

He paused outside the door for a moment. He stood there as if hesitating, glanced at the sack in his hand, then pulled open the door. "Hi, Amy."

"This is a nice surprise." I ran over and gave him a warm hug.

"You may want to rethink that nice part," Derek replied enigmatically.

"What is that supposed to mean?"

"Only a joke."

"How's the cut?" I gently ran my fingers along the bandage on his chin.

"It's fine. The bandage gives me a rugged look, don't you think?"

"Definitely," I said. "Very sexy."

He hefted the bag. "I brought lunch."

"So I see. Jessamine's," I said, reading the side of the bag. "Smells delicious."

"Shall we eat in the kitchenette?"

"We can't. I'm the only one in the store right now. I like to be up toward the front in case a customer comes in."

Derek did a three-sixty. "The sales counter? You've got a couple of stools, right?"

"Yes, but I have a better idea." I ran behind the counter and pulled a throw blanket from the bottom shelf. We kept it there when we needed something to take the chill off. I flapped the blanket in the air and laid it on the floor near the entrance. "We'll have a picnic."

Derek chuckled. "Works for me."

I grabbed us a couple of teas, and we settled down on the throw. Lunch consisted of fried green tomato sandwiches on jalapeño cornbread with a side of boiled peanut hummus on spicy flatbread.

Afterward, I settled my head against Derek's warm chest. "That was delicious. Feel free to surprise me with lunch every day."

Our lunch had not been interrupted by a single customer. I decided to look at that as a good thing. My bank account could argue otherwise later.

I felt Derek's laughter vibrate against my head and spine. "Actually, there is another reason for my coming."

I twisted around, making eye contact. "Care to explain?" I ran my fingers along his chest. He had removed his jacket and hung it on the coat tree by the door. "Or demonstrate?"

Derek cleared his throat. "You aren't making this any easier, Amy."

"I'm trying to make it as easy as can be," I purred, moving my hand along his neck.

Derek stilled my hand. "She insists on getting a restraining order."

"Who does?" And why were we interrupting a romantic moment with talk of restraining orders?

"My ex."

I stiffened. His ex has that effect on me. "On who?"

Derek hesitated before answering my question. "You, I'm afraid."

"Me? What on earth for?"

Derek frowned. "She says you are a bad influence."

"Well, I never—"

"She also says she is afraid for Maeve's safety when she is with you."

"That's ridiculous!"

"I agree. But Amy—I mean, my ex—thinks that because of your snooping—"

"My what?"

Derek threw up his hands. "Her word, not mine."

I dug my fingernails into my biceps.

"Anyway, she thinks that you attract a bad element, a dangerous element." He shook his head apologetically. "And after she heard about how you'd been taken captive by Alan Spenner, well..."

I buried my face in my hands. The woman was not wrong. In the time I had been back in Ruby Lake, I had found myself in the company of cold-blooded killers and been thrust into dangerous situations on more occasions than I cared to count.

"What do you think, Derek?" I whispered through my hands.

"I think she's wrong," Derek assured me. "And that's what I told her. Besides, I told her there was no way a judge would give her a restraining order against you on the basis she was suggesting."

Kim's advice bounced off the walls of my ear canals. *Tell him about his ex and Lani. Tell him about his ex and Lani.*

I couldn't do it.

I rubbed my face to wipe away the tears.

"You're crying?"

"Sorry." I snuffled.

"Look, my ex-wife is a little crazy. She gets carried away. Sees problems where there are none." Derek chuckled. "Believe me. I know from personal experience. Why do you think we are no longer married?"

"Why are you no longer married? We never really talked about, you know, what led to your divorce."

A sad smile crossed Derek's face. "We wanted different things, I guess. I wish we could have stayed together for Maeve's sake."

He toyed with the big ring on his finger. It was his collegiate ring from Wake Forest University. "Then again, she's doing fine now." He patted my hand. "Trust me. You're an asset, not a liability."

"You are not exactly Mr. Romantic today, are you?"

"Sorry," Derek replied. "Shall I quote Shakespeare? Compare thee to a summer's day?"

"That's better than comparing me to Lucretia Borgia." I pulled him closer. "Give it your best shot."

He did.

* * * *

I was just turning the sign on the door to Closed when Lani Rice came strutting up the walk dressed in blue jeans and his black leather jacket.

I thumbed the lock. "Sorry," I said through the glass. "We're closed."

He banged his fist on the door. "Come on, Ms. Simms. Open up. We need to talk."

"About what?"

"Maybe I've been too hard on you." He lowered his chin. "I'd like to apologize."

I hesitated, my finger on the lock.

"Please?" A vaporous cloud spread a fine film over the glass.

"Fine." I unlocked the door and pulled it open. "You can come in, but only for a minute. I'm really rather busy."

"Thanks." He wiped his clunky motorcycle-style boots on the mat.

"Did you mean it about wanting to apologize?"

"Sure." He stuffed his hands in the pockets of his leather jacket and looked around the quiet store. "Are we alone?"

"The workers are in the storeroom," I lied.

He nodded. "Nice place."

"Thank you. And thank you for the apology." His hands remained in his bulging pockets. Was there a gun in one of those pockets? I retreated a step. "Was there anything else you wanted?"

"You know that Amy Harlan woman?"

I narrowed my eyes. "Yes, I do. Why?"

"She's nuts, isn't she." He said it as a matter of fact, not a question.

"You tell me. I hear that you and she are an item."

Lani threw back his head and laughed. He raised the lid of the shelled mixed seed and berry blend and grabbed a fistful.

What? Was everybody going to start following Jerry Kennedy's bad habit?

He tossed the handful into his mouth and chewed. "You know how we met?"

"At some bar in Charlotte."

"Huh?" He scratched his head. "Who told you that?" When I didn't answer, he did. "Phil. He thinks all blondes look alike." He reached for a second helping, but at a stern look from me held back. "Sorry. No, I met her at the diner across the street. Actually," he smiled at the memory, "I was talking up some chick at the counter. Giving it a shot, you know?"

I held my tongue. Lani and Yvonne seemed to have come from different parents and different planets.

"Anyway, after the chick ditched me, this Harlan woman comes up, plops herself down on the stool beside me, and says she could use my talents."

"What was your response?"

He shrugged. "I made a play for her. She shot me down and said that wasn't what she meant. She's a cagey one. She wanted to talk in private. She suggested we meet later."

"And did you?" I resisted saying that I knew they had. The only reason I knew was because I had been spying on him.

"Sure. At the cabin."

"What did she want?"

"She wanted to give me a thousand bucks."

"That's a lot of money. She doesn't strike me as the philanthropic type. What did she want for her money?"

Lani grinned. "She wanted me to seduce you." He aimed his thumb at me.

If this was a seduction, it was a bad one. Far worse even than Jerry Kennedy's lame attempt in high school.

"I told her no." He moved to the bookshelf and flipped through the pages of a beginning birder's guide. "I mean, no offense, but if I want to seduce a woman, I'll pick her myself."

"How commendable." I watched a couple passing by on the sidewalk.

"The question is," Lani said, "why would she want me to make a play for you?"

I knew the answer: to separate me from her ex.

Lani's eyes danced mischievously. "I mean, she really does not like you. Again, no offense."

I forced a laugh. "None taken." I moved toward the front door, hoping he would follow. He did. "So you don't blame me for your sister's death any longer?"

"Nah." He waved his hand in the air. "The police got their man. For what he did to Yvonne, I hope he fries."

I opened the door, and Lani stepped out.

"I only wanted to clear the air," he said. "And to tell you that you might want to watch your step. This is one freaky town, and that Amy Harlan is one freaky lady."

"Tell me about it," I quipped.

He had more to say. "She's the one who told me about you and the Lord of Death you gave my sister. She said you knew it was cursed and were up to no good."

"That's so not true!" I recoiled. "In the first place, I don't believe in voodoo curses. In the second place, I gave her a bluebird house. My friend gave her the statue."

"Hey!" Lani held up his hands. "I'm just saying. Let's not get all worked up again, right?"

I took a deep breath. "Right."

"Besides, we don't have to worry about the Lord of Death anymore."

"I wish."

"No, seriously. Me, Teddy, and Phil turned him into toast."

"What do you mean?"

"We tossed him in the fireplace with a few sticks of firewood, some kindling, and an old newspaper and whoosh!" Lani waved his arms overhead. "The guy went up in flames!" He chuckled. "Nothing left of him now but dust and ashes."

"Good riddance."

"Yeah." Lani settled back on his heels. "I hear you got the cabin that belonged to that guy in the wheelchair."

"Mr. Samuelson, yes."

"You want my advice?"

I didn't say yes or no.

"Sell it. You don't want to live in a place with all that negative energy."

"Negative energy? I thought you didn't believe in such things?"

"I don't mean anything supernatural. But that bunch out there at that pond, they are all nutty, if you ask me."

I had a feeling they would have said that and more about Lani. "Does that mean you don't intend to keep your sister's cabin and call Ruby Lake home?"

"Not a chance." Lani zipped up his jacket. "I'm talking to a realtor. Even after funeral expenses, I should be left with a pretty penny. Enough to get me set up on the Big Island. Make some music, ride some waves."

"Watch out for boiling lava?" I quipped.

"Yeah, there is that." Lani grinned broadly. "Come visit sometime. I promise not to seduce you."

Lani winked and strutted down the walk to his van.

I wasn't sure what to make of the young man. Like all of us, I suppose he had some good and some bad qualities.

I secured the door, turned off the lights, and retreated to my apartment for some peace and quiet.

And alone time.

Lani had given me a lot to think about. Amy-the-ex seemed to really have it in for me these days. Where was she hiding her good qualities?

First, she tries to get a man to seduce me, and then she tries to get a restraining order against me—what would she try next?

I pushed open the apartment door. A dark, moving gray shape caught my eye.

I screamed.

26

"Have you lost your mind?" the dwarf-sized gray shape that was Esther the Pester screamed back.

Her hair was wrapped up high and tight in bright purple curlers, and her cheeks and forehead held big white blotches of face cream—either that or the poor dear had fallen face-first into that tub of buttercream frosting in the back of my fridge.

"Esther?" I watched as she glided around the room. "What are you doing in my apartment?"

"Barbara asked me to water the plants for her while she was gone." Esther dutifully tipped a bit of water from the jade-green jug in her hand to the potted mums on the table near the window.

"Why didn't she ask me?"

Esther held the watering can over a flowering orange pepper plant. "Would you have remembered?"

I didn't bother to respond. We both knew the answer, and it wasn't going to make me look good. "Why is there an open bottle of Jack Daniels on the kitchen table?"

"Watering makes my mouth dry."

I knew I should not have bothered asking. I fetched a clean glass from the kitchen and poured myself a shot. With a sigh, I fell onto the sofa, drink in hand.

"What's the problem?" Esther asked as she carried the watering can to the kitchen sink and left it there. "Wait, I'll be right back."

Esther went down the short hall and helped herself to the bathroom. When she reappeared, her face was freshly scrubbed, and the curlers had disappeared.

"How do I look?" Esther asked, patting her gray curls.

"Um, lovely?" I cleared my throat. "I mean, really nice, Esther."

"Thanks," she replied without cracking a smile. "I'm trying something new."

If by new Esther meant the Shirley Temple look, she had nailed it.

"I think it is very becoming." I figured if I repeated it enough times, it just might be true.

Esther retrieved her small glass from the table and sat in my dad's old recliner. She pulled the lever and tipped backward, carefully and skillfully managing not to spill a drop of liquid gold.

I got the uncomfortable impression that it wasn't the first time she'd done it. How many times had she been in my apartment previously without my knowledge? Drinking my whiskey and watering my plants?

And where had she stashed her curlers? Did she keep them in my bathroom?

I took a sip of whiskey to forget the myriad questions swirling around in my head. I really did not want to know.

"If you really want to know," I swirled my drink, "the problem is Yvonne Rice's murder."

"No suspect?" Esther pulled the throw off the back of the chair and down onto her shoulders. "Karl says Chief Kennedy is positive that it's that Alan Spenner." Karl was Karl Vogel, the former chief of police.

"Plenty of suspects, including Mr. Spenner." I sipped and felt the accompanying burn down my throat. "But no good ones, if you ask me. And no real motives. Again, at least no good ones."

"Spenner could have been lying to you. You are the gullible type."

"What is that supposed to mean?"

"You don't want to know," Esther snapped.

Suddenly, I wanted very much to know, but that could wait for another day.

"Why not just let it go? Let Chief Kennedy handle it. He says he got his man, and the state police agree." Esther bobbed her shiny chin. "Let it go."

"I can't." I frowned. "The whole thing just doesn't feel right."

"You got one of your feelings, huh?"

I couldn't tell if she was making fun of me or not. "Too many things don't make sense."

Esther thrust her right hand between the seat cushion and the side of the chair. She pulled out a pair of knitting needles attached to a square of buttery-yellow yarn that was itself connected by its umbilical cord to its mother ship, a baseball-sized ball of yarn.

What else did she have squirreled around my apartment?

"Well, don't just sit there with your mouth hanging open," Esther said. "Tell me about it."

I gaped at her. Esther was crotchety, wrinkly, snoopy, stubborn, and wily—and those were her good qualities. "Okay." I set my drink down and tucked my legs under me. "I will."

I proceeded to tell Esther everything. I explained about the two deaths and what I knew so far. I told her about all the players as well, including Lani and his most recent visit to Birds & Bees.

At her prodding, I replayed my conversations with everyone who could remotely have been involved in some way with the recent deaths.

I had talked so long I'd gotten a sore throat. Either that or it was the strong alcohol burning away the lining of my throat.

"That's about it," I sighed. "Spenner told me he didn't do it. And why does Ross Barnswallow appear to be protecting the man who nearly beat him to death?"

"Hmm."

Esther's eyes had closed midway through my recitation, so hearing some sound, even a meaningless one, come from her lips, was encouraging.

I'd thought she had drifted off.

I forced myself up, muscles stiff, retrieved the bottle of JD, and refilled our glasses.

"Thanks." Esther stirred her drink with her pinky, then licked it dry. Her gnarly fingers made come-hither motions. "Tell me about Gar's death again."

"What the devil for?"

"Precisely."

"What?"

"Boy, you can sure go on and on without really saying anything, can't you?"

I eyeballed the Pester. Was she drunk? Had her senility kicked up a notch? "Okay," I began slowly. Maybe it was me. Maybe *I* was drunk.

"The Baron did it."

"Oh, Esther." I rolled my eyes. "Don't tell me you believe all this Lord of Death voodoo spirits stuff, too?"

She shrugged her bony little shoulders and tugged at her skirt. "I'm just saying."

"That's no help at all."

Things got a little fuzzy after that. When I woke up, the sun was stinging me in the eyes, and Esther was gone.

I looked under the chair cushion. Her knitting was still there.

* * * *

I met Derek for coffee in the morning across from his office at C Is For Cupcakes.

The quaint bakery holds a dozen or so small tables. The employees' uniforms are pink and blue. The pine-topped counter is flanked by two long glass cases filled with every flavor of cupcake imaginable and then some. The bakery's walls are painted in stripes of pastel pink and blue. The floor is wide-plank yellow pine.

Every table was filled. The bakery was a popular place to be in the morning.

"Enjoying the cupcake?" Derek asked with a smile.

I licked cream cheese icing from my upper lip. "Yep." I had ordered a cherry cheesecake cupcake with buttercream and cherry topping. "Did you get a chance to reread Gar's will?"

"I did." He reached into the briefcase on the floor at his side and pulled out a file folder. "Here's a copy for you."

"Thanks."

Derek sipped his coffee and offered me a bite of his cupcake. He had selected a mocha cupcake with an espresso-infused filling and espresso-buttercream frosting—his favorite.

I took a small bite. I mean, it would have been rude not to.

"Did you find anything at all in his will that would give some indication of who might want him dead?"

"Nope. Sorry. Everything he had in life was that cabin and Pep. And everything goes to you."

"And since I didn't kill him, that means nobody had a motive to murder him."

"So maybe it was an accident?"

"I find that hard to believe." I licked my foil wrapper. My stomach called for a second cupcake, but my waistline vetoed the call. I settled for a sip of coffee. "It just seems like too much of a coincidence."

"Is that it, Amy?"

"What are you trying to say?"

"I mean," Derek tugged his collar, "maybe you don't want to believe Mr. Samuelson's death was an accident because you would like it to be something more."

"That's absurd!"

"Sorry." Derek reached out and patted my hand.

"I would never wish for anything nasty to happen to anyone!"

"I know. I know. I only meant that you, well, you do seem to like finding mysteries. I mean, you have to admit—"

"I do not like finding mysteries," I sputtered. "They find me." I folded my arms over my chest and looked longingly at the display case filled with freshly baked cupcakes.

Derek chuckled. "That they do. Still friends?"

"Of course." I smiled. "Besides, if you think I let my imagination get the best of me, you should hear what Esther has to say about it all."

Derek pulled his wallet from the pocket of his charcoal gray suitcoat and laid a tip on the table. "Like what?"

"I tried talking to her about everything, and her less-than-helpful reply was to say that the Lord of Death was responsible."

Derek laughed as we stood, and he handed me my coat. I picked up the bag of cupcakes I had selected for the store.

Derek held open the door to the bakery, and I stepped out. "I'd like to be there when Chief Kennedy arrests that little voodoo doll and reads him his rights."

"See you tonight?" Derek's lips pushed against mine. I tasted espresso. We agreed to have dinner at my place.

I glanced across the street. "Is Mrs. Edmunds back?" I asked as casually as possible.

"No, I'm afraid I'm stuck with the ex for a few more days."

My lips grazed Derek's warm cheek. "Say hello for me."

Derek gave me the oddest look, then walked over to his office. I tried not to think about Amy-the-ex ensconced behind the reception desk.

I wondered if I could throw a cupcake that far.

Then again, why waste a perfectly good cupcake even if I could?

27

Kim surprised me by showing up for work on a scheduled day at her scheduled time. I hung my coat on the coat tree and handed her the paper sack.

"What's this?"

"Ammunition," I quipped.

Kim opened the bag and stuck her nose in. "Cupcakes. Great." She headed for the kitchenette, then spun around accusingly. "Hey! Ammunition?" She shook her head. "I just got that."

As she stomped off, she added, "My cupcake-throwing days are over, I'll have you know."

"Glad to hear it."

The last thing I felt like doing was scraping cupcake guts off the floor— or, worse, the ceiling and maybe out of the birdseed.

Since she appeared to be in a munching rather than launching mood, I joined her. "Lani came to see me yesterday."

"That creep?" Kim set a strawberry cupcake on her plate. "What did he want?"

I grabbed a chocolate cupcake, and we carried them to the front counter while I explained what he said was the reason for his visit.

"So you really think he wanted to apologize?"

I shoved a stool next to hers and peeled back the wrapper of my cupcake. These were mini-cupcakes, so I didn't feel guilty at all about having another so early in the day.

Well, not very.

"It would seem so. Frankly, I'll be happy to see him gone."

Kim sucked the frosting off her cupcake.

Personally, I like to start from the bottom up, saving the frosting for last.

"I think Dan will be glad when Lani and his friends leave, too."

"Why do you say that?"

"Dan says the police have fielded a few calls about them getting a little rowdy around town."

"For instance?"

"They played a set at the biergarten last night. Paul got upset."

"Why?"

"Because they didn't ask permission. They simply set up out in the courtyard and started jamming."

I laughed. "I wish I'd seen that. I don't suppose you sat in as vocalist?"

Kim picked up what was left of her cupcake. She looked at it, looked at me, and arched her eyebrow.

I got the meaning. "Sorry."

"You'd better be," Kim grumbled as she stuffed the tiny cake in her mouth. She swallowed. "It was Amy-the-ex who talked to Lani and turned him against you?"

"You sound surprised."

Kim smiled. "I guess I shouldn't be. Have you told Derek yet?"

"No, and I'm not going to."

Kim's eyes grew wide. "Why not? Amy, you've got to tell him. That woman means you no good."

"Because as much pleasure as that might give me, I know it's wrong." I tossed my wrapper in the trash and wiped my hands on my apron front. "Amy's problem is with me. I can't have her getting mad and fighting with Derek."

"Why not? I'd pay to watch that."

"I do not want to be responsible for them not getting along." I just wished she and I could manage to get along. "Besides, it wouldn't be fair to Maeve. It's bad enough her parents are divorced. I don't want to be the reason that they are fighting."

"I suppose," Kim grudgingly admitted after a moment. "What are you going to do about the cabin?"

"I have no idea. I wish I knew what happened the night Gar Samuelson died. I don't think I can even begin to think about what to do with it until I know the truth. I still can't imagine Gar driving himself off his dock."

"The word is," Kim grabbed my shoulder, "and you did not hear this from me..."

"Spill."

"The police are pretty sure he was murdered."

"Why?"

Kim shrugged. "There was something about the wheelchair and the brakes. I don't know. Dan was telling us a little bit about it. I confess, I was only half listening."

John Moytoy, a local librarian and recent convert to backyard bird feeding, pulled open the door to the store. "Hi, ladies."

He was dressed comfortably in dark trousers, a black chamois shirt, and gray moccasins. His jet-black hair was pulled back in a crisp ponytail. He could trace his family back to the Cherokee Indians who had lived on these lands long before European settlers arrived and staked their claims.

"I'll be right with you." I waved. "There are fresh cupcakes in back."

"Thanks." John went in search of sugar.

"So everything is going okay with you and Dan and—" I hesitated to say the name of She Whose Name Shall Not Be Spoken, so I said, "Dan's houseguest?"

Kim actually smiled, and it didn't seem forced or sarcastic at all.

"It's sweet really, I mean, after everything that's happened," Kim was saying. "We've been hanging out."

"You and Paula?"

"The three of us. They are being so nice to me."

"Sure, be nice to the crazy lady."

Kim's mouth fell open. "Oh, no," she groaned. "That's what it is, isn't it? Be nice to the crazy woman who throws cupcakes."

"Don't forget 'and sees a psychologist.'"

Kim frowned. "Thanks for reminding me."

"Hey," I said, sliding off my stool and going to see how I could help John, "what are friends for?"

"That's what I'd like to know." Kim grabbed her purse and left.

I frowned. One of these days I would learn to keep my big mouth shut.

"Are you looking for anything special today, John?"

"I'd like to get one of those birding journals," John replied. He was stooped over, perusing the bookshelves. "I thought I should get more methodical about what I see and when, if I am going to take this hobby seriously."

"Wrong aisle." I helped him up. "Come on, John. The journals are this way. Do you want—" I stopped suddenly.

John slammed into my back. "Sorry, Amy." He massaged his nose.

"That's okay. My fault." I moved in slow motion to a rack of bird journals of varying sizes and designs.

"This looks good." The librarian grabbed a thick, spiral-bound book with a brown cloth cover. "Is everything all right, Amy?"

"Gar Samuelson kept a diary."

"The man who drowned?"

"He told me himself. He said that the world comes to him and that he writes it all down." I shook my head from side to side. "Or something like that."

"Is that important?"

I scratched the top of my head. "I'm not sure. I don't remember seeing a diary when I was in his cabin the other day." Then again, the place was a mess. And I had not been looking for anything specific.

Maybe it was about time I did.

"Hopefully, the birds will flock to me, and I can jot them down in here." John thumped the book against his palm. "It will save me a lot of walking."

28

Kim returned to work a couple hours later. We were pleasantly busy, but the thought of Gar Samuelson's diary never left my mind. Where it might be and what it might contain nagged at me like a splinter under my fingernail.

It was late afternoon when I finally had some free time.

Kim promised to hold down the fort. I wanted a second look at Gar's cabin, soon to be my cabin.

I still had the keys on the hook by the back door. I grabbed them and headed out in the van. Waiting for the light to change so I could turn onto Lake Shore Drive, I noticed a police car. I slid my sunglasses down my nose for a better look.

Officer Larry Reynolds was parked at the curb outside Otelia's Chocolates. Every officer on the force knew that Otelia has a soft spot for the town's men in uniform. They had helped her through a rough patch, along with my assistance.

Any time one of them had a sweet tooth, they parked outside Otelia's shop. Sooner or later, she was bound to come outside and offer up a free treat.

The light changed, and I parallel parked behind Larry and climbed out.

Today had been no exception. An open half-pound box of peanut butter–dark chocolate fudge sat upon on the passenger seat of the squad car.

Larry's window rolled down silently as I approached. "Hello, Amy. Have you got a sweet tooth, too?" He handed me the box.

"Always," I confessed, taking a medium-sized piece. "But it was you I was coming to see."

"Me?" Larry squirmed.

I leaned against the car door and bit into the soft fudge. "What's the latest news on Ms. Rice's murder? Has Spenner broken down and confessed?"

Larry unbuckled his seat belt and lowered the volume on his radio. "You didn't hear this from me?"

I rested a hand over my heart. "I never do. Promise."

"Okay." Larry looked up the road before saying anything further. "The chief got a telephone call from the state police. Alan Spenner couldn't have shot Yvonne Rice."

"What? Why not?" Even though I had had my doubts, I was expecting—hoping—to be proven wrong.

"Spenner was attending a cockfight in another county."

"A cockfight? Are you sure?"

"Yep."

"That's disgusting."

"That it is," Larry said. "But it's also true. The man was there in front of a dozen witnesses."

"Reliable witnesses? I mean, what kind of people attend cockfights?"

Larry shrugged. "Reliable enough, apparently. Spenner is on his way to a maximum-security prison cell."

"Which puts us back at square one." I chomped down on my fudge.

"Us?"

"You know what I mean. What about the gun that was used to shoot Yvonne Rice? I don't suppose it has turned up."

"Nope." Larry popped a square of fudge on his tongue and rolled it around from cheek to cheek. "A gun was found, but it wasn't the murder weapon."

"Really?"

"It belonged to Yvonne's brother."

"Lani?"

"Yeah. It was the weapon he said had gone missing. He gave us permission to search his property. The chief found the handgun buried in Lani's van." Jerry chuckled. "That and a bag of weed."

"Uh-oh. Lani stopped by the store yesterday. He didn't say anything about being in trouble for drugs."

"He's not." Larry's tongue was coated in chocolate.

"I'm surprised."

"Me, too. Chief Kennedy is not arresting Lani, because of what he's been through. He gave him a stern warning, though. Besides, he claimed he was leaving town, and I think the chief would just as soon he did."

I nodded. "That confirms what Lani told me yesterday. I don't think he's warming up to our town."

"I can't say that I blame him, can you?"

I couldn't and said so. "You've got a little fudge on your upper lip."

Larry rolled his tongue awkwardly around the outside of his mouth. "The chief isn't too happy either. Especially since he's got nothing on Barnswallow. The state police are coming tomorrow to take a crack at him. The chief is convinced that Barnswallow holds the key to everything."

It was beginning to look that way.

"He's not cooperating?"

"He's talking plenty. The chief doesn't believe a word he says." Larry held out the fudge to me. I declined. He popped a square in his mouth. "Barnswallow has a criminal record himself."

"So I heard. Maybe he's reformed."

"Maybe," Larry agreed. "But a man can't be in two places at once."

"What do you mean?"

Larry bobbed his chin. "Speak of the Devil."

I turned to see Ross going into the post office next door. He was bundled up in a floppy brown suede coat and baggy blue jeans. Pep was not with him.

Larry refastened his seat belt. "I've got to get back on patrol."

I banged on the roof of the car. "Thanks for the fudge."

Larry waved as his foot stomped down on the gas, revving the engine as he deftly pulled into the line of traffic.

I was parked a little too close to a fire hydrant, but Ross was too close to pass up and the cabin could wait. Besides, I'd only be a minute.

I strolled inside Ruby Lake's small post office. Ross stood in line behind several other customers. Only one clerk manned the counter. Ross didn't notice my approach. "Ross, what a surprise." It was toasty inside. I unbuttoned my jacket.

"Amy, hi." He held a letter in his hand. I couldn't make out who it was addressed to.

"I was just talking to Larry. You'll never guess what he told me."

"Who's Larry?"

"Officer Reynolds."

Ross nodded and rubbed the letter against the bridge of his nose.

"He said that your friend, Alan Spenner, has an alibi for Yvonne's murder." I realized too late that I probably should have kept Larry's name out of the conversation.

Ross frowned as if he'd just swallowed dirt. "Alan Spenner is not my friend."

The people in line in front of us and now behind us looked at us with questioning eyes and big ears. Ross noticed, too. He pulled me out of line, through the inside door and out to where the rental PO boxes and a weighing device were held.

"What do you want, Amy?"

"Nothing. I came to buy stamps."

Ross's response was a dubious look.

"Okay, I'd like to know who killed Yvonne and why. I'd like to know how Gar ended up in Webber's Pond." I folded my arms across my chest. "And I'd like to know what your relationship to Alan Spenner is."

Ross shifted uneasily as a customer opened her PO box, slid out a couple pieces of mail, then relocked the box and left.

"How can you be friends with the man who almost beat you to death?"

"I told you, he's not my friend," hissed Ross. He shoved his letter inside his coat.

"Then why did you protect him?"

Ross sighed and leaned against the bank of PO boxes. "Because I loved his daughter." He hung his head, avoiding eye contact. "I owed it to her."

"His daughter?" I thought back to what Jerry had told me. "So you and Spenner's daughter were lovers, and Spenner didn't want you seeing her anymore. That's when he beat you up."

"That's the gist of it. Carrie and I were going to run away together. Start fresh. Spenner didn't like it. He didn't like his little girl moving away."

"Where is she now?" I inquired softly.

"Dead," he whispered.

"I am so sorry." I squeezed Ross Barnswallow's shoulder.

"Carrie left a letter," Ross said, sounding almost like he was in a trance. "She couldn't bear living with him, and she couldn't bear living without me."

"She killed herself?" I pulled my hand away and noticed that I had left behind a fudgy handprint on his coat.

Ross nodded. "In her letter, she asked that her father and I make amends. You cannot imagine how much I hated him." Barnswallow's eyes were tearing up. "But I loved her more. When her father showed up at my cabin, I had no choice but to hide him. For her."

I felt a sudden chill. "Do the police know all this?"

"Yes, I told them everything. Chief Kennedy would like to pin Yvonne's murder on me." Ross smiled. "But he can't."

"You have an alibi, too?"

Ross sniffed and wiped his nose with his coat sleeve. "I was on the phone with Polly."

"Who's Polly?"

"Polly Christian. She's my girlfriend. She works at the medical center. She called me when I returned from Yvonne's housewarming party. Polly had been unable to go because she had a shift that night. We spoke for a good forty minutes."

"No offense, Ross, but these days, with portable phones, you could have been talking to her from anywhere, including Yvonne's house."

"I'm old school. I have a cell phone, but I have had a landline out at the cabin for years. That's the number we talked from. My reception at the cabin isn't so great, anyway."

Bird poop.

Ross's phone cord would have had to stretch pretty far to reach from his cabin to Yvonne's. Another fish had slipped free of the hook.

I was flummoxed. Alan Spenner and Ross Barnswallow had alibis for Yvonne's murder. If they were innocent, who was the murderer?

Misreading my face, Ross said, "You can ask her if you don't believe me."

"That won't be necessary." Besides, I was certain the police would have taken care of that little detail.

29

The sun was chasing toward the western horizon as I followed the now-familiar circuitous detour to Webber's Pond.

Madeline Bell looked like a moving art installation standing in the middle of her fenced-in garden. She held a rake over her head, brought it down quickly, then repeated the process.

It seemed a bit late in the day to be working in a vegetable garden, hacking away at weeds. Smoke trailed from the chimney of her cabin.

I waved a hello as the rake slashed downward. I had no reason to stop. The van bounced down the track toward Gar Samuelson's cabin.

Moving deliberately along, I spotted Kay Calhoun seated in a weather-worn rocker on her front porch. She sat all alone.

I shot her a wave, too, but she signaled for me to stop. I cut the engine, not bothering to move off the unpaved road. I couldn't imagine there being any traffic at all unless the deer were using it in their daily commute.

"Evening, Kay."

"Hello, Amy." She patted the arm of the chair beside her own. "Join me."

I clambered up the steps and took a seat. "It's so peaceful here," I exclaimed, gazing out over the darkening pond. A half-dozen small birds flew lazily across the water, then disappeared into the forest.

"Yes." Kay rocked slowly, taking a sip from a chipped, brown cup that had no handle. She turned her head toward me. "What's that expression? Still waters run deep?"

"Something like that." I smothered a yawn. All this tranquility was making me sleepy. "How do you mean?"

"Oh! Where are my manners?" Kay Calhoun unfolded herself from her chair and went inside the cabin. She returned a minute later with a second cup. She sat and picked up a bottle off the porch on the opposite side of her chair.

I was somewhat surprised to see that it was Jamaican rum. Rolling a sip around in my mouth, I tasted orange peel and brown sugar. "It's very good."

Kay nodded. "It's Warren's favorite."

"Warren?'

"My husband."

"You are married? I didn't know."

"Oh, yes." She got up quickly and went inside the cabin.

Kay returned with a faded photo in her hand. She handed the framed photograph to me.

The 8x10 photo showed a handsome younger man against the backdrop of Webber's Pond, though there were fewer trees then.

"He is very handsome," I remarked. I handed her back the photograph, which she set gently on the porch.

A yellow porch light flicked on across the pond. Ross Barnswallow stepped out onto his porch wearing his red hat and brown coat. Pep ran into the front yard and began chasing shadows.

Barnswallow looked our way, arms hanging at his side. He clapped his hands, and Pep obediently returned to the porch. Man and dog disappeared through the front door.

Kay poured a little more rum into her own cup and settled back. Her unremarkable beige coat was pilled. The frayed edges of a navy shirt peeked out at the chest and cuffs. The material of her brown corduroy trousers had grown shiny, and the heels of her boots were unevenly worn. "He's gone now."

"Has he been gone long?" I asked. A few insects braved the cold to make themselves heard. Somewhere far away, an owl was making itself known.

"He has been gone for quite some time." Kay set her cup in the folds of her coat.

"I'm sorry," I said. "I didn't mean to bring up old hurts."

Kay turned to me with a small smile. "That's all right, Amy. I expect him to come back," she said matter-of-factly before raising her cup to her lips.

I pressed my feet to the sagging porch boards and rocked slowly for a minute. What did she mean? Was she expecting Warren to return from the dead? Maybe she was expecting to die soon herself and join him?

Kay was looking at me as if expecting a reply. I struggled for something to say or ask. Nothing came to mind. Asking her if she was crazy seemed impertinent. After all, I was a guest at her home.

Besides, the answer was becoming more and more evident each time I visited with her.

"Did you ever miss anybody, Amy?" Her Southern accent lent a dreamy quality to her words.

Maybe it was the setting, maybe it was the rum, but I was beginning to get woozy. And a little weirded out.

"Of course. My mother is gone, and I miss her," I stated.

"I see."

"But she will be back," I clarified. "Definitely. She's vacationing in New Orleans. She isn't dead."

"That's nice. Gar is dead, you know."

"Yes, I know." I creased my brow. Had she forgotten that we had already had this conversation? "I was just on my way to his cabin." I had a sudden thought, albeit an insane one. "Kay, did you see or hear anything unusual the night Yvonne Rice was murdered?"

"Do you mean her killer?"

I cleared my throat. "I suppose so..."

Kay shook her head side to side. "No. I didn't see or hear anything. I rode home with Murray and the others. We had a drink at Murray's, and then he took me and Madeline home.

"I went to bed. I was so tired," she said, as if feeling a need to apologize for not being more help. "It wasn't until the next day that I learned of Ms. Rice's death."

"Did Murray give Ross a ride home too?"

Kay thought a moment before answering. "No, only to his place. Ross walked straight home from Murray's the minute we got back to the pond."

She leaned forward, resting her arms on her legs. "The two men don't really socialize with each other much. I do not believe they much like one another."

Could Ross have run back to Yvonne's cabin and shot her before talking to his girlfriend on the telephone? Murray had told me that he would have heard if Ross had driven off in his noisy truck.

But he wouldn't have heard if Ross had gone running past.

Kay licked her lower lip. "Amy, do you think the Devil shot Ms. Rice?"

"I don't think the Devil uses a handgun," I quipped. "I'm not even sure the Devil has a license to carry."

"You know," Kay rested her head against the back of her chair and looked across the pond, "I only saw the Devil once before."

"You-you saw the Devil?"

"Yes, I told you, dear." Kay patted my hand. "Remember? It was the Devil that took Gar away."

"Yes, I remember now. You said it was the Lord of Death."

"Isn't that the same thing?"

"Not exactly." But it was close enough.

"Do you want to know what I think?" Kay eyed me slyly.

"Yes."

"I think Ms. Rice must have known that she was going to die."

"You do?"

Kay nodded solemnly. "She knew that she was going to die. She wrote *I am murdered.* The Lord of Death was right there on the mantel. Looking at her." She pointed at her eyes. "And then he took her."

"But she was shot," I reminded her.

She shrugged. "The Devil uses whatever is handy. Maybe Ms. Rice owned a gun and the Devil used it against her."

"I guess it's not impossible." I meant the part about Yvonne owning a gun and somebody using it against her—not the part about the Devil being the shooter.

My thoughts were swirling. My head was a fishbowl filled with rum. "You said you saw the Devil another time. When was the other time?"

Kay didn't stop to think. "I saw the Lord of Death the night Warren disappeared." She pulled her coat tighter across her chest. "Of course, I didn't know it was the Lord of Death then. But I knew it was the Devil."

A waft of cold air wrapped itself around my feet. "Did the Lord of Death, the Devil, take Warren?"

I knew it was a crazy question. I also knew that Kay wouldn't think it was half as crazy as I thought it was.

"Oh, dear, Amy." Kay's voice cracked. "I hope not." She rocked faster.

"Me, too. How long has Warren been gone?"

"Let me see." Kay tilted back her head and closed her eyes. When she reopened them, she turned to me and said, "It must be going on ten years now. Right before, no, right after Ross Barnswallow moved in."

"Ten years is a long time."

Kay clicked her tongue. "Life everlasting. What's ten years when you've got life everlasting?"

What indeed.

If I stuck around here long enough, I'd end up as crazy as my host. I stood. "Thanks for the rum, Kay." I set my glass carefully on my chair.

"You're welcome. Come visit me again."

I drove a few hundred yards farther to Gar Samuelson's cabin. The porch light at Ross Barnswallow's place went out.

I felt better knowing that the empty Fritsch cabin at the end of the road truly was empty and that Alan Spenner was under lock and key somewhere.

I strode out onto the pier and gazed down at the inky water. A stiff, cold breeze ruffled my hair and clothing.

How had Gar ended up here? I refused to believe it was an accident. He'd been up and down that pier hundreds, maybe thousands of times before.

I still had the keys to the cabin, and I let myself in. I hit the light switch. The interior was still a mess, but Derek had set up a couple of lamps the last time we'd been there. Both were working.

I rummaged through the books on the floor. No diary. I scanned the bookshelves on either side of the fireplace, although few books remained there.

Still no diary.

And I had no idea what it looked like.

A pair of hunting rifles sat in an open cabinet opposite the kitchen table. They had been untouched. A deadly-looking bow and a quiver full of arrows sat on the floor beside them.

I dug around the cabin haphazardly, searching the floor, the nightstand, and the dresser in the bedroom. I even lifted the plush dog bed at the foot of the bed and felt around the thick foam padding. Nothing.

Not even a flea.

In the tiny galley kitchen, I checked the cabinets and the refrigerator and freezer compartment.

Tired, cold, and hungry, I was about to give up when I noticed a metal reaching tool tucked in a corner next to the kitchen door behind a tall plastic trash bin. It was a big, heavy-duty grabbing tool, folded in three. He probably used it to place and retrieve items in the upper kitchen cabinets.

Then it struck me: So far, because Gar was wheelchair bound, I had been focusing my attention on those places I thought he could reach. After all, if he did keep a diary, it would have to be someplace fairly easily accessible.

But what if he had wanted to hide it from prying eyes or searching hands?

I pulled out the reacher tool and extended its arms. With the joints locked, the sturdy aluminum reacher extended approximately eight feet. There was a black pistol grip at one end. At the grabbing end, a pair of tongs had heavy-duty rubberized grippers.

I tried it out in the kitchen and had no trouble grabbing a box of oats from the top shelf. Even for someone seated in a wheelchair, the grabbing tool was more than sufficient for the task. If anything, Gar would have been better off with a smaller one.

So why such a long tool? I had seen shorter versions in the stores and on TV.

Assuming there really was a diary, that whoever had tossed the place after Gar's death had been looking for that diary, and that it was still here someplace in the cabin, I looked around the cabin with a fresh perspective.

I moved from the kitchen to the main room of the cabin. It was the only space high enough to accommodate the full length of the grabber tool.

I tried the rafters first, running the tongs inch by inch across their unseen surfaces.

No luck.

Keeping it extended, I moved toward the bookshelves and fireplace. There was no place to use the reacher. Not even a wobbly stone in the fireplace that I could pull loose.

Or was there?

A large flat river rock hung out just an inch or two past the others. For the first time, I noticed that the edges of the stone were smudged black.

I stood on the hearth and peered up at it. Stepping back down, I slowly maneuvered the grabber's tongs around the rock and squeezed the pistol grip. "Gotcha," I whispered.

I gave the stone a jiggle. It moved. Carefully, I brought the stone to the hearth. I set the reacher on the floor. I examined the stone. The edge was black, but it wasn't soot.

I stepped back and peered up. I couldn't see a thing. I switched on my flashlight app and tried again. The beam of light reflected off something golden.

I picked up the grabber tool and tried to fish it out. The tongs were too clumsy, however, at least for me, with my lack of experience with the things. All I had succeeded in doing was pushing whatever I had seen farther back, like an angry possum retreating into its lair.

I threw the reacher down on the sofa and grabbed an ancient kitchen chair. I still couldn't reach the recess from the ground. Knowing it was stupid and that it would serve me right if I broke a leg, I hoisted the chair up onto the hearth, wedging it as best I could into the fireplace for extra support.

I put my hands on the seat of the chair to keep it from teetering. It was rickety, and it would be hours, if not days, before anybody found my broken body if I fell, but I wanted whatever Gar had seen fit to put in that cubbyhole.

Squeezing my fingers around the fireplace stones, I eased myself up. The chair legs bobbled. So did my legs. My fingers found the hole. I grunted and thrust my hand inside.

I felt something cold and hard. Hopefully not the bones of a dead rat. Please, please, not a living rat!

I managed to work my fingers around the object and pulled it down. The chair shifted and popped free from the fireplace. I lost my balance and leapt feet first, figuring it was better to possibly land on my feet than definitely on my head.

My feet hit the hardwood floor, and my legs gave out. Balance and grace had never been two of my strong points. I tumbled head over heels, rolled across the room, and hit the big recliner chair in the corner.

30

I sat there a minute, trembling and seeing double, leaning against the front of the cold brown chair. I shook my arms—all four of them: check. I lifted each leg: Again: check. I turned my neck from side to side: perfect.

Well, no more creaks than usual.

Satisfied that I was alive and had all my significant parts in working order, I hoisted myself up onto the cushy chair.

That was when I noticed that I had something clenched in a death grip in my right hand. I peered at it—happy to see that my vision had returned to normal and that I was seeing only one hand.

I urged my fingers to open. Finally, and under protest, they did. I was holding a gold watch.

I sighed.

So much for Gar's diary.

I peered overhead, where the big head of a stuffed brown bear peered right back down at me. Its ugly, honed yellow teeth seemed to be fixated on my tender, exposed neck.

"What are you looking at?" I leapt from the chair.

Not because I was afraid of a dead bear. I just felt like getting up.

I examined the watch. There was nothing special about it. It was a simple man's watch with a black face and a broken gold band. The crystal was milky and contained fine cracks. Neither of the watch's hands moved. I saw no inscription on the back.

Perfectly ordinary.

Perfectly useless.

I bounced the heavy watch in my palm.

Why had Gar kept it hidden above the fireplace? It could not have had any value beyond a sentimental one.

I turned to my hungry-looking friend. "I don't suppose you know where your master kept his diary, do you, big guy?"

Was it my imagination, or were the bear's glassy black eyes mocking me?

Feeling the strain of defeat and the call of a hot bath and a hot cup of tea, I set the watch on the mantel. Time to call it a night.

I flipped off the lamp switch and turned the doorknob. "For a bear head on a wall, you sure are useless," I snapped at my furry, silent friend.

I waited for a snappy reply, but since none was forthcoming, I left, slamming the door shut behind me. I took one step, then a second.

Then I stopped. Something niggled at the back of my brain.

Gar called the story he had written his buried treasure. What if he had been toying with me? What if it wasn't a buried treasure but a *bearied* treasure?

I threw open the door and strode back inside, flipping the light switch with a flick of the wrist. The glassy-eyed bear was laughing at me.

"Laugh all you want, bear. Your laughing days are numbered."

I crossed the room. The bear trophy was just out of reach. I climbed onto the lumpy recliner and extended my arms. My fingers touched fur. If I could just curl some of it in my fingers…Then the bottom of the chair fell out!

I fell too.

That's how science works. My chin struck the top of the chair. It was a good thing it was well padded. Nonetheless, I was seeing stars for the second time that night, and both times I had been indoors.

I studied the pile of rubble that was once Gar's chair. Now my chair. So at least I wouldn't have to pay for the damages.

Overhead, the bear continued to mock me.

But I was determined to get the best of him.

I retrieved the grabber tool from the sofa where I had earlier tossed it. I waved it at him. "You're mine now, bear!"

I thrust the grabber upward, placing the tongs on either side of the bear's snout. I squeezed the handle and pulled gently.

I expected something of a fight. Bears can be stubborn. Besides, the head looked heavy. Instead, to my surprise, it came down quite easily. It had been hung on the wall with a metal hook, not nailed or screwed into the logs.

The bear's head wasn't stuffed at all. In fact, the trophy head was completely hollowed out inside and was supported by what seemed to be a fiberglass cast.

"No wonder you couldn't talk." A dark leather-bound book was stuffed in the bear's snout. "And here I thought you were just being rude."

Was I looking at Gar's story slash diary?

I set the trophy head on the busted chair and peered at the book. It was about an inch or two thick and maybe five by seven inches in size. It had a cover of cobalt-blue lizard skin. Fake, I hoped. I'd never seen a lizard that blue, except in cartoons.

I poured myself a glass of lukewarm water from the kitchen tap and carried it to the table. I fetched a candle from the shelf and set it on the table for extra light.

I unsnapped the leather clasp and carefully opened the book. I flipped through the lined, yellowed pages. The ink was deep blue. Each page was filled with Gar's tight, small handwriting.

I began at the beginning.

The title on the first page was a doozy. And it caught me by surprise. *What Happened to Warren?*

Gar's prose was dark, rambling, and sometimes raving. He told a tale about what had happened the night Warren Calhoun disappeared from sight. If not what happened, his suspicions of what might have happened.

And it was chilling.

Maybe an hour later, my glass empty, my throat parched, my head throbbing, I leaned back in the hard wooden chair. Gar believed that somebody at Webber's Pond had murdered Warren Calhoun.

He wasn't quite sure who. He suspected the newcomer, Ross Barnswallow. As for why, well, that was a surprise too.

According to Gar, Ross was likely having an affair with one of their neighbors: Madeline Bell, of all people. Stiff, stodgy, and oh-so-prim and oh-so-proper Madeline Bell.

Was it possible?

Gar also had a hunch where the body was buried. It seems the old stables over on Yvonne's property had burned down in a forest fire and been rebuilt right around the time that Warren went missing.

A deer track ran through the woods at the back of Webber's Pond and heading in the general direction of Yvonne's property. Folks in the area often used it to travel from their homes to the old Stenson homestead, which Yvonne had purchased and which now belonged to her brother.

That was where Gar had found the wristwatch two days after Kay had reported Warren missing, half-buried in the undergrowth.

Gar was certain the watch belonged to Warren, but he had kept the find a secret from Kay, because of her already fragile mental state.

Could what Gar suggested be true? Could Warren Calhoun be buried somewhere under that foundation?

I massaged my neck while my little gray cells went into overdrive. The myriad pieces of this thousand-piece puzzle were beginning to come together. Not all, but enough to see the general picture.

Gar's theory would explain Yvonne's murder. She had said she was going to tear those stables down. That meant there was a good chance that Kay's missing husband's body would be found.

I had a hunch of my own as I played over what I knew about both Yvonne and now Gar's death. Gar didn't know what I knew. He couldn't have known, and not knowing had likely cost him his life.

I knew who the killer was.

The front door opened. The candle on the table flickered.

But it wasn't Ross Barnswallow who let himself in.

31

"Hi, Amy. I saw the light on."

"Hello, Murray."

I saw a sliver of silvery moon as he moved inside and shut the door behind him.

I slid the blue lizard-skin book off the table and wedged it between my thigh and the seat of my chair.

Murray Arnold took a long stride toward the broken chair in the corner with the bear's head on top of the heap. "What happened?"

While his head was turned, I took my eyes off him just long enough to slip Gar's book into my purse, which was lying at my feet.

"Whoever trashed this place must have yanked the trophy head off the wall. Don't ask me why. And busted the chair in the process," I said.

"But—"

"Yes?"

"But I can't imagine who might have wanted to burgle the home of a dead man." Murray picked up a couple of books near the fireplace and set them sideways on the shelf. His eyes moved upward, but if he noticed the gap in the fireplace rocks, he didn't show it. "It's so disrespectful, senseless."

Murray straightened the sofa, its legs scraping the floor and sending a chill up my back. "I'll bet it was those kids that Madeline says have been hanging around." He turned to me. "What do you think?"

"I think it has been a long day." I stood, stretched and yawned. "I was just about to lock up." I picked up my purse and slung it over my shoulder.

"It's been a very long day," Murray agreed. He moved toward the front door. "But I don't think you should leave just yet."

Murray reached into his right-hand coat pocket and pulled out something shiny. He extended his arm. From his fingers dangled a watch, a busted watch.

My eyes flew to the mantel where I had left it. Gone.

Murray knew!

I flew for the door. I was fast, but Murray was faster and closer.

He threw himself against the door and spread his arms. "I don't think so, Amy."

I trembled.

The jig, as they say, was up.

"It was you, wasn't it, Murray? You did this." I waved my arms at the mess. "After you murdered Gar."

Murray was shaking his head. "You can't prove that. You can't prove anything. In fact," he took a step toward me, "you won't even get the chance."

I jumped to the other side of the sofa and grabbed the reacher tool. I waved it in front of his nose. He made a snatch for it. I hit him in the arm.

"Damn!" He rubbed his upper arm. "You'll pay for that."

I had no doubt that I would if he had any say in the matter.

"Where did you find the watch?" Murray was smiling, which made him appear all the scarier. "That was very resourceful of you. I turned this place upside down looking for it."

"You knew about the watch?"

"Not until I saw it on the mantel. I recognized it immediately. Warren never went anywhere without it. Well," Murray stroked his chin, "except his final resting spot, apparently." He chuckled. "Kay said he even wore it to bed."

"It was hidden in the stones above the fireplace."

Murray nodded. "And the notebook?"

"What notebook are you talking about?"

Murray's eyes flared, and he lunged toward me. I moved out of reach behind the table. "Don't toy with me, Amy!" He took a deep breath and said more calmly, "I do not like being toyed with. I know you found the notebook, and I want it." He held out his hand. "Now!"

I gulped. "It's in my purse."

"Bring it out, and give it to me. Slowly."

I threw my purse at his face, turned, and dashed for the kitchen door.

Murray howled and followed in close pursuit. My fingers fumbled with the chain on the door. Murray grabbed my shoulder and spun me around. I kicked him high between the legs.

It wasn't a direct hit, but close enough. He howled and let go.

I ran to the kitchen. Murray tackled me and pulled me to my feet. We were both breathing hard. I leaned over, hands on my thighs.

"Please, Murray," I begged. "Give it up. Haven't enough people died?"

Murray's unshaved face was mottled purple. He threw open the kitchen drawers one after another until finding something to his liking.

What he liked was a serrated knife with a wooden handle and a nasty-looking tip. "Let's go."

He jabbed. I moved.

"Pick it up." He gestured at my purse on the floor, its contents spilling half out. The blue-skinned book was visible. "Is that the book?"

I nodded.

"Hand it to me."

Seeing that I had no choice, I did.

Murray grunted. He clumsily flipped through Gar's book while training the knife on me with his other hand. "Gar. The fool told everybody that he knew what happened to Warren. That one of us killed him. And that he knew who it was and where he was buried. Bragged that he had written it all down and hidden it where no one would ever find it. He said that if anything ever happened to him, the truth would come out."

"He was bluffing," I said. "He thought it was Ross."

Murray snorted. "That loser? I wouldn't count on him to give a cockroach the heel of his boot."

"But it was you."

There was a prolonged silence but for our breathing.

"Yes, it was me. What made you suspect?"

"I didn't," I admitted. "Until I read that." I pointed to Gar's tale of Warren's disappearance. "Then it all came together. The housewarming party. *I am murdered.* Kay's seemingly crazy ramblings. She told me the Devil or the Lord of Death or something pushed Gar into Webber's Pond."

"What? You don't believe in evil spirits?"

"No. I believe in evil people." I slowly maneuvered myself to the side of the sofa. "Clever of you to write *I am murdered* instead of *You are murdered.*"

"That would have been rather obvious, don't you think?" Murray's eyes never left me.

"What Kay saw on the dock the other night was you." I waved my finger up and down. "Wearing that. The burgundy pea coat. That red hat on your head. She probably got a pretty good look at both under the lights at the end of the dock." Each dock had a pair of overhead lights at the end on tall metal poles.

"Ross has a similar hat and a not-so-dissimilar coat."

"Yes, but he has a distinctive limp. Kay told me she saw the Lord of Death running down the dock, pushing Gar in his wheelchair. That leaves only you, Murray. You pushed Gar Samuelson into Webber's Pond. You killed him."

"Very clever, Amy. Gar said you were clever." He stroked his chin some more. "Too clever, really."

"You probably shot Yvonne, too."

"Why would I do that?" As he talked, he pulled a pair of leather gloves from his coat and slipped them on.

"Because she was going to tear down the stables, and you couldn't let that happen. Because that was where you had buried Kay's husband, wasn't it?"

Murray smiled. "Like I said, you are clever."

"Yvonne told us what she planned to do with the stables. The contractor was scheduled to come the very next day. What if he started digging around?"

I was babbling, but at least I was breathing.

Murray quietly flexed his fingers.

"So you murdered her. But things didn't work out, did they? You overhead Lani in the diner saying that he was going through with the project after all. What I don't understand is, why kill Gar? Why not kill Lani?"

"Gar was getting too curious. Snooping around. The whole episode had been dead and buried for years. Yvonne's murder had stirred him up again.

"I was afraid that sooner or later he would figure things out. Maybe even guess where the body was buried. I couldn't let that happen. I couldn't let him tell anybody. I was afraid he might have said something to you.

"As for Lani, I figured I could handle him the same way I handled his sister, if it came to that. I do what I have to do, Amy.

"I was hoping to make this look like an accident." He dropped the knife on the table. "But maybe it's better you disappear." Murray slid a handgun from inside his coat and aimed it at me. "Nothing personal."

I held up my hands. "Wait. Murray, please."

Murray shook his head.

"At least tell me how all this started. Why murder Warren?" It was the one thing that still made no sense. What had been at the root of this whole sordid tale?

"I'm surprised you haven't figured it out." Murray lowered his arm ever so slightly. "I loved her."

"Kay?"

"No!" Murray's scream frightened me. He slammed his empty fist against the wall. "Not Kay! Madeline. I was in love with Madeline."

"I-I still don't understand."

Murray wiped the spit from his lips. "Don't you see, Amy?"

I shook my head no and inched my way a step farther from him. He was losing control.

"I was in love with Madeline. I still am. I always will be. But she loved him!"

My thoughts were flying furiously. "You mean Warren?"

Murray jerked his head up and down. "They had an affair. It was disgusting. The two of them, right under Kay's nose. Madeline deserved better than him. And Kay deserved better than having a lowlife, cheating husband. I confronted Warren. He laughed at me. Every day he laughed at me."

Murray began pacing. I moved closer to the front door, my hand stretching backward, fishing blindly for the metal handle. "I hated that man. Madeline deserved better." He thumped his chest with the muzzle of his weapon. "I could have given her everything."

"I'm sure—"

"Kay deserved better, too." With his free hand, he picked up the rock I had extracted from the wall over the mantel. He hurled it at a glass-covered photograph of Gar and Pep on the wall.

I flinched as the glass shattered and flew across the room. "Does Madeline know?"

"That I strangled Warren? No. I'm sure she suspects, though."

I wondered why she had never come forward with her suspicions, but love and friendship sometimes lead to strange behaviors.

"Finally, I had had enough. I confronted Warren at the edge of the woods one night. He was on his way back home to Kay from Madeline's house. I cursed him and begged him to stop.

He laughed at me again, like he always did. I strangled him with these." He looked at his hands.

"I used Gar's electric cart to move the body to the stables. I wrapped him in a tarp, dropped it in a deep hole prepared for the foundation, and covered it with gravel. The next day, it was buried under several feet of concrete."

"And Warren's watch?"

"When I was wrapping him in the tarp, I saw the pale markings on his skin and realized the watch was missing. I went back and looked for it with a flashlight but couldn't find it. Several times, I continued searching for it, but I never found it. I had almost forgotten it until tonight."

"Kay must have seen you and Warren arguing. She said she saw the Lord of Death the night her husband went away."

"Poor Kay." Murray actually sounded like he meant it. How twisted had the man become—all because of his love of a woman he could not possess?

"There is still something I don't understand. Both Madeline and Kay told the police they were with you at the time Yvonne was shot. Why would they lie for you?"

"They were with me, as far as they knew," Murray replied. "I spiked their drinks with a quick-acting sleeping medication. It only took me five minutes to drive to Yvonne's house. I let myself in. I shot her before she even knew what was happening." He sounded almost proud of what he had done.

"But she telephoned nine-one-one."

"Did she?" Murray replied in a surprisingly falsetto voice.

"*You* called the police from her phone to give yourself an alibi for the time of the murder. Where's the phone now, at the bottom of Webber's Pond?"

Murray jerked the handgun at me. "Why don't you tell me? You'll be there yourself soon enough."

32

The blaring of a loud horn split the air.

Murray turned toward the window and tugged at the curtains.

I ran for the door and threw it open. He was going to kill me, so I had nothing to lose if he shot me in the back rather than the front.

Pep leapt through the air. Murray fired. A loud bang filled the air, followed by a deep growl and continuous barking. I glanced over my shoulder. Pep was tugging at Murray's trousers. Murray struck the dog in the head, knocking the poor animal toward the fireplace.

I slammed the door and tumbled down the wheelchair ramp leading from the front door and raced to my van. Murray was on my heels.

I tripped on the front tire and threw out my arms. Something dark whooshed past my ears.

I covered my head and cried out.

I heard two gunshots, maybe more, and scrambled to my feet. I grabbed the door of the van and threw it open. There was no key ring dangling from the ignition.

Just my luck, the one time I remembered to take my keys out of the van, I could have used them. But no, the keys were in my purse, and my purse was in Gar's cabin. Murray was between them and me.

Murray tapped his gun against the glass. "Step out of the van, Amy."

I lifted my hands to show I was complying. Murray stepped back, but not far enough. I kicked the door open savagely, catching him smack in the middle of the chest. The gun flew from his hand.

I jumped down. Murray's hands found my neck, and he began squeezing. I fell to my knees, digging my fingernails into his hands, but he was wearing leather gloves, so he was doing more damage to my neck than I was doing to his hands.

A dark shape rounded the corner of the van and struck Murray down. I sobbed and grabbed the earth. For the third time that night, I was seeing stars. But this time, when I looked up I was seeing something—rather someone—else.

"Kay!" I gasped.

Kay Calhoun stood behind Murray, looking not like the Devil but like the angel of my salvation. She was wielding a double-barreled shotgun, which she held by the steel barrels rather than the wood stock.

"I saw the Devil coming." Kay held the shotgun at the ready, high above her head like a club. She trained her hate-filled eyes on Murray. "Where's Warren, Devil?"

Murray hoisted himself up on his elbows and raised his hands protectively over his face. "No, please! No!"

I pulled myself off the ground and dusted my knees. Pep ran between my legs and licked my hand.

"I called the police!" Ross Barnswallow was a dozen yards back, limping toward us.

Kay looked at us all uncertainly. She still held the shotgun at the ready. I prayed it wasn't loaded.

"Give me the shotgun, Kay." I held out my hand.

Ross called Pep to his side. "I saw Murray. Then I saw Kay. What's going on?"

"The Devil is running loose," Kay waved her weapon at Murray. She ever so slowly lowered the shotgun, planting the butt of the stock on the ground and holding onto the barrels for support.

"It's okay," I said to Kay. I ripped Murray's cap off his head. "This is your Devil."

33

Two days later, the world was back to normal. Well, back to as normal as normal gets in Ruby Lake.

Mom and Aunt Betty had returned from their vacation. Their mouths gaped and their eyes bulged as I gave them the lowdown on what had been happening in our fair town since their departure.

It was nine in the morning, and Birds & Bees was open for business. The whole team was present at the front of the store: me, Esther, Mom, and Kim.

"It certainly has been quite exciting around here, hasn't it?" Mom fussed with my hair. She always complains I don't get the part straight. "I worry about you, Amy."

"I'm fine, Mom." I gently pulled her hand away and shook my head so that my hair could find its natural balance, adjusting for the spit, of course.

"Did you mention that you almost got shot to death?" Esther had to ask.

I frowned at her. "Yes. I did."

"I didn't hear it."

"That's because you went for coffee."

"Hmph!" Esther snorted. "He could've shot Amy right in the heart." She dug a hole in her chest with her index finger even while balancing her mug. "Can you imagine? Just like that Yvonne Rice woman."

"That's enough, Esther," I begged.

"Yeah, don't upset the murder lady," Kim quipped.

"I am not the murder lady. I run a bird lover's store."

"It seems to me I'm the one who does most of the running." Esther flashed me a look.

"Okay, okay," Mom interrupted. "It sounds like you could use a vacation, Amy." Mom rubbed my back.

"What she needs, what both these girls need," said Esther, "is to put in a good day's work here in the store."

I blushed. She wasn't wrong. Working in Birds & Bees would seem like a bit of a vacation after all I had been through.

"You know—" began Mom.

"Wait a second." I stilled Mom with a hand on her shoulder. "I'll be right back." Forgoing my coat, I darted out the door and ran across the street. Amy Harlan was strolling into Ruby's Diner. She may have been going for a piece of pie, but I wanted a piece of her.

Her conniving could have cost me my relationship with Derek—or worse. Not to mention, she was using Maeve in her twisted attempts to drive a wedge between me and her ex-husband. Derek was mine, and he was going to stay mine.

I threw open the diner door and went straight for her.

"Hello, Ms. Simms." Amy Harlan sat at the counter, drawing attention to herself in a slinky, red wool dress and matching pumps. "I was about to order a biscuit and coffee. Care for something?"

I grabbed her shoulder and swiveled her around to face me. "What I care for is for you to accept that you are divorced."

She batted her long lashes at me. "Of course, I'm divorced," she said evenly. "Everyone in town knows that."

Tiffany set a cup and saucer on the counter in front of Amy Harlan, but her unsettled eyes were on me. "Hi, Amy. Anything for you?"

I shook my head no, and she retreated. "Derek and I are in love. You need to accept that."

"Has he told you that? That he loves you?"

I felt my cheeks burning red. "That's beside the point. You need to move on with your life. Better yet, move on to another town."

Tiffany returned and placed a small blue plate holding a freshly baked biscuit on the counter.

"Where's the gravy?" Amy Harlan demanded.

"Coming right up." Tiffany faded into the background once more.

"I'm serious, Amy. Leave Derek alone. And stop trying to bribe strangers to hit on me in some demented scheme to break me and Derek up."

"I don't know what you're talking about."

"I am talking about you minding your own business. If you don't, you'll be sorry."

"Is that a threat, Simms? Because if that is a threat—"

"Here you go, Ms. Harlan!" Tiffany hurried over carrying a small gravy boat and a spoon. The waitress tripped on the rubber mat under her feet. She managed to hold onto the porcelain cup, but the hot gravy flew across the counter. The thick gravy struck Amy Harlan's chest and oozed down her stomach.

"My dress!" shrieked Amy-the-ex. She leapt off the bar stool, grabbed a wad of napkins, and dabbed wildly at the fabric.

"Sorry," said Tiffany. Her face said otherwise.

"Derek is going to hear about this," Amy Harlan snarled. She flung a ball of damp napkins over the counter.

"You bet he is," I replied. "From me."

Amy Harlan grabbed her coat from the rack at the door and sped off in her Lexus.

"Sorry about that, Tif. She left without paying."

"Are you kidding? Worth every cent. In fact, that's the kind of entertainment folks around here pay good money for."

I suddenly realized that the eyes of everyone in the diner were on me. A couple of folks even applauded. A blush ran from my toes to my nose. I smiled weakly.

A busser appeared from the kitchen bearing a mop and bucket. He went to work on the dirty floor.

"I have to get back to the store," I said.

Tiffany picked up Amy Harlan's uneaten order. "Take the biscuit."

"I don't have any money. I left my purse at Birds and Bees."

"Don't worry. I'll stick it on Amy Harlan's tab the next time she's in."

I ate the warm biscuit as I crossed the street. Even without gravy, that was the best bite I had ever eaten in my life. Nothing like a little backbone to whet the appetite and sharpen the taste buds.

"What was that all about?" Mom asked when I returned to the store.

I explained about my little run-in with Amy Harlan. This elicited a round of laughter.

"You're gonna be the talk of the town, Amy," Esther cackled with delight.

Sadly, she was probably correct.

"What about this Lani and his friends, Amy?" Kim asked. "Are they staying in town?"

"Last I heard, Lani said he wasn't sure. I ran into him last night at Brewer's. He, Phil, and Teddy were performing again."

"I thought Paul told them to stop?"

"He seems to be tolerating them. Plus, they don't charge him, and they pay for their own drinks."

"Sounds like Paul's favorite kind of people," I replied.

"What are you going to do with that cabin you inherited?" Esther wanted to know. She had a cup of coffee in one hand and a bagel in the other.

"Sell it," I announced. "The money will go to charities." I had several in mind, from senior citizen organizations to animal welfare and rescue services and, of course, bird conservation.

Ross had agreed to care for Pep. Both man and dog seemed happy with the arrangement.

"Are you sure, Amy?" asked Kim. "Because if you're looking for someone to share your inheritance with..."

"I'm sure." I had no use for it, and the money was better spent on others. Besides, I'd be happy if I never laid eyes on Webber's Pond again. Everybody who lived there seemed just a touch crazy.

Maybe it was something in the water.

"I think that's a wonderful idea, Amy," Mom replied. "What do you think, Esther?"

Esther chomped down on her rye bagel and chewed a moment. "It's not the dumbest thing Amy's ever done."

Kim giggled.

I did not.

I glanced out the window. Two familiar figures were walking up the path. "Look who's here, Kim." I pointed over her shoulder.

Kim spun. "Dan and Paula? I wonder what they're doing here." She reached for her purse under the counter and pulled out her tiny mirror and makeup kit.

"Maybe Dan needs more birdseed," Esther said greedily.

"Maybe Dan's going to propose to you," I suggested. I hadn't forgotten Kim's story about how the spirits had told her he would soon be requesting her hand in marriage.

"Propose? What's this all about?" Mom asked.

The door flew open before any of us could explain.

Kim raced from behind the counter. "Dan! Paula!" She gave each a friendly hug, followed by kisses. "What brings you to Birds and Bees?"

Kim gave Paula a measured look. No doubt seeing what I saw. Paula's long locks hung from beneath a blue and white ski cap, and there was a rosy glow to her cheeks. Her matching sweater was just tight enough so that you couldn't miss her assets.

Speaking of assets, her jeans hugged all the right places, leaving nothing to the imagination but the imagination.

Dan grabbed Kim's hand. "We wanted to give you the good news."

Kim tilted her head and held out her left hand. "What good news is that?"

Oh, brother.

Was Dan actually going to propose marriage? Here and now inside Birds & Bees?

That would be newsworthy for our monthly newsletter. Except for the recent sighting of our yellow cardinal, stories had been rather stale of late.

"I've put in for leave." Paula smiled.

Oh, sister.

"Leave?" Kim asked. She looked at me for a clue.

I threw out my arms to show I had none.

"That's right," Dan explained. "We know you've been having a tough time." He moved closer to Paula. "Paula has decided to stay and help out."

"Help out?" Kim was pale as a swan.

"Sure. You're always saying how tight money is now that you've quit your real estate gig. No offense, Amy," Dan said for my benefit.

"None taken," I replied. I knew how little money there was in the pot to go around. And that pot wasn't big to begin with.

Dan wasn't done yet. "And how you've always wanted a roommate."

"Roommate?" Kim was foundering. I propped her up.

"You know, to help cover the bills," Dan said.

"I'll be happy to pitch in." Paula's sexy smile wasn't helping Kim any.

Kim struggled for words. "But, Dan, when I said roommate, I was thinking—"

I for one knew exactly what my best friend had been thinking. She had told me how she'd been hinting around with Dan about how nice it would be to have a roommate, ostensibly to help cover her bills.

Of course, she was really hoping that roommate would be Dan.

And that roommate would be synonymous with husband.

As for the bills, Kim has never been one to worry about whether she had enough money to cover her expenses.

It looked like her little scheme might be backfiring, and I was helpless to change the course of coming events.

"Thanks, Dan, but—" Kim grabbed Esther's coffee and gulped it down fast. "You see, I was thinking—" She shoved the mug back into Esther's hands.

Dan's kiss on Kim's lips put a stop to her voiced objections. "No need to thank me, babe. Your happiness is all that counts." He pulled up his sleeve, looked at his wristwatch, and yelped. "I've got to get to the station. I'll catch up with you later."

Dan practically flew out the door on a cloud, having done his good deed for the day.

Kim was looking mortified.

Paula took Kim's hand. "How about showing me around the store?"

Kim looked at me for a lifeline.

What could I do? This was a store filled with bird-feeding and bird-watching supplies. It was not a marine supply store. There was nary a life preserver or lifeboat in sight.

Besides, Paula's money was as good as anybody's. Maybe we'd make a nice sale.

I watched as Paula led Kim arm in arm, down the center aisle. "Did I mention that Chief Kennedy suggested there might be an opening with the Ruby Lake PD?" I heard Paula say.

"Huh?" Kim's lurch was followed by what sounded like an orc taking a direct hit to the gut from a battle axe—Derek had recently talked me into watching the Lord of the Rings trilogy.

Kim cranked her head around and smiled at me, though that smile did not reach to her eyes. "You didn't forget Amy's present, did you, Barbara?"

I turned my attention from Kim as she rounded the bend—both physically and mentally, I feared—with Paula and redirected myself to my mother. "Present?" I asked brightly.

What can I say? I like getting presents.

"Yes, I almost forgot." Mom hoisted a huge shopping bag from the floor. Inside were several presents. "For you, Esther."

"Thank you, Barbara." Esther set her cup on the counter. She tore into her package, leaving shreds of purple and green wrapping paper and thin red ribbon all over the floor.

"Careful," cautioned Mom, looking uneasy.

Esther set her gift on the counter and carefully opened the lid. Inside, sat a big, brightly decorated dessert with purple, green, and yellow icing. "It's a cake."

"Not just any cake," explained Mom. "It's a Mardi Gras king cake. They are a New Orleans tradition. It's made from brioche and is filled with nuts and fruits. And a tiny baby."

Esther screwed up her face. "A baby?"

Mom chuckled. "A plastic baby. It's supposed to be lucky. Whoever gets the piece with the baby in it will be king, or queen, for the day."

"Thanks." Esther was genuinely pleased. She picked up the cake box. "I'll cut us some slices and put the rest out for our customers."

Mom handed me a tall package. There was a shorter remaining package at the bottom of the sack. Mine was biggest—I'm just saying.

I slowly pulled away the wrapping and ribbon. Somebody had to show a little restraint and set an example for neatness around here.

As the owner, it was my duty.

I positioned the box on the sales counter and scooped out some packing peanuts, catching a glimpse of black and red. I got a grip on the top of whatever it was and extracted it.

I don't know how to explain it other than to say my entire body turned into a block of ice the moment that I saw that sardonic face glaring defiantly at me.

"Do you like it?" Mom asked, pulling anxiously at her pearl necklace. "I do hope you like it."

"It's...I—" I gulped and winced in pain. It felt like I'd just swallowed a sheet of coarse-grain sandpaper.

"Baron Samedi," smiled Mom.

"But...why?" This one was dressed in a black tuxedo and top hat with a blood-red vest featuring skull and crossbones buttons. But it was him all right. The Lord of Death.

My Lord of Death.

With a pasty white face and dead black eyes.

"Kim called me at the hotel."

"Yeah?"

"Yes. She told me how much you missed having a doll of your own and suggested I get you one."

Mom was beaming.

I was not.

"So I did. I bought Kim some pralines," Mom added. "What do you think? I hope you think he's as nice as the one you had before."

I didn't know if it was the Lord of Death talking or me, but somebody said, "I'm going to kill her."

ABOUT THE AUTHOR

    In addition to writing A Bird Lover's mystery series, novelist and musician **J.R. Ripley** is the author of the Maggie Miller mysteries and the Kitty Karlyle TV pet chef mysteries (written as Marie Celine) among other works.

    You may visit JRRipley.net for more information. Visit JR on Facebook at facebook.com/JRRipley.

CPSIA information can be obtained
at www.ICGtesting.com
Printed in the USA
LVHW041925211019
634862LV00002B/294/P